Also from Ken Vanderpool

KILL THE MUSIC

KILL THE MUSIC

Ken Vanderpool

ISBN 978-0-9903655-2-5

Printed in the United States of America

Cover and Interior Design
by Sandra Vanderpool

Dedication

For his ongoing assistance and energetic support throughout each of my Music City Murders novels, and for his rigorous editorial advice. ***Kill the Music*** is dedicated to Dew Wayne Burris.

Chapter 1

The Cole Home
Nashville, Tennessee

Beware the one who calls you *friend*.

Brooke Cole's audit uncovered the truth, but the question remained. What measure of treachery is required for a veteran bank employee in a position of authority to betray his employer and embezzle more than a million dollars?

Initially, although thinking it doubtful, she'd assumed the oversight could have been hers. It was not. She couldn't help but feel insulted that the culprit, a fellow worker for four years and she thought her friend, would think she could miss this pedestrian attempt at deception.

Brooke pulled her left hand from the steering wheel of her aging Honda Accord and held it to her throbbing chest as she considered her compelling question. Her doctor taught her how to interrupt and calm her symptoms before they progressed into full-blown panic attacks.

All she could think about on her way home from the bank was the inconceivable result of today's audit. As the meticulous Manager of Internal Audit for Nashville's Davidson Savings &

Loan, one of Brooke's departmental audits had, for the first time, exposed evidence of internal duplicity pointing to mortgage fraud.

Brooke drew in another full abdominal breath and exhaled slowly as she turned the car onto her up-sloped concrete drive. She reached toward the sun visor, pushed the button on the remote garage door opener and began the sharp turn necessary to navigate the turnaround and face the rising segmented steel door. Her bare foot released pressure on the brake pedal and allowed the car to roll forward into the garage.

Safe at home, she sat frozen. Her head back against the headrest, both hands still clamped around the steering wheel. She was drained from the stress. Staring at nothing, she tried to digest the breach of trust she had uncovered today. It remained unthinkable.

She shoved the shifter into park and killed the engine. With her shoes back on, she collected her purse, her briefcase and the small plastic bag of groceries she'd picked up after work. Fresh fruit for her and chocolate for the spooky Halloween cuties who would be invading the subdivision in a couple of weeks.

Brooke climbed the steps leading to her kitchen and selected from the keyring the proper key using the only fingers not currently holding something. She pushed the wall-mounted garage door button with the middle knuckle of her index finger, and unlocked the kitchen door.

Inside the doorway, she stopped. Her four-digit access code ended the high-pitched tone of the security system seconds before the home-based siren would have been activated and the South Nashville monitoring station alerted.

She shoved the kitchen door with a firm push from her right elbow. She stepped into her kitchen and immediately headed for the granite-topped counter with thoughts of a soon to be prepared fruit salad. The usual secure sound from the metal door slamming into the jamb behind her hadn't come. She stopped, confused. Then, she turned without releasing her armload.

There, holding the door, was a man. A large man, she didn't know. The gloves on his hands and a determined low-brow stare revealed a hostile intent. He said nothing.

A rush of adrenaline surged through Brooke's body, dilating her pupils and forcing her lungs to inhale large quantities of air. Her heart rate was kicked upward once again. Her blood advanced oxygen delivery to her muscles, preparing her body to react to the danger.

"Jon, come here now!" She shouted for her husband, knowing well he was not there, but hoping her urgent appeal would cause the intruder to abandon his invasive plan.

Hearing no response to her plea, the man continued to gawk at her like a bobcat poised to pounce on its prey.

Short of breath and overcome with escalating terror, Brooke tried her best to sound forceful and in control. "What the hell? Who are you? How did you—?" She knew it wasn't working.

She surveyed the area around her for a way to defend herself and instantly thought of her husband's pistol in his bedroom nightstand. Jon taught her how to use the nine millimeter and coached her at their local shooting range.

Without taking his eyes from her, the big man shifted forward enough to slowly push the door closed behind him.

It was time to act. Brooke threw her briefcase, her purse, everything into his path. She turned and bolted for the bedroom. Her left ankle went sideways on her third step. The slender four-inch heel broke from her suede shoe. She gasped as she stumbled.

Her misstep allowed the intruder time to lunge forward and snatch a handful of long blonde waves. Her slender size-two frame was yanked off her feet and pulled backward.

She reached out with both arms for something, anything, to catch her fall. Finding nothing, she dropped hard to the floor. Her shrill scream ended abruptly and turned into a low-pitched groan as the back of her head struck the unyielding porcelain tile floor. Her consciousness faded.

The intruder dropped to his knees and straddled her slight body before she could regain her senses.

Her desperation grew with her returning awareness. The immense pressure of the man's weight crushed her abdomen. She attempted to reach up for his face, clawing her thick faux fingernails toward his eyes. She missed and scratched his arm instead. He tilted his sizable head and pulled it back, out of her reach. She screamed, praying someone could hear.

He slapped his gloved right hand over her mouth to stifle the sound. His index finger slipped from her bottom lip and dropped inside her open mouth.

She bit down.

"Bitch!" He clenched his teeth, jerked his hand free and used it to punch her in the jaw. Anger engorged his face with blood as he fought to grab her wrists. After a brief exchange of flailing arms, he was able to pull her smallish wrists together and clamp them both into his sizable left hand. He forced her arms to the floor above her head. His upper body weight shifted forward over her.

Her fear-filled attempts to scream were quieted by the considerable pressure of his body crushing hers. She was unable to collect even a half-breath.

Brooke continued to struggle, gasping and tossing her head from side to side. Tears flowed from the corners of her eyes down into her hair. Refusing to give up, she tried to kick her legs upward hoping to reach his head, but his weight pressing against her body prevented it. She fought to pry her reddened hands free, but his vice-like grip had them locked together.

Her fight and the lack of adequate oxygen accelerated her weakening. Her mouth wide in search of another breath, she struggled to scream again. The sound of her attempt was stifled to a soft raspy plea, muted by the pressure of his right hand now firm against her throat.

The attacker leaned full-forward with his clammy face intentionally inches above hers. A furrowed brow hooded his squinting eyes. Pushing downward as he smiled, he crushed her slender neck against the cooperative resistance of her kitchen floor.

Brooke's watery eye lids fluttered. Her eyes rolled up and back into her head.

Chapter 2

Cris Vega's Home
Woodmont Area
Nashville, Tennessee

Cris Vega and her partner Detective Jerry Rains were up on the Nashville Police Department's homicide rotation. The next victim was theirs. However, Rains was in California with his wife on vacation, visiting her family.

Cris went to bed last evening confident her chances were somewhere between decent and good for a normal night's sleep on this hopefully uneventful Tuesday night. She'd been asleep since just after 22:00 and was dreaming of an arrest she was in the process of completing in the area south of Broadway downtown, better known to Nashvillians as So-Bro.

Without resistance, she'd handcuffed the tanned, well-muscled, shirtless suspect and placed him in the backseat of an assisting uniformed officer's cruiser. As he sat facing her with his legs extended outside the blue and white cruiser's back door, he looked up with his magnetic sky-blue eyes and smiled at Cris.

"Detective." He tossed his head toward the empty molded plastic bench seat behind him. "There's room back here for both of us." His white teeth sparkled as he winked. "You can leave the cuffs on if you'd prefer."

She tucked a few strands of her hair behind her left ear and was about to offer up an amorous retort when the irritating alert of a cell phone interrupted her response.

"Hey beautiful, I think that's my cellphone ringing," the brawny hunk said. "Can you get it for me?" He smiled. "My phone is here in my front pocket. Reach in there and feel around. I'm sure you'll find it." He leaned back in the seat, offering her access to his bulging jeans.

Cris woke and realized the repetitive sound was actually coming from her own cell phone ringing on her night stand.

"Damn."

She slapped at the annoyance, angered by the intolerable interruption. She grabbed it up and offered a disgusted and sleepy response.

"Yeah. Vega."

"Detective, we have a body," the sergeant said.

Yeah, I had one too. Mine was alive, but thanks to you he's gone now.

"Oh, thank you, Sergeant. I thought for sure I was going to stay asleep for six or seven hours." Her sarcasm was too thick to miss. "Where is it?"

"East of Brentwood, off Edmundson Pike." He recited the street and number.

Cris rolled onto her side and using the light from her phone, she yawned as she scribbled the address onto a notepad she kept by her bed.

"Judging from the address, is this the result of a domestic altercation?"

"Not sure. The first officer says the scene looks as though the victim was surprised when she arrived home. So, it could be a home invasion, but I would say it's hard to tell for sure until you arrive."

"Who called it in?"

"The husband, I'm told."

"At 03:00?"

"Seems he's a musician. According to the first officer, he'd been playing a gig downtown and didn't get home until around 02:30. That's when the 911 call was made."

"Any idea yet what time the victim arrived home."

"No. But I'm guessing you, or the M.E., will be able to tell us all real soon," the sergeant said with his own tone of sarcasm.

Cris shook her head, glanced at the phone and said, "Tell them I'll be there in less than an hour."

"Good luck detective," he said, as he disconnected the call.

"Gee, thanks Sergeant." Cris couldn't help spewing the whispered sarcasm as she returned her phone to the nightstand. "You have a wonderful morning, Sergeant." Cris gave a large sigh and fell back onto the pillow.

"Jerry," she mumbled to her vacationing partner, "I sure hope you are enjoying California."

Careful not to wake her housemate in the bedroom across the hall, she propelled herself from the bed and immediately dropped to the floor for sessions of stretching and three sets each of squats, sit-ups and push-ups. At 38, Cris was still obsessive about conditioning. She would not allow herself to skip morning maintenance of her body's enviable firm tone.

She had a reputation within the department as the most well-conditioned female officer. At five feet-five inches, she was not the tallest female in the Metro Nashville Police Department, but she was by far the toughest. Her quickness and skills in hand-to-hand combat had put more than a few male officers, and detectives, on their heels. Some, on their asses.

She'd moved up the departmental ladder to detective even faster than her supervisor and mentor, Sergeant Mike Neal. However, she had benefitted from some unnecessary nepotism. Unbeknownst to all but four members of the MNPD leadership, Homicide Captain Alberto Moretti was her mom's older brother.

The crazy thing was, according to Sergeant Neal, Cris would have accomplished all she'd achieved even without her connection.

"She didn't need the favoritism," Neal said. "She only needed opportunity."

Showered and dressed, it never took Cris long to get ready. Her mocha Latina complexion framed by her thick raven hair required little makeup.

She watched as her morning citrus concoction dripped from the juicer into the plastic tumbler. She wondered if the orange she'd used came from anywhere near where Jerry was vacationing. She frowned, wishing she was the one in sunny California.

She recalled the hunky suspect from her interrupted dream as he looked up from the backseat of the car. Those blue eyes. Those ripped and tanned muscles. His smile and irresistible invitation.

She grunted and pulled the container from the juicer's platform when it stopped dripping. She spooned in a heaping scoop of protein powder and some crushed ice. With the plastic lid secured, she shook the container violently up and down as she continued her focus on the remnants of her dream. She lifted the frothing mixture ceremoniously, as if making a toast.

"To the day when I'm on call, my cell phone remains silent and the incredible hunk comes back to complete my dream." She took a large gulp as she grabbed her car keys from the kitchen counter. "As if that'll ever happen."

* * *

Cris pushed the shifter into Park, climbed from the dark blue unmarked sedan and started for the house, already bathed in flashing blue and red strobes. The wooden barriers and yellow crime scene tape were up and uniformed officers were in place around the property's outer perimeter. The crime scene access table was in position at the street near the home's brick mailbox and the log was being manned per departmental procedure. It looked as if the First Officer and those who followed had done their jobs.

"Vega, Homicide." She flashed her credentials at the officer who was manning the crime scene log.

"Who's the First Officer?" Cris asked as she scratched her information onto the log sheet and then pulled two shoe covers from the small box on the table.

"Goodrich. He's somewhere in the back of the house."

"So, why are all these fine cars and people out here on the street? Is somebody having a party and forgot to invite us?"

"They said the husband is an up and coming performer, songwriter, musician, whatever. They said he called his manager as soon as he hung up from making the 911 call."

"And?"

"His manager must have called everyone with a financial interest in the guy. Based on what one of the men there next to the Mercedes said, he's becoming quite popular and several folks have a lot riding on him and his career. I guess they're afraid of what this could do to their plans for *his* future—and *their* income."

"Hmm. Where *is* the husband?"

"Sergeant Hill or Goodrich can tell you. I would assume he's with one of them." He pointed his thumb over his shoulder toward the home.

"At least the media's not yet got wind of this. That's when the circus begins."

"Ain't it the truth," the officer agreed.

Cris scanned the well-groomed middle class homes along the street as she climbed the driveway. She saw movement in her peripheral vision and turned to catch sight of two large white vans with mounted satellite dishes atop their roofs. The mobile units were from competing local television channels.

"I guess I spoke too soon." She turned back to the officer. "Listen, make sure nobody who's unauthorized gets inside the outer perimeter. With all these wealthy rubberneckers, it may get crazy here in a bit. We don't need any additional distractions."

"Will do."

She glanced again at the expensive cars and their owners who were now quiet and staring at her as if waiting for an update on the status of the incident.

The expanding crowd of huddled neighbors along with the arrival of the media convinced her. She was going to call for investigative assistance. She wasn't looking forward to it, but she knew she needed to wake up her former partner who was now her boss, Sergeant Mike Neal.

Chapter 3

Mike Neal's Home
Green Hills Area
Nashville

His brow grimaced in response to the irritating sound even before he woke. He wrapped the long goose down pillow around his head in an effort to suppress the annoyance. When it failed, he raised his head with squinted eyes seeking the source of the commotion that disconnected him from his sleep.

His senses peaked for an instant. His head dropped hard on the pillow as he realized the sound was produced by the vibration of his cell phone as it tugged at the charger cord allowing it to dance, reaching out toward the edges of the nightstand. He rolled onto his left side, moaned his frustration and grabbed it. His initial desire was more to stop the obnoxious noise than to discover who'd stolen his bout with sleep.

Without looking, he dragged his finger across the phone's screen and, with significant effort, exhaled his name, "Mike Neal."

"Mike. I'm sorry to call you like this."

"Cris? Hey, what's up?" Mike said, trying to sound as though he was wide awake. His mouth stretched to its limit as he yawned without making a sound.

"I got a call. You know Jerry is on vacation?"

"Yeah. I remember," Mike said, attempting to push the cobwebs from his mind and confirm what he thought she was telling him.

"I caught a case tonight. It could, uh—be a problem. I think I'm gonna need some help."

"Sure. I told you to call me if you needed to."

"I know, but I'd hoped it wouldn't be necessary. Sergeants require their sleep too."

"Don't we though? So, what's the story?"

"The scene is east of Brentwood, near Edmundson Pike. When I got here there were several people standing by a line of expensive cars parked near the crime scene house. The broadcast vans from the local channels have already started arriving. I have a feeling I'm going to need some help handling the interviews and such."

"What's driving all this attention so soon? Have you identified the victim?"

"I haven't spoken with any of the family yet, but I'm told she's the wife of an up and coming country music singer."

"Really? That'll pull in the media. Who is he?"

"I don't know his name yet. I'm just now walking to the rear of the home. I still need to talk with the first officer, but I can already tell all this is going to turn into a circus if we don't have enough investigators here to deal with it."

"Do you have plenty of uniforms on site?"

"I think so. The first officer appears to have done his or her job. More officers are arriving every few minutes. One of them told me Sergeant Hill is here somewhere."

"Okay. Text me the address while I get ready."

"Thanks, Mike."

"No problem. Keep everyone busy, on task and away from your crime scene. I'll see you shortly."

"10-4."

Mike disconnected the line.

As he placed his phone back on the nightstand, he noticed the time—03:56. He pushed himself up and off the bed. Once standing, he stretched and grunted audibly in response to a sharp pain in his lower abdomen. He instantly attempted to suppress his voice so as not to wake Carol. Then, he remembered. His fiancé was out of town helping with her sister's newborn.

Carol didn't normally stay at Mike's house every night, but the nights following his proposal were special. They were both excited about their new status and excited to get together.

Only days after Mike's proposal, Carol's younger sister gave birth to a healthy six pound, seven ounce little girl. Her first. But, shortly after arriving home with her baby, she began to experience symptoms of postpartum depression. When Carol's brother-in-law called, she dropped everything and flew to Kansas to be with her sister.

The last time Mike spoke with Carol on the phone, her sister's doctor remained unsure of how long the situation might take. Carol, now 41 and herself the product of a failed marriage, shared with Mike her concerns involving her sister's and brother-in-law's relationship. The doctor told Carol the driving force behind being able to move past PPD was a strong positive and supportive marital relationship. So far, according to Carol, that relationship wasn't so evident.

With little more than half the sleep he'd planned, Mike pushed his eyelids together and rubbed them in an attempt to clear his vision. He rotated his neck all the way to his left and then to his right. He tilted it sideways to his left until he heard the audible crackle and pop from his adjusting cervical vertebrae. He stretched various muscles as he trekked toward the hall bathroom.

He stood before the mirror, scratching his one-day beard and still stretching, as he waited for the water to heat up for his shave. Mike's fast-approaching membership in the half century club was not yet evident in his physique. He kept himself in shape, running as often as possible and working out in the MNPD gym at least twice a week.

Lately he'd begun to experience an annoying pain in his lower abdomen. Maybe he'd pulled a muscle during one of his workouts or an extra-competitive racquetball game. The price, he speculated, of the inevitable condition known as middle-age.

It was only two weeks since he'd prepared a romantic dinner, served a premium cabernet and delivered his marriage proposal right there in his living room. He'd never seen Carol so happy or surprised. Such a special night.

He and Carol Spencer had been violating MNPD Homicide Captain Alberto Moretti's fraternization rule and seeing each other as often as possible for years. Mike decided it was time they made their commitment to each other a more permanent, and public, one. But before their plans became common knowledge, he would request a meeting with the captain to bring things into the open.

In the last week he'd begun to envision what it would be like to raise a family in this highly desirable, vintage and peaceful Green Hills area of Nashville. In the years since his promotion to detective and subsequent home purchase with his VA loan benefit, property values had nearly doubled. However, the issues driving home values skyward were also changing this portion of Music City in other less attractive ways. Traffic was congested in Green Hills six days a week from dawn until the stores and shops closed their doors at night.

As he tucked his shirttail inside his pants, he rubbed the spot on his lower abdomen where the annoying pain had been grabbing his attention. This time he recalled the pain he'd suffered a year ago from a stubborn kidney stone. But, that pain started in his lower back.

Before turning off the bedroom lights, he snatched his phone off the nightstand and gave a cursory effort toward making the bed. This, only because he knew Carol would expect it.

It was one of many things he was trying to get used to, now that he was going to be sharing his bed, his home and his life. He knew, after living alone for so long, the coming changes would not be easy for either of them.

Chapter 4

The Cole Home
Nashville, Tennessee

Cris keyed the location's address and her expression of thanks into a text message and forwarded it to Mike. She pocketed her phone and pulled on the pair of shoe covers she'd taken from the box on the crime scene log table.

She took a pair of black nitrile gloves from her jacket pocket and tugged them on as she followed the concrete drive around the end of the home. She stopped in front of the crime scene tape stretched across the garage door opening. The kitchen door was standing open a few inches. A red Honda was parked in the garage and a uniformed officer was in place outside the barrier tape to protect the scene and prevent unauthorized access.

"Vega." She showed her ID. "Homicide."

"Yes, ma'am."

"Don't call me ma'am."

"I'm sorry?" the officer said, with a confused apologetic tone.

"It makes me feel old when you say *ma'am.*"

"Uh. Sorry. I'm from the South. You're not old and my mom taught me to show respect to all ladies, regardless of their age."

"That's a hard one to argue with, Officer—." She checked his name tag. "Goodrich."

"Yes ma'am. I mean … ."

"Forget I said anything, Goodrich. Thanks for the chivalrous intent."

"Yes ma'am." He winced as the last syllable passed his lips.

Cris gave him a big smile. The officer's features caused her to believe he too may have some Latino blood. If so, with a name like Goodrich, it must be from his mother's heritage.

"I'm from the South as well," she said, "likely farther south than you. I'm from Houston, originally. I've been with the department here about a dozen years. I'm surprised we haven't met." Cris locked on to his large brown eyes.

"I've been working out of the West Precinct for two years."

"That could be it. My partner and I don't seem to get so many calls from the West. It's nice to meet you, Officer Goodrich."

"Same here, Detective. Houston, huh? I'd say that's pretty far south."

"It's about as far as you can go without getting wet."

Goodrich laughed.

Cris admired his striking smile. "You're the First Officer?" She made a closer inspection of the officer's well-groomed appearance. The more she studied him, the more he began to look like her hand-cuffed and shirtless beefcake from this morning's dream.

"I am. I arrived at 02:48." He pulled a small spiral notebook from his back pants pocket as if he knew already what Cris wanted to hear.

Cris continued to admire the young officer's professionalism as he brought her up to speed on the details of his early discoveries.

"When I arrived, I came through here," Goodrich indicated the garage. "I entered the home through this door." He pointed toward the kitchen.

Cris nodded as she followed Goodrich's report. "Is there a security system?"

"Yes."

"What was the status when you arrived?"

"Green light. It was off."

"Okay. I'll call the service company to get usage on the last twenty-four hours." Cris made a note.

"The victim, Mrs. Cole, was where she is now, on the kitchen floor. When I checked for a temporal pulse, I could tell by her body temp she'd been deceased for a while. The EMT, who arrived shortly after me, also checked her. He said she'd been dead for hours. The victim's husband remained in the driveway out here wandering around in circles and talking on his cell phone.

"Not long afterward, my backup showed up and while we were putting up the cones and tape barriers the people in all those cars out front started arriving. We were able to run the secondary tape along the front of the property and keep them outside the perimeter. I notified Sergeant Hill and called for more backup when I saw how fast and how many people were showing up. Those folks have been asking a lot of questions and wanting to see the victim's husband. They say they are his friends and business associates and they'd like to make sure he's okay."

"I understand. You've kept him away from them and his wife's body?"

"Oh, yes ma'am. He's been out there on the patio alone, since I arrived. Well, I asked Officer Logan to stay with him until we're given new instructions."

"Did you speak with any of the mob out front?"

"Just enough to keep them in place out there to allow you and the crime scene folks room to work. I didn't answer any questions except to assure them Mr. Cole was okay. Considering, of course."

"Sounds like maybe the husband could be hitting the Country Music scene big time?"

"I guess so, or at least he's headed for it," Goodrich said. "The folks out front seem worried about him."

"So, has anyone been inside the house other than you and the victim's husband?"

"Just him, me and the one Nashville Fire EMT. He immediately came back out. Didn't touch or move anything. I watched. The husband hasn't been back in the house since I got here. I've tried to keep the crime scene intact for you guys."

"Good thinking, Goodrich. I'll have some more questions in a minute. I want to get a look at the victim and the immediate scene."

"Gotcha. I'm pretty sure since the kitchen door was open when I arrived, it was likely the access and egress point for her killer. If you'd like, you can see the victim and the immediate area around her by entering through the sunroom out by the patio. I got the husband to loan me his key so I could unlock it. I was sure you guys would want access other than the kitchen door there."

"Thanks. The criminalists should appreciate it as well. We'll talk more in a few minutes."

Cris stepped toward the patio and acknowledged officer Logan with a wave. She saw the victim's husband sitting at a table with his head in his hands. He was dressed in jeans, western boots and a multicolored plaid western style shirt. Typical stage attire for the lower Broadway music venues.

"Mr. Cole?"

He looked up. "Yes."

"Mr. Cole, my name is Detective Cris Vega. I am truly sorry for your loss sir. I'm here, along with several other officers, to try and determine what happened and why, as well as who did this."

He nodded.

"May I assume we have your approval to search all your property and everything on it in an attempt to locate pertinent evidence and determine who was here and who may have reason to harm your wife?"

"Yes. Whatever you need. It's fine."

"We'll be obtaining a search warrant since it's standard procedure, but it could take a little while. In the interest of time, we like to get your verbal approval."

"I understand. You have it."

"Thank you. I'd like to ask you some questions, but first, I want to get a brief overview of the inside, if you don't mind. I'll be back with you shortly."

"Okay." He leaned forward. With his elbows on the patio table, he lowered his head into his hands again.

As Cris passed by Officer Logan, she spoke. "Stay with him. Let me know if he needs anything."

"Sure thing," Logan said.

Moving through the darkened sunroom and into the large and well-lighted family room, Cris could see the evidence of a struggle in the kitchen. She pulled out a notepad and pen and began to make notes as she surveyed the area from her current perspective at the edge of the large family room. Her note pad was lined on the front for notes and graph paper was printed on the backs of the pages for crime scene sketches.

Cris was approximately six feet from the victim. The young woman's body was face up on the tile floor, her long blonde hair splayed in multiple directions. Her eyes, partially opened, revealed blood-red sclera and petechial spotting beneath the lower eye lids, likely the result of some method of asphyxiation.

Cris mouthed a prayer of thanks the body had not yet begun its journey through putrefaction. The indescribable stench of decaying human viscera was a common impediment of her job, but its absence at a fresh crime scene never disappointed her.

Several contusions on both sides of the victim's neck, as well as a large one on her left cheek and temporal area, were reddish in color.

Her arms appeared to be reaching out perpendicular from her body, left and right. Her wrists were covered in various shades of red to purple contusions, but no blood could be seen anywhere on, or near, her body. Her legs extended straight downward in a normal fashion with her heels on the floor.

The toe of her right shoe, still on her foot, was pointed upward and outward at a forty-five degree angle from the floor and her left foot was similar in the opposite direction, but bare. The missing shoe was approximately ten feet from her body with the heel broken away and lying near the wall.

Her white blouse, ripped from two of its buttons and pulled from the waistband of her gray skirt, revealed a portion of her pale flat abdomen. Cris noted the blouse appeared, from this distance, to be made of silk or a material made to look like silk.

"Hey, Cris."

She turned back toward the sunroom entrance to see Carlos Padilla, a photographer from the Crime Scene Unit, paused outside the doorway with his black bag on wheels full of camera equipment.

"Carlos. Glad you're here. As always, I need you to get video of the surrounding area outside as soon as possible. But first, there are numerous expensive cars and people out there on the street with a couple of our uniforms."

"I saw them. Nice rides."

"I want to be sure we capture all of them on film, including their IDs and each of their car's plates before any of the cars are allowed to be moved. Take an officer with you and make sure no one leaves before you can get these shots and the data. Okay?"

"Got it." He unzipped the large black canvas bag, pulled his video camera from the foam insert and began adjusting the settings as he crossed the patio and started for the street.

After making an initial sketch of the home's area near and around the victim, Cris noted the locations of numerous items in the vicinity of the body which appeared out of place. She exited the home back through the sunroom and walked to the garage area and Officer Goodrich.

"My boss, Sergeant Mike Neal, will be here shortly. He and the Crime Scene Unit are the only ones who can enter the home without my approval. No one else. Okay?"

"Got it."

"Thanks, Officer Goodrich."

"Yes ma'am." He smiled as if proud he got away with his show of respect.

Cris nodded her acceptance, turned and walked back to the patio to begin collecting information from the grieving husband.

Chapter 5

The Cole Home
Nashville, Tennessee

Fifteen years as one of Nashville's top homicide detectives had taken Mike Neal to virtually all corners of the county. But, he didn't recall investigating a murder or a suicide in this area.

The homes in this area of town appeared to be well cared for and likely maintained a respectable rate of increasing value. The people here must value home life and their possessions. They seemed to have invested themselves into their lives, built and maintained homes, not just houses.

As Mike approached the active crime scene, the quantity of blue strobes convinced him Cris was correct in her prediction of escalating activity. The collection of first responder vehicles was larger than he'd expected. He decided to park his Chevy Impala a block or so from the crime scene and walk the rest of the way.

As he was attempting to park, one of the more senior patrol officers, who'd worked with him on various occasions, flashed his powerful flashlight at Mike. He recognized his car and him. Mike lowered his window.

"Hold right there, Sergeant." The officer grabbed two fellow uniforms and told them to move the marked units, which were positioned grill to grill in order to block the street and crime scene access by anyone other than first responders and the investigative teams.

As he drove by the senior officer, Mike slowed.

"Thanks, Chuck."

"Good luck, Sergeant." The officer waved a casual salute.

Mike gave him thumbs up. He appreciated all the patrol officers' deference, but he did not expect it. Mike felt he was one of them. He'd served his years on patrol and knew all about the job they were asked to do. He felt he was just another police officer, only with a different task. They respected him for the quality of his work, the way he treated them and the example he set for their department.

Mike spotted the collection of big-ticket cars and SUVs parked end to end along the street opposite the crime scene home. The owners of the vehicles appeared to be huddled in discussion until they saw him approach the log table.

"Your friends?" Mike asked the officer at the log table.

He smiled as he handed Mike the log sheet. "My friends don't drive those. Like me, they only look at them in magazines."

"Me too. Is Detective Vega around?" Mike snatched two shoe covers from the box.

"She should be in the rear of the home with the victim's husband."

"Thanks."

Mike scanned the area around the home as he pulled on his gloves and shoe covers. Ever concerned with altering crime scene evidence, he walked slowly along the edge of the driveway where no one was likely to have stepped. With his small high-lumen LED flashlight, he scanned the drive and the area alongside it as he walked, looking for potential evidence or anything out of the ordinary.

He approached the back corner of the house and spotted a uniformed officer.

"Have you seen Detective Cris Vega?" Mike held up his ID.

"Yes sir. She's out on the patio back there." He tossed his head to his left.

"Thanks."

"Yes sir, Sergeant Neal."

Mike looked back at him. He didn't know the sharp looking officer. And there was no way he could have read the information on his creds so quickly.

"Do you know if we've checked the neighborhood for citizens' outdoor security cameras?"

"I was told it's being done now, Sergeant."

"Thank you, Officer Goodrich." Mike read his name plate.

"Yes sir."

He spotted Cris with a man sitting at a round metal patio table. The young man looked to be in his late twenties or, at most, early thirties. Another uniformed officer was standing nearby.

Cris stood when she saw Mike approaching. "Sergeant Mike Neal, this is Mr. Jon Cole."

Cole pushed back his chair as he stood and reached to accept Mike's hand.

"Mr. Cole, I'm sorry for your loss."

"Thank you. You can call me Jon."

"Thank you, Jon."

"Sergeant Neal is here to help us sort all this out," Cris said, and turned to Mike. "Jon was beginning to tell me where he was prior to returning home this morning."

"Okay." Mike pulled out a patio chair and sat. He adjusted it so he was positioned where he could comfortably see Jon's facial expressions and body language as he spoke.

"Do I smell of cigarettes and beer?" Jon asked.

"Oh no. I wasn't moving away. I wanted to be able to face you while we talk."

"Oh. Okay. I know after spending a few hours in the club the smell of cigarettes and beer sort of permeate my clothes. Brooke always hated the smell." He looked down at his hands for a moment.

"You're fine. Go ahead. I'll catch up," Mike said.

"Well," Cole looked from Cris to Mike, "as I was telling Detective Vega, my band and I played a gig tonight—last night I guess it is now—at the Country Tradition. It's a club downtown. We wrapped up the last set around one thirty and then packed up our equipment like always. I declined the guys' invitation to meet up for breakfast at Paradise Park. I knew Brooke was here alone. She wasn't a fan of my being away at night." He paused, pursed his lips and bowed his head. He shook his head slowly.

"Take your time, Jon." Cris laid her hand on his arm. "There's no rush."

Mike took the opportunity to scan through the rear windows at what he could see of the home from their position on the patio. He looked back at Jon when he heard him sigh.

Jon took in a deep breath and blew it out slowly. "The guys like to go to Paradise Park after downtown gigs to wind down a bit. I wanted to get home, so I left them around two o'clock. It takes me about fifteen to twenty minutes that time of night to get here from downtown. When I got here—." He paused and exhaled. "Sorry."

Cris looked at Mike. Neither one spoke, but waited for Jon to continue.

"When I got here, I opened the garage door, as usual. I could see her car was sitting where it always was. I noticed the door to the kitchen was standing open. I knew something was wrong because Brooke would never leave the door open, not even in the middle of the day or on weekends." He looked at Mike and then Cris.

Cris nodded as she looked up from her notes. "Go ahead."

"I didn't pull inside. I opened my door, left the car and shouted for Brooke as I walked through the garage. There was no answer. I came up the steps and—." He forced out a breath and paused. "I became lightheaded when I saw her." His brow wrinkled and his chin quivered. "I called out to her. I thought maybe she'd fallen and hit her head. I couldn't believe—."

"Did you enter the kitchen?"

He nodded. After a moment he said, "Yes. I went to her. I knelt down and bent over her. I put my ear to her mouth to check for her breathing. I couldn't feel anything. Her lips were cool. I knew it wasn't good. I checked her pulse in front of her ear," he put his fingers to his temple, "but I couldn't find one, so I checked her wrist. I still couldn't find one, so I pulled out my cell and called 911."

"What time was it?" Mike interrupted as Jon's speech began to quiver.

"Maybe two-thirty? I'm not sure. It could have been a little later."

Cris noted the time.

"What did you do then?" Mike asked.

"I—kept trying to get her to wake up. I pushed on her chest

several times like the 911 operator told me. I blew into her mouth." He cried. "I should have been here. I just should have been here."

Cris offered him a tissue from her pocket.

Both detectives waited and allowed him to collect his emotions.

"Do you remember whether or not you moved or altered anything in the kitchen?" Mike asked.

Jon looked at Mike as though he wasn't sure what he was asking. "I'm sorry?"

"Did you alter anything with your movements into and out of the kitchen and around your wife such as when you caressed her or gave her CPR. Did her position on the floor change from the way you found her when you first came in?"

"I—when I reached under her to hold her," he moved his hands as he spoke, "her arms were sort of up like this, sort of reaching above her head." He held his arms in the air.

Cris made notes and asked, "Anything else? Do you think you may have moved anything else? Even accidentally? We try to recreate the original scene as best we can."

"Not that I can recall. I wasn't in there but ten, maybe fifteen minutes. As soon as I realized she wasn't coming around, I called 911. I did what they said, but—." He bowed his head and began to sob.

Mike looked at Cris. "Are we getting photos yet?"

"Yes. Carlos should be shooting his video inside." She looked at her wristwatch. "He may even be doing stills by now."

Mike nodded. "Please excuse me. I'll be right back."

Mike walked to the garage door opening. "Officer Goodrich, is our photographer inside?"

"Yes sir. He's been coming back out to his bag there for different lenses, evidence markers and things."

"Carlos," Mike shouted as he stuck his head inside the sunroom door. "Estas aqui?"

"Si, mi amigo." The response came from inside the home. "Un minuto, Sargento."

"Tome su tiempo," Mike said, letting him know he could take his time.

Mike stepped up and into the sunroom. He scanned the kitchen area for anything that could tell him something about what had happened hours earlier. All evidence, both on the victim and around her, pointed to an unevenly matched struggle which ended in her being overpowered. The fact the victim's briefcase, purse, bag of groceries and its contents were on the floor around her, told him it was likely she was surprised by her assailant upon her entering the kitchen. The assailant could have been lying in wait inside the home or may have followed her in.

"Hey, Mike." Covered in white Tyvek from head to toe, Carlos Padilla entered the den from the hallway at the far end of the family room. His mask softened his words.

"Carlos. Are you shooting me some quality photos?"

"Always. I've completed my videos and I've got shots of what look like the suspect attempted to locate valuables throughout the home. An open and virtually empty jewelry case, a lot of open drawers, ransacked closets, and such."

"How much do you have left to do before Cris and I can come in for our walk-through?"

"Give me twenty, maybe thirty minutes. Then, I'll finish these room shots and take my close-ups of the body."

"Bueno."

Carlos was one of the only people with whom Mike was comfortable when speaking Spanish. He didn't fear being judged or corrected if he used the wrong word or pronounced a word incorrectly. Carlos was not hesitant to help him. He knew Mike was trying his best to learn the native language of many of Nashville's newest citizens. Crime was increasing in Hispanic neighborhoods as rapidly as in others and making connections for the sake of the victims and the investigations was critical in his effort to gather the facts.

Mike stepped back out to the patio where Cris was still talking with Jon Cole. He listened as Cris asked Jon questions.

"You said Brooke worked for the Davidson Savings & Loan," Cris said.

"Yes, she was their Manager of Internal Audit. She's been there for about four years. She expressed her interest in working her way into upper management. So, when one of the bank's Assistant Vice Presidents announced he was taking a position with another bank next month, the bank's president added her to the list of those up for the job. She was being considered along with two others from the bank."

"Where is the bank office located?"

"It's near downtown on Church Street."

"Do you know of any issues out of the ordinary she was experiencing at work or anyone she was having trouble with? A customer or another employee?"

He thought for a moment. "Other than the possible promotion, I can't imagine."

"The other two up for the Assistant VP job, do you know their names?" Cris readied her note pad and pen.

"Yes. Brooke told me about them. Marc LeBlanc and Darin Gray."

Cris wrote down the two names and looked up at Mike, likely thinking the same thing.

The listing of potential suspects had begun.

Chapter 6

The Cole Home
Nashville, Tennessee

"Let's talk about your day yesterday, your evening, and your arrival here this morning," Mike said, as he opened his notepad and clicked his rollerball.

"Well, the last time I talked with Brooke—was yesterday morning, before she left for work. We played downtown Monday night, like last night, until one thirty. I got home a little before two thirty and went straight to bed. She was asleep. I got up to go to the bathroom around seven the next morning and saw Brooke collecting her things, getting ready for work. We shared a quick hug and a kiss and—."

"Did you talk?"

He collected his emotions and finally said, "No. When we see each other in the mornings, we normally just hug with no discussion. If we talk, lately anyway, it's during the day on our cellphones once I'm up. We also sometimes text each other."

"Why?"

"In the mornings, I'm barely awake and she's watching me go back to bed as she's leaving for work, so neither of us is in any condition or mood to intelligently share our thoughts."

Mike wrote in his notebook and said, "Go ahead."

"I uh, got up around eleven and ate a small breakfast. I worked on a new tune I've been writing. Then, I got ready and met the guys down at Scott's place in Franklin."

"Scott?" Cris asked.

"Sorry. Scott Lindsey. He's my manager."

"What time was it?"

"Two, two fifteen?"

"And?"

"We ran through some covers Scott wanted us to consider adding to our set."

"Covers?"

"Other people's songs."

"When did it wrap up?"

"We finished around five thirty or five forty-five and went to grab some grub before the show."

"What time did the show start?"

"Our first set starts at eight o'clock."

"So, were all the band members together from two o'clock when you gathered at Scott's until eight o'clock?"

"Uh, let me think." Jon stared at the patio floor, apparently searching his memory. "I don't remember anyone leaving during that time. Scott could probably verify it. I know he was there the entire time. We left his place and then all hooked up at Jack's Barbecue for dinner."

"Can I assume you went to dinner in separate vehicles?"

"Three. Scott's SUV, Bill's car and my car. I knew I would likely be leaving right after the last set."

"Who's Bill?"

"Bill Sands. He's my lead guitar and band leader. He's been with me since Tyler, Tyler, TX. Bill and I went to the same school and played in bands together before we came to Nashville."

"How did you get to the club after dinner?"

"We park in one of the garages or lots downtown and walk. The Country Tradition is only a couple of blocks from Jacks."

"Were you all together at the club? Did anyone leave at any point, maybe during a break?"

"Uh." He thought for a moment. "I don't remember anyone

leaving. Again, you could ask Scott. He was there. He pays more attention to those things. You don't think one of my band members could have—."

"We don't know, but we must check out all possibilities. It's what we do."

Jon gave an accepting nod. "She looks as though she fought her attacker. I know Brooke. Believe me, she fought in whatever way she could. I hope she didn't suffer a lot of pain." He paused. "Can you tell me something?"

"If I can," Cris leaned toward Jon.

"Was she—? Was she raped?"

"We can't be sure yet. We're expecting the Crime Scene Unit any minute and soon afterward the Medical Examiners team. They'll tell us for sure when they get back to the lab and run their tests. It's the only way to know for certain."

"Okay." Jon put his elbows back on the table and his head in his hands. He began to cry.

"Take a minute, Jon. Then we'll continue."

Mike took the opportunity to text Sergeant Hill to see if the Crime Scene Unit was in transit.

"Do you recall anything different about the appearance of your home's interior when you went into the kitchen?" Cris asked.

Jon squinted his brow. "What are you talking about? I guess I wasn't thinking about it at the time."

"Did you notice your wife's things on the floor in the kitchen area?"

"No, I—I didn't. What things do you mean?"

"Her briefcase, purse and some groceries were all scattered across the floor."

"All I noticed," he hesitated, "was Brooke lying in the middle of the kitchen floor looking as if she'd lost a fight. That's all I saw." Jon pressed his lips together.

In order to observe his reactions, Mike watched Jon closely as Cris asked questions.

"Did you or your wife have any high value items in the house which might have attracted attention from someone visiting your home?" Cris asked.

"Brooke owned a few items of jewelry. Her engagement and wedding rings, a few gold items with small stones like necklaces and such she received as gifts from her dad. One necklace was her mom's."

"Are her wedding rings still on her finger?"

"I don't know."

"We'll check. What about you? Did you have anything of value in the home?"

"Not here. All I have worth anything are my guitars and my amp. They're all locked up in the back room at The Country Tradition."

"Did you or your wife own any electronics equipment, computers, and such?"

"Brooke had a laptop and cellphone, both provided by the bank. I have an inexpensive cellphone. The officer there has it." He pointed to Officer Logan.

"Did your wife keep her laptop and phone with her?"

"Yes. She had to, because of work."

"Okay, we'll have the CSU look for them here in a few minutes.

"Did your wife have credit cards?"

"Yes, two."

"You should call and notify the card companies tomorrow," Cris said.

"Oh. I just remembered. I have a 9 millimeter Smith and Wesson semi-automatic pistol in my nightstand. I guess it would be worth something."

"Yes, I'd say so. Do you know the serial number?"

"I have it written down. Yes."

"We'll need it." Mike finished his notes and said, "You can take a break for a few minutes. We're going to make an initial walk-through of your home and we'll be back with some more questions. Let the officer here know if you need anything."

"Thanks."

The two detectives stepped inside the sunroom and closed the door. This was their first opportunity to speak in private.

"Do you believe she surprised a burglar?" Mike asked.

"I don't think so. I called the security company to determine what time the system was armed and what time turned off. It was armed at 13:45 when Jon entered his code and left the house. It was disarmed at 19:03 when Brooke Cole entered her code. Looks more like the killer entered the home after she did."

"So," Mike began, "did you get anything helpful before I got here?"

"Yes," Cris said, "but whether or not it points in the direction of her killer is yet to be determined.

Based on what he's told me, we have a list of people to talk with. He named maybe a dozen folks with enough ties to her or him to require an interview. How many of them had motive or opportunity will require investigation. He gave us permission to search his property while we wait for the warrant."

"Good. I spoke with Carlos while you were talking with Jon." Mike checked his watch. "He should finish soon with his close-up stills. When he does, we'll complete our walk-through so the criminalists can get started when they arrive. How much of the sketches have you done?"

"The primary crime scene area in the kitchen is mostly done. I do need to complete some measurements."

"Okay, Sergeant," Carlos said, as he entered the family room from the hallway. "I'm finished. It's all yours."

"Gracias, mi amigo."

"Let's walk the home now. Afterward, you can finish up your sketches before the criminalists move in to hopefully collect some usable trace evidence."

Chapter 7

The Cole Home
Nashville, Tennessee

Mike moved through the sunroom and into the den like he was navigating a newly discovered Iraqi minefield. Cris was stretching to carefully step inside, or near, his footsteps. Both detectives wore gloves and shoe covers and pulled on their disposable dust masks before moving further into the home. The paper-like masks were worn primarily so the two could talk without concern of depositing their saliva throughout the crime scene.

Everything in the area outside the kitchen appeared to be pristine.

"She, or her housekeeper, is quite thorough." Cris scanned the large room. "Makes me wonder how long it's been since it was cleaned. It could have an effect on the criminalists' work, especially prints, hair and fibers. We'll ask."

Mike pulled out his personal digital recorder and turned it on. He began his monologue notes to himself as they moved toward the kitchen and the victim.

"Ceiling light is on in the kitchen area." Mike's head rotated. "The switch looks to be by the door to the garage. No lights were on in the sunroom when we entered. Carlos Padilla, MNPD photographer, said as he'd moved through the home, he discovered some of the overhead lights in other rooms were already on. These remain on as we enter the home.

"The victim is lying on her back in the kitchen area near the great room. Her head is toward the east which is the direction of the kitchen door to the garage. Her extremities are extended out away from her body in a natural way. Her face reflects a significant contusion on the left cheek, and red markings on both sides of her throat. Petechial hemorrhaging is present beneath the eyes and both eyes show much of their sclera are bright red."

Mike pressed on the victim's body in several places to check for the progress of rigor mortis. The coolness of her body and the progressing stiffness moving from head to toe told him she'd been dead more than eight hours.

"Rigor is well into its cycle," he said. "Her small size will quicken the process."

In the next two to four hours, her slim body would stiffen and remain so for as much as eighteen hours.

"Livor mortis is already complete. The backs of the victim's arms, her hands and the backs of her legs and heels are reddened by the pooling of her blood."

Mike pressed on Brooke Cole's right calf in the area of the red wine colored livor mortis. The failure of the area he pressed to turn white, or blanch, in response to the pressure also verified it had been at least eight hours since her death.

Mike pulled his digital camera from his jacket and took more than a dozen pictures of the body from various angles. He extended the camera out above the victim. Aiming downward and using both hands to stabilize the camera, he began at her head and moving toward her feet no more than twelve inches at a time, he shot ten more close-ups from no more than twenty-four inches above the body.

Mike knew Carlos would capture plenty of high quality photos of the crime scene, but he still preferred to also have his own shots.

He stood. Looking at the back of the camera, he scanned the photos he'd taken. When finished, without moving from his current position, he snapped fifteen more shots of the kitchen-den area around the body where the odd items such as a purse, briefcase and various groceries were located.

He turned to Cris. "We'll need to discover which grocery she stopped at on her way home. They may have cameras so we could see if she was there alone or possibly if she was followed when she left."

Cris made a note.

He squatted near the body and held his position motionless for minutes, inspecting the head and torso area. He pocketed his camera and recorder, then pulled from his shirt pocket a slim high-lumen LED flashlight about the size of a ballpoint pen. Once he'd pushed the button at the rear of the flashlight, he aimed the bright narrow beam across the body. The bright light illuminated the surface area of the victim's torso, but did so at an oblique angle causing anything that might be attached to, or extending from, her clothing to be highlighted.

"Do you have a paper evidence envelope on you?" He asked Cris without looking away from the victim.

Cris patted her pockets. "No, but I can make you a bindle from a sheet out of my notebook if it'll be large enough."

"Good. It'll work."

Cris tore a sheet of paper from her pocket notebook and folded it into a paper receptacle.

Mike tugged on the cuff of his glove to tighten the slack in the fingers. He retracted into a fist all but his index finger and thumb on his right hand. In a slow and determined manner, he again angled the flashlight with his left hand and scanned across the body, his eyes following the light. He reached toward the victim's white blouse, but did not touch it.

Looking as though he'd missed whatever he reached for, Mike pulled his hand back and away from the victim as he stared at his find in the light. He extended his hand toward Cris and her bindle without taking the light or his eyes from his discovery.

Cris pressed the edges of her folded paper causing the top to separate and open.

Mike loosened his closed finger and thumb and allowed the hairs to drop into Cris's improvised evidence envelope.

"Hairs?" Cris asked.

"Three. All similar. Two to three inches long." He slowly shook his head. "Wrong length. Wrong color. Wrong person."

"Excellent," she said.

"I hope so. Seal it and ID it. Put it in one of CSU's envelopes when they arrive. Make sure Wendy gets it and knows where it came from."

"Got it."

Mike scanned the kitchen counters, the cabinets and the floors once more before deciding to proceed through the rest of the house. The random locations of the victim's personal items as well as groceries added supportive evidence to the victim's involvement in some degree of violence prior to her death.

"Okay, are you ready to look through the rest of the home?" Mike gestured toward the hallway exiting the den.

"Sure. Lead on, boss." She chuckled. It was a running joke between Detective Norm Wallace and Cris. Both were partnered with Mike in years past and knew him well enough to joke. He hated being called boss or treated like a typical boss.

He walked slowly as he pulled his recorder out again.

"The first room off the left of the hallway appears to be a guest room. It's been searched for valuables. Dresser drawers are open and the closet has been tossed.

"The hall bath across from this bedroom looks to have been searched. Some drawers are open. Some closed. Possibly looking for drugs. The eighteen inch tiles could produce some usable shoe prints.

"The next room on the right looks to be a multi-purpose room with a desk, lateral file cabinet and two pieces of exercise equipment. Some of the desk drawers are open. The desk has a laptop docking station, but there is no computer, only a small printer, keyboard and mouse."

Mike stepped into the room at the end of the hall.

"At the end of the hallway is a door to the master bedroom. Both the dresser and chest look to have been searched. Drawers are open and the contents are on the floor. Two of the drawers have been pulled from the dresser and are also on the floor. Their contents, mostly clothing, are scattered across the carpet. The jewelry box on top of the dresser looks to be virtually empty. Some pieces of costume jewelry are on the dresser and—." He stopped the recorder and stood staring at the framed photograph on the dresser's top.

"What is it?" Cris asked.

"This older couple. They look familiar."

"How?"

"I'm not sure. Somehow, I know them."

"We'll ask Jon. They may be his parents or her parents."

"Okay."

"Look." Cris stepped toward a small table separating two antique reproduction Queen Anne chairs. She bent down for a closer look at a silver-framed color photo of Jon and Brooke on their wedding day. "She was a beautiful lady."

Mike stepped up next to Cris. "Definitely. Nice looking couple."

Cris shook her head. "Sad."

"Okay." Mike turned his recorder back on. "Both nightstand drawers are open. If there was anything of value in them, it's likely gone. The pistol Jon Cole told us about is not here. The closet door is open. Boxes are open and scattered across the floor as if they were once stacked on the top shelves and were pulled to the floor. Contents of the boxes look to be normal off-season clothing, shoes, boots, sweaters and such."

As they left the master bedroom, Mike turned to Cris. "I'm sure there's an attic of some sort. There. There's the access," he said, pointing to the pull down stairs in the hallway ceiling. He pulled down the collapsible stairs and extended them to the hallway floor. "Be my guest." Mike gestured toward the attic.

Cris climbed the steps until she stood inside the attic. She shined her flashlight from one end to the other and back.

Mike held his recorder high in Cris's direction to capture her words.

"We can inspect it more thoroughly, but it appears to have been rarely used," she shouted down to Mike. "Everything is covered in dust. I see one large long box labeled 'tree', a few smaller cardboard boxes labeled decorations and there's a long zippered clothing bag hanging from a nail high on one of the rafters. Duct tape securing the bag closed at the top of the wooden hanger. Wedding dress, I'd guess."

"Okay. Good," Mike said.

Cris backed down the stairs. Mike collapsed the stairs and lifted them back to the ceiling.

"Is there a basement?"

"Based on the look of the structure and the property's sloping angle, I'd say there's a half basement." Cris began to carefully open closed doors in the home's hallway. After locating a small linen closet, she opened another door. A light, controlled by a motion sensor, came on over a set of steep unpainted wooden stairs leading downward. She looked back at Mike and said, "There is a basement."

She started down the shallow steps, shining her light and questioning the staircase's stability as she went.

"Smells musty, like a basement," Mike said, as he took in the damp stale air that thickened with each step. "Is that a light switch there on the left?" He shined his flashlight.

Cris flipped up the white wall switch when she reached the bottom of the stairs. The small basement was poorly illuminated by a row of single sixty watt light bulbs mounted on three of the floor joists. A black bug of some type with several legs scampered across the floor and away from Cris.

"Smart move." She made sure he was gone before continuing. "Looks like the usual basement junk."

Lawn chairs, a kayak, and fishing equipment were hung from the joists. Numerous boxes of various sizes were stacked in one of the room's spider web-infested corners. Most of the items in the basement were covered in a layer of dust, but the stacks of brown cardboard boxes appeared to be cleaner than everything else.

Cris walked to the boxes as Mike checked out the rest of the dimly lit room. She pulled her assisted-opening pocket knife with a four inch blade from her front pants pocket and sliced easily through the packing tape on one box. She pulled back the flaps and pushed aside sheets of tissue paper revealing a tall stack of colorful posters with a photograph of Jon on stage; and an advertisement for his concert tour with a list of at least thirty or forty U.S. cities with dates. She opened a few other boxes containing rolled up posters in tubes and T-shirts with similar images and tour information.

"Mike."

"Yeah."

"Come over here a second."

Mike crossed the small space and stood next to Cris. "Hmm. Posters and flyers for his upcoming concert tour. Nice photograph. Looks like Jon's going to be a star."

"I'm not so sure," Cris said.

"Why do you say that?"

"Look. The concert dates on all this promotional material— they're for last year."

Chapter 8

The Cole Home
Nashville, Tennessee

As Mike and Cris exited the sunroom they spotted Wendy Egan and Kim Sellers, criminalists for the MNPD Crime Scene Unit. They were outside the garage talking with Officer Goodrich, preparing themselves and their forensic equipment for evidence collection.

"Hey Mike, Cris," Wendy said.

"You ready to get started?" Mike asked.

"Almost." Kim tugged at her Tyvek coveralls.

"It appears, since the sunroom here was still locked when the first officer arrived, the suspect likely entered the home after the victim, through the garage and kitchen doors," Cris said. "His exit path was likely similar, but the overhead garage door was down when the husband arrived, so he must have used the entry door next to the overhead."

"Got it," Wendy said.

"The primary scene is the kitchen area. It appears the struggle took place there and it's where the husband says he found his wife. Several areas throughout the home have been tossed."

"Carlos has finished inside," Mike said. "Let me know when you folks are done. We'll likely be outside with the husband."

"Will do." Wendy and Kim turned back toward their equipment.

Mike and Cris returned to the patio and Jon Cole, who'd crossed his arms atop the patio table and was resting his head there.

"Jon, after walking through your home, we have a couple more questions."

Jon Cole sat up straight and wiped his eyes with his handkerchief.

Mike sat in the patio chair and again leaned toward Jon. "Did Brooke do the housekeeping or did you have a cleaning service?"

"Brooke hired a service that came in each week, on Mondays. Brooke didn't have the time. Her job kept her busy. She was able to log into the bank's mainframe from here so she worked from home a lot."

"I understand. The place looks quite nice. Do you know if the home was cleaned this past Monday?"

"I'm sure it was. The maid comes every week, without fail. She has her own key."

"Okay. We'll need the number for the service."

"It should be in Brooke's phone. If not, I'll try and find their invoice. It should have the number."

"Cris, ask Wendy to check the area for the phone, please."

Mike added this information to his notes. "We walked through your home for a look at what might appear to be disturbed or out of place. We found your basement and located several boxes of promotional items for a U.S. tour. The photos are flattering, but the dates looked to be for last year. Did you tour all those cities last year?"

As Mike formed his question, he could see Jon's realization of what was coming shown in his eyes as he looked down and took his time to answer. "I, uh—I didn't get to tour last year."

"Oh? It appears the graphic promotions were ready."

As she returned to her seat, Cris leaned toward Mike and whispered. "Wendy is checking his wife's phone for fingerprints."

"Thanks."

Jon hesitated, but finally looked up and answered. "Everything was planned. The promotion was falling into place, radio ads and print ads for all the performance locations were bought and in production. It was ramping up to be an awesome tour. My first album was set to be released a couple of weeks before we were to start the tour." Jon acted as though he was ashamed of something.

"What happened?" Cris asked.

He stared down at the patio table. "Brooke. Brooke made me cancel it." He spoke the words like a little boy whose mother told him he couldn't play football because she was afraid he'd be injured.

"What do you mean Brooke made you cancel it?"

He was obviously distraught by her murder and now he had to divulge this distressing fact.

"She demanded I cancel the tour." He looked up at Cris. "She said, if I loved her, I wouldn't do the tour."

"Was she not supportive of your music?"

"To a point." He hesitated. "Brooke liked to be in control of things. She wanted events happening her way and on her schedule." Jon rubbed his hands together as if washing them.

"This sounds as though it may have been predictable," Mike said. "Is this a topic the two of you have butted heads on before?"

Jon nodded slowly. "More than a few times."

"Can I assume she knew all the preparatory work was already done and a large amount of money invested by several folks?"

"Yes. She knew. She said she couldn't help it. She'd changed her mind and didn't want me to go. She'd originally been okay with it, but the closer the date got, the more she was against it."

"I wonder if your supporters weren't upset with you?" Mike asked.

Jon took in a deep breath. "They weren't happy. Scott handled their complaints and bought us some time."

"Time?" Cris asked.

Jon rubbed his face. "Time to develop a plan B; time for Scott to do damage control with the promotors, the venues and all the support people affected by it."

"It must have been an expensive decision for several of your people. Some of them had to have lost a lot of money," Mike said.

Jon nodded. "It was especially costly for Scott. He'd invested several grand already in promotion, fees, deposits and such. He's a great manager and a good friend. I can't believe all the things he does for me."

"He's paid well isn't he?" Cris asked.

"Well, he will be. But he's not compensated until I start making some real money. He's risked quite a bit for me. He believes in me. He's convinced I have a real future in this business." Jon hesitated. "Without the money he's fronted for my sake, I couldn't begin to make things happen. I owe everything to him, and at some point, I will repay him all he's invested on my behalf."

"How much is that?" Mike asked.

"I'm not sure, but it's probably close to a half million dollars, possibly more."

"Seriously?" Cris asked, as she and Mike shared a look.

"Very much so," Jon assured her. "This is an expensive business. I have to move my career along and get the money coming in as soon as possible in order to start paying Scott and the others back for all their support."

"What about your performances such as the Country Tradition?"

"That money barely pays the guys in the band enough to stick with me. Several of them are required to work session gigs on the side to survive. If I didn't pay them first, I wouldn't have a band. These guys are good, but so is everyone else in Nashville."

"That's amazing," Mike said. "I guess, getting started, you need folks like Scott, around to support you. Can I assume Scott is one of the people parked out in front of the house?"

"I'm sure he is. He drives a black Corvette."

"Do you know who else is out there with him?" Cris asked.

"No. He's the only one I called. I've grown accustomed to relying on Scott for so much. I knew he was the one call I had to make."

"Do you have any family here in the Middle Tennessee area?" Mike asked.

"No. All my folks are in Texas. Tyler, Texas."

"Have you spoken with them yet."

"No sir. Not yet."

"Okay. In a while, we'll give you some privacy so you can call home and speak with your family."

"Thank you." Jon nodded. "The officer there has my cell phone."

Mike looked at the uniformed officer who held up the phone. Mike reached out his hand and accepted the phone. He examined the front of the phone. There were close to two dozen missed calls and voicemail.

"Looks like several folks have been trying to reach you. I'd prefer you not respond to them until we let you know it's okay. It"s standard protocol."

"Yes, sir. I understand."

"I won't be able to give your phone back until at least tomorrow. You may want to share this fact with your family when you speak with them."

"Uh. Okay."

"Cris, why don't you go out there and give Jon's friends an update. Make sure we have the names and contact data for all of the ones waiting there. Give them the minimum about what's happened and let them know Jon is in good hands. Tell them we'll talk with each of them in the next twelve to twenty-four hours and for them to stay available and in the area. If there are any conflicts, let me know. Also, ask them to not try and contact Jon. He'll contact them once we let him know it's okay."

"Got it." Cris turned to leave.

"Oh, and Cris."

She turned back toward Mike.

"When you've finished, ask Scott Lindsey to stick around for a few minutes."

"Copy that." Cris turned back toward the driveway and almost ran into an MNPD uniformed officer and a seventy-something grey-haired man casually dressed in khakis and a light Tennessee Titans jacket.

"Detective?" The officer spoke to Cris.

"Yes?"

"This is Mr. Oberleas from two doors down. He says while walking his pup tonight, around seven thirty, he saw a man he'd not seen before walking on the street. He was coming from this direction."

Chapter 9

The Cole Home
Nashville, Tennessee

Mike stood when he overheard what the officer said to Cris.

"Excuse me a minute, Jon?" He started toward the neighbor, listening as he walked.

Cris glanced at Mike as he approached.

"Mr. Oberleas, this is Sergeant Mike Neal."

"I'm pleased to meet you," Oberleas said, as he accepted Mike's handshake.

"Likewise, sir. Thank you for coming forward with this information and sharing it with us. Don't let me interrupt."

"Go ahead, sir." Cris gestured toward Oberleas.

"I was taking my little Susie out for her evening pee. We'd just rounded the far end of our house where it's real grassy. She likes it out there. I keep it cut short 'cause she's short and she don't like the tall grass. You know what I mean?"

"Yes sir. Go ahead."

"Okay. Well, Susie squatted and she started her little growl when we both saw some movement near the street light in front of the Albert's house here, next door between us and the Cole's. I was standing in the shadow of our house so the man couldn't see me, but Susie was out there in the light. It didn't appear he saw her either. At least he didn't pay any attention to her."

"Can you describe this man?"

"Well, he was pretty far away, but I could tell he was wearing black, or at least dark, clothes and he was a big man. Not just tall, but sorta muscled up. Thick. Broad shoulders. Big arms. You know. And he had a full beard. Frankly, he reminded me of one of those wrestlers on the WWF."

"What else could you tell about him, Mr. Oberleas?"

"He was too far away to tell much of anything else. Big, and muscles. That's all I can be sure of. Oh. He was carrying a book under his arm."

"What kind of book?"

"It was hard to tell, but it was a fairly large book, like a coffee table book or an encyclopedia. Not thick, but large. You know." He used his hands to mimic the size of the book.

"Could it have been a computer?"

"Oh, no. It was much too small to be a computer."

"Mr. Oberleas, do you know what a laptop computer is?"

"A what?"

"Laptop. They're small, thin, light weight. About the size of a large book, yet usually much thinner."

"Oooh. Yeah. I've seen those in Sam's Club when my wife and I go shopping. Well, now that you mention it. It could have been one of those things."

"Okay. Good. Anything else you may have noticed and forgotten?"

Oberleas paused, apparently attempting to recall any remaining details. "I don't—. Oh. His shirt had some kind of logo or light colored writing on the left chest area." Oberleas patted above the left side of his chest.

"Could you see the color or shape of the writing?"

"He was too far away."

"Okay. Anything different about his walk? Maybe a limp? Type of shoes he was wearing?"

"No. Pretty normal I'd say. Couldn't see his shoes."

"What time would you say it was when you saw the man?"

"Oh. I'd say—." He paused. "I'd say it was between seven thirty and seven forty-five. Somewhere in there."

Mike gently took the old man's arm. "Let's take a walk and you show me where you were when you spotted this man and where he was. Okay?"

"No problem." The old man started toward the street with Mike.

"I'll talk more with Jon," Cris said.

"Great. Thanks."

"Are you sure you've never seen this man before here in the subdivision?"

"I would remember someone like him. Someone that large."

"Could you tell if he was black, white or Latino?"

"Oh, I'm pretty sure he was a white man. Light skin. Dark hair. Dark beard. I forgot to tell you, didn't I?"

"I didn't ask yet. How long was his hair?"

"Hmm. It wasn't long. Wasn't really short, either. It was hard to tell."

"I understand." Mike scribbled in his pad.

"Do you think you might be able to pick this man from a lineup of several photos?"

"I—uh." He shook his head slowly. "I doubt it. I wasn't able to see his face well, the beard and all, plus he was quite a distance away." Oberleas stopped. "This is our house."

They walked up the driveway and stood at the rear of his home.

"We walked out the back door there next to the garage and stopped here at the end of the house. I was standing there when I saw him." He pointed.

Mike stood close to Oberleas and scanned toward the street. Dawn was approaching, but the street lights were still on. He estimated the distance at approximately seventy to eighty feet.

"Is this the way it looked to you then?"

"Yep. Pretty much like this."

"He was walking in this direction?" Mike pointed right to left.

"Yep."

"Did you watch him until he went out of sight?"

"No. When Susie was done, we went back inside. I didn't think much about the guy at the time. No real reason. We have new families moving in and out. I assumed at the time he was new."

"I understand. We investigate all potential leads. After tonight, if you see anyone resembling this man, I need you to call me.

Would you mind if we exchange phone numbers in case something comes up or you remember something?"

"I reckon so. You are the police."

Mike smiled and handed the elder Oberleas his card.

"You ready?"

"Go," Mike said, as he readied his cell phone. He noted the old man's number in his contacts list. "Thank you, Mr. Oberleas. We appreciate your thoughtfulness. I'm sure Jon Cole will as well."

"Jon and Brooke seemed to be pretty good neighbors. They kept to themselves for the most part. I didn't see either one so much. I'm home most all the time and they seemed to be gone most of the time, other than at night. Brooke is there at night. Well, was there."

Mike nodded.

"Except for the one night, we've never had any trouble with them."

"What night, sir?"

"Yeah. Maybe I shouldn't say anything since Brooke is gone. You're not supposed to talk badly about the dead, you know."

"What do you mean?"

"Well, I found out later. She was upset."

Mike looked at Oberleas without speaking. He tilted his head as if to say "Go on."

"I was told they had a fight. There was a lot of yelling and screaming. I turned up the TV. My neighbor next-door told me Jon came outside to get in his car. She followed him and continued her complaining. One of our other neighbors got a little overly sensitive and called 911."

"When was this?"

"Last year sometime. Honestly, I don't remember the month. It was warm weather, though. It's been a while. You could ask Jon. Well, maybe not."

"Did you find out why they were arguing?"

"I talked with Jon a couple of weeks later when I was mowing the grass and saw him in the back yard. He walked over and apologized for the disturbance. He said he and his wife had a disagreement over his road tour. Nice kid. Respectful. He must have been raised right."

"I hope so."

Chapter 10

The Cole Home
Nashville, Tennessee

"So, Jon. Was Brooke content at work, or do you know if she was dealing with any kind of stressful issues there? Anything she may have alluded to that was bothering her?"

"She didn't say anything about any kind of trouble. I know she was being considered for the upcoming assistant vice president position I told you about."

Cris nodded as she made notes.

"Otherwise, I don't know of anything unusual."

"So, she was ambitious?"

"Yes. Very much so."

"Did she say anything to you about her relationship with the other two candidates?"

"She's said in the past they seemed to always treat her with respect, but she'd begun to question their motives. She was concerned her gender might play a role in her chances of acceptance for the position."

"Oh? Why?"

"Brooke has a young friend, a guy, Lee Parrish, who's in training at the bank. He's a couple of years out of college, a fellow alumnus of hers from University of Alabama. An accounting major, she said. She texted me the other day to tell me Lee overheard the two candidates talking in the men's room. He was confident they were talking about her although they did not call her by name. He said he recognized their voices. He also told Brooke he couldn't be sure, but he understood them to say something involving the phrase, 'it should take her out of the competition'. Lee told her their conversation stopped abruptly soon afterward. He thought they must have realized someone was in one of the stalls and they quickly left the restroom."

"Was this the first time she'd mentioned anything like this occurring at work?"

"She'd talked about the upcoming vacancy and her interest in the job ever since she heard of the opening coming up. This is the first time she'd mentioned anything about the competition for the job possibly becoming heated."

"Did Brooke share any type of social relationship with these two or any others at work?"

"I'm not sure to what degree. I know she's gone out after work for dinner or drinks with some of her fellow workers, but who they were, I'm not sure. I've heard her speak several times of another lady she liked who works there, Patti Woods, I think."

Cris noted the name. "Good. Did Brooke drink much?"

"Rarely. She enjoyed white wine, Pinot Grigio was her favorite. She told me once she was concerned about what happens to a person's discretion when it's bathed in alcohol."

"She was right. Inhibitions have been known to disappear, along with good common sense, as the result. What about drugs?"

"I'm sorry?"

"Did Brooke ever use drugs of any kind?"

"She had a low dose prescription for Xanax. She'd had it since shortly after her mom passed. Brooke had a history of panic attacks. The Xanax helped her when she took them, but she rarely took them anymore.

"She was afraid she would have an attack when I wasn't here to help calm her, so she kept the prescription in her purse. I was concerned about it too, but the doctor explained to us both what she should do if it happened."

"Is Xanax the only drug she used?"

"Other than over-the-counter meds, yes."

Cris added to her notes.

"Did you ever meet the two guys she was in competition with for the promotion," Cris read from her notes, "LeBlanc and Gray?"

"Not that I remember. I generally didn't attend bank functions that called for a spouse's attendance. I could tell Brooke wasn't so anxious for me to get involved with her corporate life. I'm more the blue jeans type. I went to a banquet with her a year or so ago and she ended up getting real upset and we left early."

"Why? What happened?"

"After dinner when everyone visited the cash bar and began to marinate in their chosen poison, the socializing began. A crowd sort of accumulated at our table and she became annoyed by it."

"Let me guess," Cris said. "From your appearance, I'd say they were all, or mostly, young women?"

"Yeah. Brooke didn't care for it. She never understood, I can't push this kind of attention away. It would be a death knell for a person with a performing career. The people who spend the most money on artists like me are people like those young women.

"So, after we stepped away from the table to 'get a breath of fresh air', I got her calmed down enough to talk about it. Once calm, she gave her bosses the old headache excuse and we left. She was never one to enjoy sharing me or my time with anyone."

"Was this part of her motivation to demand you cancel the concert tour?"

"I guess so. Brooke wanted a husband with a normal job who worked in the daytime, like her, and then came home at night to sit, talk and share the day's issues."

Cris nodded.

"She was never happy with anything having to do with my music career. The fact so many experienced people felt confident of my chances to be a success had little impact on her. I don't believe she wanted me to be successful. She knew the more I accomplished, and the more money I made, the less time I would be able to spend at home with her."

"Didn't she realize all this before you were married?"

Jon hesitated. "Honestly, I don't think she ever truly believed I would become successful. She knew about all the thousands of talented people who come to Nashville and never make it. She saw me as one of them, facing high levels of competition and low chances of success. I believe it's what she wanted to see. This way I would give up, get a normal job and be home with her at night and on weekends."

"But, you didn't give up."

"No. I couldn't" He shook his head. "And, I owe it all to Scott Lindsey. I wanted to give up and end the bickering with Brooke. It was taking a toll on me and our relationship. Scott's commitment and devotion wouldn't let me.

"He believed in me from the beginning when he heard me sing one of my songs. It was at an afternoon get together by a bunch of music industry folks down in Leiper's Fork. After my song, he asked me to talk with him. I liked what he said and somehow I knew he was what I needed to take my career forward."

"You write songs as well as sing and perform?"

"Yes, ma'am. I enjoy writing. Scott has exposed several of my tunes to some pretty successful folks in town. A couple of my songs are set to go on the next albums of two popular country recording artists. Scott asked me not to talk about them until we're sure they're on the song list."

"I understand. Congratulations."

"Thank you. I'm awfully proud. Kinda gives me credibility."

"For sure." Cris made more notes and looked up to see Mike come around the end of the house and head toward the patio.

"Jon, please excuse me a minute." Cris approached Mike so they could speak in private.

"Did you learn anything from the neighbor?"

"Yes. Mr. Oberleas described the man he spotted walking away from the area earlier last evening as tall, muscular and probably two fifty or more. Dressed in black or dark clothing, with dark hair and a beard.

"If this large man is our suspect and he was involved in a scuffle with the victim, even though she is much smaller, he is likely to have worked himself into a sweat. I know from experience it doesn't take much for big guys like Norm to get hot and sweaty. If the man he spotted is the guy and he did sweat, there's a chance we may be able to collect some trace evidence of sweat on the floor around the victim or even on her clothing."

"It's worth a shot," Cris said.

"I'll ask Wendy to make sure those searches get added to her plan of action. Also, Mr. Oberleas shared some interesting information about the Coles and their past."

"Oh, really?"

"Seems they had an occasion when one of their marital confrontations came outside. Several of the neighbors were able to hear the exchange and one even called 911."

"Did it get physical?"

"No evidence it did," Mike said.

"Jon doesn't seem the type to manhandle his wife, but then we've seen them all."

"Yes. I've been fooled by people more times than I care to count. However, evidence has always been honest with me."

"People can lie," Cris said, "evidence doesn't."

"Scott," Jon said, as he sprang to his feet, pushing his chair back from the patio table.

Mike and Cris watched as Jon walked toward his manager's outstretched arms.

"Hey, buddy. I am so sorry." Scott Lindsey held Jon as he began to cry again.

"I can't believe this. Why me? I should have been here. This wouldn't have happened."

"Jon, this could have happened to anyone. It could have happened even if you were here. You could have been killed as well."

"She always wanted me here with her at night."

The two men released their hug, but Scott kept his arm around Jon's shoulder.

"You could have been caught in traffic and late getting home. Any number of things could have come into play. It's not your fault."

"Do *you* know yet what happened?" Scott looked at Mike.

"Scott—this is Sergeant Neal and Detective Vega," Jon said. "Detectives, this is my manager, Scott Lindsey."

Jon wiped his eyes as Mike and Cris shook hands with Scott.

"We can't be certain yet, but a good bit of the house was tossed as if the suspect may have been looking for valuables. It could be the primary motive and it could be an afterthought. Our criminalists are going through the home now searching for any evidence which can tell us more than we now know."

"Scott, I get the impression from Jon you are the closest thing to family he has in the Nashville area."

"That's probably right." Scott looked at Jon. "He's definitely a member of my family."

"Since we can't allow him to stay here tonight or possibly even the next few nights, can he stay at your house? If not, we can get him a hotel room."

"Oh, no. It won't be necessary. Jon's always welcome at my house. And, if he likes, I have a friend who has an apartment house. He always has vacancies."

"Is it okay with you, Jon?" Mike asked.

"Yes, sir."

"Okay. We're going to want to talk with both of you some more tonight before we can let you leave and maybe again in the morning at our office in the Criminal Justice Center. Do you know where it's located?"

"I'm not sure, but if you give me the address, I'll find it."

"Cris can text Scott the address."

"Copy that," Cris agreed.

"Can I get some clothes from my bedroom closet? I need some jeans and a few shirts."

"Jon, if you'll tell me which items you need, after our CSU and Medical Examiner's team are finished, I'll bring them out to you. But, it may be a while."

"Thanks, detective."

Chapter 11

Jon Cole told Cris he knew of no one whose appearance matched the description given by his neighbor Mr. Oberleas.

Jon was now at the Crime Scene Unit truck, currently parked in his driveway, providing Wendy with a buccal swab of his DNA, his fingerprints and several head hairs, some pulled out and some cut. While Jon was occupied, Mike and Cris took the opportunity to talk with Scott Lindsey on the patio.

"Scott, Cris and I appreciate you giving up sleep and hanging with us while we try to determine what's happened here, who's involved and if possible, why it happened."

"No problem. Jon is a great kid. He's like a son to me. I can't imagine what he must be going through right now. I wish there was something more I could do to—."

"Maybe there is. According to Jon, you two are pretty close. Sounds like you admire him as much as he looks up to you. You may know things, without realizing it, which can help us figure all this out."

"I hope so. Believe me."

All three took their seats at the patio table.

"Tell us about Jon and his wife. How long have you known them?"

"I met Jon about two years ago at Luke Kilgore's place down in Leiper's Fork. I assume you both know who Luke is?"

"Everyone knows country music's most prolific hit song writer," Mike said, as Cris nodded her agreement.

"Luke's got a hundred and eighty acres of mostly cleared pasture land where he runs a small herd of Santa Gertrudis, a few dozen head of Black Angus and some quarter horses.

"Luke likes to throw these Texas style barbecues, pit-cooking entire hogs and half a steer. Then he impresses everyone with how he's recreated the Kilgore family home place here in Tennessee and moved his momma up here to live with him and his family.

"A friend of mine, who spotted me walking through the festivities, grabbed me and introduced me to Jon, the young lady he was with and a couple of others who were gathered there in a huddle. Jon told me weeks later, Luke heard he was from Tyler, TX and that's all it took. He sent word to invite him."

"Is Luke from Tyler, too?" Cris asked.

"No, Luke's from Longview. But, they're only thirty miles apart. 'In Texas,' Kilgore told me, 'that's next door neighbors.'"

"What happened then?"

"That afternoon a few of us, maybe a dozen or so, were sitting around a couple of picnic tables in the shade drinking Jack Daniel's and telling our wildest stories about this crazy business. Somebody pulled a guitar from its case, shoved it at Jon and asked him to sing one of his songs. By the time he hit the song's chorus the second time, I started looking around to see if the other artist managers were anywhere close by. Luckily none were near us. I knew he and I had to talk. Sometimes, after you've been around a while, you can tell. At least I can.

"Shortly after his song, I asked him to walk with me down to the barn so we could get a look at Luke's horses. He knew I wasn't going to talk about horses. Two days later we signed an agreement."

"That simple?" Mike asked.

"That simple."

"I can't believe no one else had wrangled him in. I guess I was lucky. Right place. Right time. Karma. Blessing from above. Whatever it was, I still give thanks when I say my prayers."

"Tell me," Mike said. "Who had the most to gain from Brooke's death?"

"Hmm." Scott sat silent for a moment. "That's a hard one to answer."

"Why?"

"I don't know all the folks who might be in a position to benefit from Brooke's passing. I don't know much about her family situation, as far as parents and siblings and such. I've met Brooke several times, but she was always quiet, spent considerable time distracted by her cell phone and frequently acted as though she'd rather be somewhere else. Other than that, all I know about her is what Jon's told me."

"What's he told you?" Cris asked.

"According to him, she was driven, especially in her work. Always busy. Liked to control things; have things happening her way. Kinda sounds like positive traits for a bank auditor, but maybe not so much for a marriage partner."

"What else has Jon told you?" Mike asked.

"Not long ago, he mentioned she was in consideration for a new job at the bank. Assistant VP, I think he said. Jon wasn't surprised, based on her diligence. He said her boss, the president, always thought highly of her. Anything else, I guess you'd need to ask Jon."

Cris was documenting more of their discussion when Mike said, "So, tell us about the music business and if the ugliness we hear about it is actually the way it is."

"I'm not sure what you've heard, but the odds are if it's ugly and unbelievable—it's likely true. In general, the public only gets to see the glitz and the glamour afforded the upper crust, the top five percent or so of the stars. This is the bait causing so many to sell their souls for a chance at stardom.

"For the most part, the ugliest portion of the business, the underbelly as they say, stays hidden beneath the carcasses of all those who searched for fame and failed. Sadly, those poor bastards are in the majority."

Mike was beginning to suspect he was going to get more in response to his question than he'd anticipated, or wanted. He decided to continue the topic in hopes it could move the investigation forward.

"Like all industries, ours is out to make a profit. Not just as much profit as people deserve, but as much profit as possible, regardless of who gets screwed to generate it. Don't get me wrong. There are good and honest people in this business. But, there are not enough of them."

"It's sort of sad," Cris said.

"Yes, I agree. I have tried my best throughout my career in this den of thieves to retain my integrity and be one of the honorable ones. Sometimes, when you find yourself up against one of these slick-skinned reptiles with fangs and venom at the ready, you have a decision to make. Either you find a way to alter your methods in order to compete with theirs, or you and your client learn to lose. It's my responsibility to take care of my clients and move them toward their goals. I'm not afraid to get down in the mud and fight for them. I've been there. I've won, and I've lost. It could be one of the reasons I'm still in the business and I've never had to want for clients to represent."

Cris nodded. "No doubt. What are your primary responsibilities as an artist's manager; and who else is involved in helping to make Jon successful?"

"As his manager, I am primarily responsible for making decisions on about anything Jon does daily that supports and promotes his success and his future."

"How do you make sure you are doing that?" Mike asked.

"I've been at it long enough. I'm able to rely on my gut instincts and twenty-two years of artist management experience."

"That's a lot of experience."

"More than most. Some of my experience has come from success and some from failure. But today, in our business, much of what each artist goes through has been done before, many times. Both the artist and I, as their manager, learn from our successes together and hopefully, I can help them learn vicariously from my, and others', past failures so they don't go through it themselves. I've managed almost three dozen artists over those years. Some have been successful, some have found moderate success and others have found little beyond disappointment. Like many other managers, my score is about fifty-fifty.

"Some of my clients' success has been driven by significant talent and some has been attained through sheer fortitude along with only above-average talent. It takes all kinds. Charisma is huge. It's one of the reasons Jon has been able to recover from the loss of last year's tour dates. He knows how to connect with an audience better than anyone I've ever managed, or ever met for that matter. He could hold classes on it. The guy is simply lovable."

"He seems like a good kid," Mike said. "Do you think his dream has been affected much by all the stress from the lost tour, not to mention now his wife's death?"

"It's difficult to say how much. Only he knows for sure. So far, he seems to have handled it better than most. He's a pretty strong-willed young man. He grew up in a farm family where playing music was as much a part of life as fried chicken for Sunday dinner. His family is a typical Texas salt-of-the-earth music-loving family. I've met them a few times. They're good people. They know how to raise good kids and teach them standards. I believe he'll be okay. He needs to grieve a while and realize he can still do this and achieve his dream. I'll be there to help him. Like always. My money is on him, in more ways than one." Scott smiled.

Cris looked up from her notes. "What about all the other people Jon's had to deal with? What are they like and what effect have they had on him? Is there anyone with whom he doesn't, as they say in Texas, 'gee-haw'?"

Scott laughed. "Well, Jon has several folks supporting him and his career. Some through financial investment; some simply because they care. He doesn't appear to have any negative issues with anyone I'm aware of.

"I try to keep a concerned eye on everything Jon is involved in. Sometimes it's difficult, but fortunately Jon and I trust each other and he makes a point to involve me in any discussions or decisions made concerning his career."

Cris continued her notes, then stopped with another question, "Who on Jon's list of supporters is most likely to be confrontational?"

Scott chuckled. "Record company people can be aggressive—downright irritating too. You have to watch out for them and know who you're dealing with. Frankly, they're famous for shafting their new artists in order to increase their profits. Some of this is purely intentional deceit on the part of the company's lawyers or management. These are the ones who don't even know the artists.

"Part of it is the fault of some artists themselves, their excitement on getting a record deal, their overall naiveté and their inexperience with contract negotiations. Some of these kids don't even consider their representation until long after they've been signed and screwed. Fortunately, Jon and I hooked up before he and his recording company did. I was able to guide him through their agreement and a few others. He's safe.

"Also, record companies are known for adjusting sales numbers in order to withhold a portion of the artist's royalty money to cover expenses that should have been theirs to pay. There are so many ways in which the artist's royalties can be modified, held back, or used to pay off a fabricated debt. Some would view these methods as unethical, but most of these terms, good or bad, are laid out in the contract. Too often, they are agreed upon and signed by the unsuspecting and ill-prepared, poorly managed, artist."

"I'm getting the impression trusting almost anyone can be a big mistake for a new artist," Cris said.

"There are lessons to be learned in this business. Some are learned quickly and painfully. They're all best learned through the successes and failures of others. The neophyte artist has to have an experienced manager who has already made the journey and knows the way to success."

Chapter 12

The Cole Home
Nashville, Tennessee

"How often do managers like you come across an artist with what you see as Jon's potential?" Mike asked.

"Rarely. But, when you do, you need to recognize the potential quickly before some other perceptive manager takes hold of them and gets them under contract.

"It's kind of like buying a young Thoroughbred race horse. If you know what bloodlines, traits and conformation to look for, you can claim an advantage and make an informed selection on a colt with plausible potential winnings in their future."

"Tell me about the ramifications of last year's tour cancellation following Jon's wife's demands," Mike said. "How do artists, venues, record people and promoters deal with something like this? This had to piss some people off, maybe enough to seek retribution?"

"In most situations, the concerts are not cancelled. They're postponed and rescheduled. Unfortunately, in our case, the dates *had* to be cancelled. We weren't in a position to know what our future options were at the time.

"It's not something taken lightly and the people affected don't forget. Since it wasn't a last minute type of cancellation, some folks were more forgiving than they would've been otherwise. There were escape clauses in some of our venue agreements allowing less painful consequences. Some venues had several months notice and they were able to rebook those dates without a substantial loss."

"Are there ever legal issues to deal with?" Cris asked. "Does Jon have a lawyer?"

"Yes. I have a music business attorney I've used for years. He reviews all our agreements with outside entities and is available to represent Jon whenever needed."

"How does something like this tour cancellation affect an artist's reputation?" Mike asked.

"Not as much if they're sufficiently contrite. Jon issued an apologetic statement on social media claiming his wife was ill and he couldn't be away from her. The way it was written, likely gained him fans rather than losing them. I don't think Brooke cared much for what it said, yet it was her fault he had to do it." Scott paused for a moment. "Last year was a good year and it could have been *huge* for Jon. Instead, he was forced to continue to play local venues, small and moderate-sized clubs in and around the South. All, so he could be at home most all nights. Brooke's demands cost Jon a year of progress, and success. And it cost several of us who believe in, and invest in, him quite a large amount of money."

"What's large?" Cris asked.

"Personally? Loss of the tour expenses cost me well over two hundred thousand dollars."

"Wow," Cris said.

"So you will know, each month, I provide Jon an accurate accounting of every dime I spend on his behalf. I need it for my taxes anyway. To date, I have invested in excess of six hundred and thirty thousand dollars in Jon's success. My commissions have totaled less than twenty-eight grand."

"Wow," Cris said.

"What about the other people on Jon's team?" Mike asked.

"I'm not certain what they've spent or how much they lost on the tour. Most of them won't talk about it. I can't say I blame them. I'm sure their accountants will see the bad news in March or April."

"No doubt," Cris said.

"Some of the tour costs were recoverable, so it helped a bit. But, all together, I'd say his label, his producer, booking agent and promoter lost a million three to a million five. That's in addition to my losses."

"Hmm. Why would Brooke make that demand of him? She had to know his growing popularity would demand this kind of thing at some point," Mike asked.

"I can't speak to all that. I was around Brooke enough to know she was not a fan of Jon's increasing popularity. She seemed to tolerate it, but I'll admit, I wasn't shocked by last year's tantrum. Somehow I'd hoped she would allow Jon his dream, much like he has supported her in her finance career."

"Did Jon ever talk about Brooke's demands or discuss anything that might help explain what happened to cause her to want him to cancel the tour?"

"No. I think, mostly, he was embarrassed by it. He wasn't one to air his dirty laundry around us. If anyone spoke negatively about the tour cancellation or Brooke he always took up for her. My guess, this was a product of his conservative family upbringing."

Cris leaned toward Scott. "With a work schedule like you've described, what about *your* personal life?"

"What personal life?" Scott smiled. "I was divorced within two years of my leap off this music business cliff. My clients are my children and their children are my grandchildren. It's simple. My work *is* my personal life. It's simply the only life I have. I'm okay with it. I enjoy what I do, especially when I can see one of my people like Jon Cole find his place and his fans. That part of it, to me, makes it worth all the negatives. And, when they're successful, I get to be successful too. It works, at least occasionally."

"I'm glad for your sake, but don't you have any downtime? Time to recharge the battery?" Cris asked.

"I try my best to carve out a few hours each week to escape and be alone. I learned a trick from a girlfriend of mine years ago. I sit in silence, cross-legged on the floor in my living room. I concentrate and leave myself. I go to another place where this crazy business doesn't exist. I shut out everything about it and I meditate. It's proven to be of high value for me."

"Well, at least you have that."

"And a bottle of Jack Daniel's." Scott laughed.

Cris smiled.

"Possibly the most difficult part of my job is trying to keep my artists upbeat when so much in their trek toward success is defeating them and bringing them down. And, when we get bad news it seems it's always me who gets to deliver it to them.

"The tour cancellation last year was devastating for Jon. Now, he's lost his wife." Scott slowly shook his head. "I hope he hangs tough. His dream is big enough to pull him through this and, hopefully, beyond. I feel certain he's sufficiently strong-willed, but we're talking about some big-time emotions, love, loss and pain, maybe even fear and anger. Who knows how he'll react?" Scott raised his hands palms up. "All I can do is be there and try to help him keep his eyes on his dream. It's all I know to do."

"Jon's fortunate to have someone like you he can trust," Cris said.

"I hope the new tour in the spring can help him get back on track, especially now, and realize his fans are still there, still wanting him and still waiting for him."

"You have a tour scheduled for this coming year?"

"Yes. It's been in the works for months."

"What about Jon's wife? What if she hadn't been killed?"

"Jon assured us he would talk to her and work it out. He said she wouldn't be a barrier to this new tour. Jon knew if anything happened to shut down this new tour, it would mean the end of his dream."

"Do you know if he'd talked to her yet?"

"I don't know for certain. He told us not to worry about it. So, I let him handle it. She's *his* wife. I give him advice daily on all aspects of his career. I can't manage his marriage too."

Cris nodded her understanding and added to her notes.

"I have a plaque hanging in my office at home. I look at it every day, without fail. I try to live by it, the best I can. It reads: *'Don't expect too much from other people.'*

"I don't know who said it, but my guess is whoever it was, he or she was in this business. This is possibly the wisest advice a person striving to make it in the music business, or any business, could get. I may sound cynical, but it's the way it is."

Cris passed him a sheet of paper. "I need the names and phone numbers of Jon's band members and the industry people you spoke of earlier who are involved in and support his career. I'll need to speak with each of them."

"No problem." He pulled out a pen and his cell phone.

"Just a couple more questions while you're listing those folks. You told us about how little you've received so far from Jon's income. How are you compensated for your services as Jon's manager?" Mike asked.

Scott pulled in a deep breath. "By agreement, I'm to receive a commission on all of Jon's income except his songwriting. The songwriting is all his, earned from his writing talent. I am currently contracted to receive twenty percent of his other income."

"Twenty percent seems like a lot," Cris said, "when you think of how much a big country star makes."

"So far, my commission has amounted to less than five percent of what I've spent out of my pocket promoting and attempting to propel Jon's career forward, hoping for future gains. We've been actively working together close to two years."

"Oh. I didn't realize."

"You see, being an artist manager truly is a gamble. You have no way of knowing if your artist will be a success. No guarantees. You put *your* money and your credibility on the line and then do all you can to make sure the odds remain in your and your client's favor. This may be the reason some people call this place *NashVegas*."

Cris smiled.

"I've invested what anyone would consider a substantial amount of money in Jon's career. I still expect to make a generous return. Otherwise, I wouldn't be in this business.

"To date, my expectations for Jon have not been met. There are plenty of reasons why and plenty of people to blame. I still feel it was money well spent."

"Okay guys, we're all set with Jon's DNA, hair and prints," Wendy said, as she and Jon approached the others on the patio.

"Scott," Mike said, "thanks for your help and also for explaining about your unpredictable music business."

"No problem. Too often, our business reminds me of a game of Texas Hold 'Em. Learning how to best play the hand dealt you and how much to risk is all you truly have control of. You have to quickly determine when to cut your losses and fold. And, when to spot a winning hand and go all in."

"Helps when you know how the game is played," Mike added.

"Exactly." Scott smiled. "Is it okay if we go now?"

"Yes, but Jon wanted to call his family in Texas. Would you allow him to use your phone?"

"Sure."

"We'll have to keep *his* cell phone for now." Mike looked from Jon to Scott.

"I don't mind." Scott looked at Jon and smiled. "He's worth it."

Jon stood and wrapped his arms around Scott, who returned the embrace.

"Thank you."

"No problem, brother." Scott smiled. "Grab your clothes."

"Come on guys," Cris said. "I'll help you get through all the traffic out here."

Chapter 13

The Cole Home
Nashville, Tennessee

Mike and Cris completed their initial discussions with Jon Cole. They sent him off with Scott Lindsey for the next few hours to get some rest and collect his thoughts before putting him through another interview later in the day.

Once Wendy had concluded her evidence collection in the areas on and around the body, the Medical Examiner's team moved in and cautiously placed the victim into a large zippered bag for transport to the Davidson County morgue.

Wendy and her crew were still inside the home, methodically going room by room, collecting all the evidence possible.

The two detectives sat on the patio reviewing the notes from their discussions.

"What are your thoughts so far?" Cris leaned over the patio table toward Mike, anxious for his take on Jon Cole.

As was normal, he took a moment before answering. "So far, Jon doesn't exactly match up with the classic spousal killer. His strong alibi and my early sense of his demeanor cause me to doubt his involvement. But, this is only my initial picture of the man. Things change."

Mike stared through the home's rear windows at Wendy in her Tyvek coveralls as she moved intently through the family room of the Cole home. "Like all of us, I've been fooled before. Hopefully, a little time and a better picture of both the Coles' contacts, and their feedback on Brooke and Jon, will tell us more."

"He seems sincere in his answers and comfortable with any question we've asked," Cris offered, "but then he is a performer."

"Yeah. There's that."

"With dozens of people around him," Cris said, "he has a pretty decent alibi. But, it doesn't mean he couldn't have hired it done."

"True," Mike agreed.

"I'm anxious to see if those hairs from her blouse tell us anything about our killer."

"Without follicles, the chances are limited, but we may still be able to get mitochondrial DNA from the hair cuticle. We can't be sure if they fell out or were cut until Wendy gets them under her microscope. Hell, at this stage for all we know, they could have been planted there as a deception."

"I don't recall ever finding this many similar hairs on a victim unless they were pulled out during a struggle, Cris said."

"It's definitely odd to have a suspect leave this many on his victim. The fact they might have fallen out, rather than being pulled out, is what's puzzling. Assuming they weren't planted, I hope when we discover whoever owns them, he has some left on his head for us to pull a match."

Cris smiled. "Could he be losing his hair and that's why we found so much?"

"Possibly."

"What could be driving it? Balding? Old age? Chemo?"

"Could be any of those, I guess. Or, something else, even more uncommon.

"Hopefully Wendy's vacuum will collect some hair the victim pulled out during her resistance so we'll have some follicles with nuclear DNA. Then we can send it to the FBI's CODIS (Combined DNA Index System) and wait our turn."

"Are you surprised it doesn't appear she was sexually assaulted?" Cris asked. "When victims look like Brooke Cole, they *are* frequently also sexually assaulted in some way."

"I'm somewhat surprised. But, attractive victims aren't always sexually assaulted. But if not, there's usually a reason. Maybe rape was not on his agenda. Maybe his goal was either robbery or murder. Did he come to rob and decide to kill her? Or, did he come to kill her and then decide to rob her?

"We may have to rely on Dr. Jamison's autopsy to tell us for sure, but she doesn't show the normal signs of having been assaulted."

Mike couldn't help thinking about his seventeen-year-old sister Connie's brutal rape and murder twenty-two years ago. Anytime an attractive young woman was the victim of a rape and murder, his thoughts took him back to the night he had to identify her body mere minutes after he arrived back in Nashville from Iraq. He tried to envision what Connie would look like today at thirty-nine.

"She was beautiful," Cris said.

Mike nodded, "Yes. She was." He thought first of his sister and then realized Cris was describing Brooke Cole.

"Could the killer have felt he might be interrupted? And, that could be why he didn't assault her sexually?"

"It could be," Mike said, his focus now back on their victim. "Maybe she was screaming and he feared someone might hear and call 911. However, based upon the next-door neighbor's testament earlier about the Cole's history, the screaming may have been ignored."

"Maybe he couldn't rape her?"

"It's a possibility."

The two detectives sat thinking for a while without speaking.

Mike pulled out his phone and began keying a text message. "I'm asking Dr. Jamison to be sure to swab the victim's entire face and neck for saliva from the killer."

Cris nodded.

"The way she was throttled, I'm confident he was in her face for some period of time. If so, we have a decent chance to recover some of the suspect's saliva."

"Sergeant Neal," Officer Logan said, as he stepped closer to the two detectives.

He'd been so quiet standing his post at the rear of the home, Mike had forgotten he was there.

The detectives turned toward the young uniformed officer. "Yes?"

"I don't mean to be rude, but I hope to become a detective one day and I'm interested in what you were saying about potential saliva on the victim?"

"You're not being rude, officer. We usually have the criminalists or the M.E. swab the victim's face in situations like this one in hopes the killer spoke to the decedent, maybe even yelled at them while in close proximity and deposited spittle on their face.

"We've had more than a few who have kissed or even licked their victims before killing them."

"Or after killing them," Cris added.

"I suspect the purpose was to taunt them, maybe scare them more than anything. I'm hoping this killer was a member of this group. We could use the additional evidence."

"This is interesting," Logan said.

"It'll be even more interesting if we find traces of his DNA," Mike said.

"Cool. Thanks." Logan held up his hand. Sorry to interrupt."

"No problem, officer. Good luck with your goal. Curiosity is a major asset for a good detective."

"And luck is another one," Cris said.

"Amen to that." Mike stood. "I'm going out to the command desk to catch up with Sergeant Hill. I haven't heard if we've located any neighborhood security cameras during our canvasing. I'd love to have a legible photograph of the big man the next door neighbor spotted."

"Good luck."

Cris was scribbling in her notebook as she strolled near the garage. Officer Goodrich stepped into her path and spoke.

"Detective Vega. Do you have a minute?"

"Sure. What's up?"

"I have a couple of questions."

"Okay." She lowered her notebook and looked up at Goodrich's handsome face.

"How is it people think they can murder someone they know and assume they will never show up on the investigator's suspect list? Isn't it common knowledge most killers are known by their victims? I wonder how many killers are actually found in the victim's phone contact list."

Cris smiled. She was already impressed with Goodrich and his interest. It was nice to see he was also inquisitive. She stood with her hands together behind her.

"Yes, in well over half the cases nationwide, killers are known by their victims. The killers' assumption of invulnerability is the same notion adopted by most criminals of any flavor, not only murderers. They honestly believe they're smarter than law enforcement and they can get away with their crimes. Fortunately, it's the advantage we enjoy."

"Advantage?"

"It's the edge we have over most all the culprits. Their assumption is usually based on an elevated self-esteem and a misguided sense of judgment."

"I see. I would assume once we hand the suspects over to our overworked justice system, the attorneys' eagerness to plea down so many of the charges, and the suspects' awareness of this fact, has to bolster the criminals' willingness to commit their crimes without feeling a normal level of risk?"

"So true, Officer Goodrich." Cris nodded.

"One more question," he said.

"Shoot."

"During my own investigation tonight, I observed that when you removed your personal protective equipment none of your fingers, especially on your left hand, appeared to be surrounded by any variety of precious metal or stone."

Cris considered asking him to repeat himself, but she'd heard him clearly. She knew she did. She simply wanted to hear it again. It had been a long while since she was approached in a manner quite so thoughtful and amusing, especially from a uniformed officer. Some didn't have the moxie to address a detective this way. She was enjoying this.

"Your point?"

"So." Goodrich's hands were animated during his speech. "I was wondering."

He scanned the area as if trying to be sure his negotiations were private.

Cris fought back the urge to give a visible reaction to Goodrich's manner. She prepared herself for what appeared to be an approaching invitation.

He looked down from his six foot one perspective directly into Cris's hazel eyes.

"Do you ever get to eat a nice dinner?"

She managed to hold back the smile she wanted to show. "On the rare occasion I'm off duty, I do sometimes consider it."

He nodded. "Do you periodically entertain the concept of being social when said dinner is consumed?"

Impressed and willing to play along, Cris said, "I have been known to experiment with the concept."

"And how did your analyses turn out?"

"I'll admit, the outcomes to many of my experiments have been, how should I say it? Disappointing."

"Mmm." He tilted his head and squinted. "Hate to hear that."

"Well. You should know, since the averages have not been impressive, my standards must be challenging for most fellows."

"I see." He nodded. "I've never been one to shy away from a challenge. So," he paused, "if your standards are up for one more appraisal, I would be willing to risk my ego and provide those standards some willing and interested subject matter."

Cris was enjoying the bilateral repartee. If he was this much fun at a crime scene, he must be a hoot over dinner. "If you're sure you're up for it?"

"Oh, yes." He smiled. "There is no doubt about that."

Cris struggled to hold back her laugh. She finally allowed herself a careful but large smile. "Give me a call in the next couple of days. Assuming we can close this case in time, I'm supposed to be off rotation one day this weekend."

"Copy that. I'll call you." He paused. "I wish you and Sergeant Neal the best of luck with the investigation. For Mr. Cole's sake, and now also for mine." He smiled.

"Thanks, Officer Goodrich."

"You can call me Adam."

"And, you can call me Cris."

"I *will* call you—Cris."

His familiar smile, and her memories of this mornings dream, caused her to ponder as she walked toward her car. She stopped in the Cole driveway, shook her head, started walking again and began to laugh out loud.

Chapter 14

Davidson Savings & Loan
Nashville, Tennessee

It was 09:00. Mike decided his visit to the offices of the Davidson Savings & Loan warranted a clean set of clothes without the crime scene smell he'd gotten used to over the years. No more than twenty minutes at his home and he was on his way.

The short list of bank employees Jon gave him was enough to get him started, and he was confident the discussions with these few would likely produce more.

Mike stepped through the double door entrance and into the large open lobby. He noticed the brushed nickel letters on the wall behind a young lady's head announcing to everyone they'd arrived at the reception desk for the Davidson Savings & Loan.

As he walked toward the receptionist, Mike spotted a man waiting in the lobby to his left and nodded a casual greeting.

The receptionist's head was angled downward as she focused on the computer monitor before her. She spotted Mike as he neared her desk and brought her gaze up to meet his. Her expression morphed from a solemn stare to what appeared to be a forced, yet courteous, greeting.

"Good morning. Welcome to Davidson Savings & Loan. How may I help you?"

"I'm here to see Mr. Thomas Green."

"Do you have an appointment, sir?"

"No." Mike handed her his card and gave her a moment to read it. "If you could let him know I'm here, I'd appreciate it. It's important." He nodded, confirming the importance for the young lady.

"Yes, sir." She picked up the handset to her desk phone.

Mike turned and approached the waiting area. He took a seat and checked his phone for messages. Few people kept him waiting for long. There must be something about keeping the police waiting that caused most folks to reorder their priorities and accelerate their response.

A balding man in his mid-to-late fifties, wearing an expensive looking charcoal gray wool suit, stepped around the receptionist's desk, briefly exchanged respectful smiles with her and followed her nod toward Mike. He extended his right hand.

"Good morning, I'm Tom Green."

"Sergeant Mike Neal, Mr. Green." He offered Green a card.

"If you'll come with me."

Mike followed Green down a lengthy hallway and along the outer hallway of a cubicle farm with twenty plus people randomly straining above their five foot walls to see who was following the bank's power to his corner office.

At the end of the hallway, Green slowed his progress, stopped and turned to face Mike.

"Here we are." He backed up against his door and indicated to Mike he was welcome to come in.

Mike took a seat in one of two high-back leather chairs fronting Green's mahogany desk.

"Thank you."

"What can I help you with today, Sergeant?"

Out of respect, Mike waited as Green took a seat in his desk chair.

"Can I assume you know about Brooke Cole?"

"I must be at a disadvantage. I know she's not arrived yet. I assumed it was due to traffic. So, I'm not sure what you mean."

Mike prepared all of his investigator receptors so he would not miss any part of Green's response, be it verbal or kinesics.

"Mr. Green, last evening Brooke Cole was murdered."

Green's brow wrinkled. He fell back in his chair. "Oh no. Are you sure? Are you sure it's *our* Brooke?"

Mike nodded. "I was at the Cole home most of the night and this morning with Jon, her husband."

Green closed his eyes and expelled through his mouth a large breath. "Do you know what happened?"

"We know *what* happened. We're trying to find out who was involved and why it happened. She was killed inside their home. It appears it happened as she arrived there from work last evening. Her husband found her around two thirty in the morning when he returned from his music venue downtown."

"Oh my. I can't believe this."

"There's a good possibility whomever she spoke with here at the bank before leaving yesterday may have been one of the last to interact with her. They may be able to help us find some answers."

"Okay." Green nodded obviously dazed by the news. "She was so nice and so smart. Her husband must be devastated."

"He is."

"At least she didn't have any kids. She didn't, did she?"

"No," Mike said. "No children."

"What can we do to help you?"

"I need names and contact data for all your team members here, or at any other location, who may have interacted with Brooke yesterday, and especially those who worked with her on a regular basis."

"No problem." He pulled a note pad from his desk and scratched a note. "What else?" He looked up at Mike. He batted his eyes and continued to periodically move his head from side to side as he listened to Mike.

"Tell me about the type of work Brooke did here at the bank."

Green sniffed, then held the back of his index finger beneath his nose. His tears were accompanied by a runny nose.

"Brooke was our Manager of Internal Audit. She was good. So good. She kept the bank on the road and out of the ditches. She was our internal police force, so to speak. Internal auditors worldwide are frequently unsung heroes for banks and corporations of all kinds. She was the best I've worked with."

"Do you know of anything regarding the bank and her work

here that could be involved with or related to someone's desire to take her life?"

He shook his head again before speaking. "Wow. I—I can't come up with anything connected to Brooke or any of her work that might stimulate anyone to want her hurt in any way. It seems so ridiculous to even be talking about this. I'm sure you deal with these things all the time, but it makes no sense to me." He held out his hands, palms up. "I can't think of anything." He pulled out a handkerchief from his pocket and dabbed his eyes.

"Was there possibly something Brooke was working on? Something she may have only recently begun to analyze? Something you may not have been aware of or haven't yet thought of? You called her your internal police force. I know what it's like to be the one who is chasing the truth. We don't always notify everyone of our investigations or our progress. Sometimes it's the best way to move through the ranks unnoticed."

"Good point. I don't know what it could have been. Most of her work was standard procedure. She worked using similar methods on comparable tasks most of the time. Fortunately, we've rarely experienced issues in the areas she's involved in.

"You see, Sarbanes-Oxley requires executives like me to certify the accuracy of the financial numbers we present to our investors and other stakeholders. If the numbers prove to be inaccurate or fraudulent, we can be held responsible. So, folks like me need talented people we can trust, like Brooke, to keep us out of the fire." He looked down. "I don't know what I'm going to do. I have no one else on staff like her. Nobody even close. She was such a rare find."

Mike nodded as he added to his notes. "Would there be evidence of her current audit in her office? Or on her computer? This could possibly answer some questions and point us in a productive direction."

"As particular as Brooke was, I would suspect she would have everything put away and her desk cleared before leaving the office. She kept everything on her PC. She used a bank-issued laptop and rarely, if ever, left here without it."

"I'll need to see her office before I leave today."

"No problem."

"Did she have a planner?"

"I'm quite sure she did. She was likely to have used a digital planner on her PC. I use one of those myself."

"Who can you think of who might benefit in some way from her death?"

"I can't imagine who it could be. I wouldn't know where to start. Surely no one here at the bank or affiliated with us would find her death a benefit. The only thing I can imagine which might produce a threat to her life is something related to her husband's friends or his business. You know, according to what I've heard from the few contacts I have in his business, some of those folks are not so trustworthy. Some even greedy. Have you talked with her husband?"

"We spoke with him and his manager at length last evening and we'll talk more as we progress through the lists of both his and her personal contacts."

"I recall speaking with Brooke on a few occasions when she had a stressed look of dissatisfaction on her face. I was concerned it might be caused by the volume of her work, but she assured me she was fine with her job. She told me she and Jon were having some discussions about his performing and being away at night. She didn't like being home alone so often. I asked if there was anything I could do to help her. She told me no."

"It sounds as though Brooke may not have been as security conscious as she should have been."

"What do you mean?"

"It's rarely a good idea for women, especially young women, to share the fact they are frequently at home alone. If this apparently innocent information is overheard by the wrong person, it can mean unnecessary risk or even worse."

"I see. I have no idea who else she may have shared it with. Is there anything else I can help with?"

"That's enough for now. I will probably want to speak with you again. May I have one of your cards?"

"Absolutely." Green handed Mike a card.

"I'd like to speak with Ms. Patti Woods if she's here. And, I'll need the listing of Brooke's contacts I asked you about earlier."

"Yes," Green said. "I'll have it for you by the time you finish talking with Patti."

"Good."

Both men stood.

"Sergeant, thank you. I hate to hear this tragic news. Brooke will be missed by all of us here. She was such a valuable member of our team." Green's eyes began again to collect tears along his lower lids as he offered Mike his hand.

"Thanks for your help. How do I get to Ms. Woods office?"

"I'll let you use one of our conference rooms and have Patti meet you there. If it's okay?"

"Yes. Thanks."

Chapter 15

Davidson Savings & Loan
Nashville, Tennessee

Jared Reed, a commercial real estate developer in Middle Tennessee, sat in the lobby of the Davidson Savings & Loan, legs crossed, reading and answering email on his smartphone as he waited to see the bank's Vice President for Commercial Loans, Patrick Nichols.

The soft chime of the front door redirected Reed's attention and he looked up from his phone. A physically fit man with short graying hair dressed in a tweed sport jacket with gray slacks approached the receptionist. Reed nodded a casual greeting as the two men noticed each other. He adjusted his phone so he could continue to read his email and also watch the new arrival. He liked to pride himself as a man who was aware of his surroundings.

It wasn't that Reed didn't trust people. He knew most weren't nearly as cagey as he was, but the trusting and unaware folks were always the ones who were easily taken advantage of. He preferred to remain suspicious and to be the one who was prepared to take the advantage.

The receptionist hung up her phone and exchanged some

information with the visitor. He thanked her, unbuttoned his jacket as he pulled out his phone and took a seat in one of the chairs across the lobby from Reed. As he sat, Reed noticed a flash of shiny gold on the man's belt. It wasn't a buckle. It was off-center, to the man's right. Too large to be a buckle, unless this guy was a rodeo cowboy. No. It was a badge.

Reed wondered briefly why a plain clothes cop would be at the bank. He stared at the email on his phone and hoped his curious concern was unfounded. He decided the odds were high that cops had bank accounts and borrowed money from time to time like the rest of us. He speculated the fact that he noticed this cop could be driven by his own illicit designs.

As Reed debated with himself about his new lobby-mate, Thomas Green, the bank's president, walked through the doorway with a reserved half-smile on his face and his right hand offered to the cop. Reed met Green months ago when he opened his commercial account at the DS&L. Reed was unimpressed.

As the cop leaned forward to stand, his right side jacket panel fell open. Scanning over the top of his phone, Reed could see the badge clearly now and, holstered next to it, a matte black semi-automatic pistol. He overheard the cop say the word *Sergeant* as he took Green's extended hand.

The two men disappeared within the bank and, after a few moments of curious consideration, Reed went back to his email.

He was again staring at his phone when Patrick Nichols stepped into the lobby to retrieve him.

"How are things?" Reed asked Nichols as he reached the doorway.

They left the lobby and started down the perimeter aisle outside the cubicles before Nichols answered. "Just another day in paradise."

"Aren't you chipper this morning?"

"Yeah. The result of yet another futile debate with my unyielding and perpetually unhappy wife."

"Why is the cop here?" Reed asked as he took a seat and Nichols shut the door to his office.

"What cop?" Nichols froze in his steps. He stared out his glass wall into the open area housing the bank's cubicle farm, searching for any sign of a uniformed police officer.

"Green just came out to the lobby to greet a plainclothes cop and take him back here somewhere." Reed waved his index finger at Nichols window. "A detective I'd say, based on his appearance."

"Seriously?" Nichols continued to crane his neck.

"Yeah. I saw his badge."

Nichols took his seat behind the desk and faced Reed. "I heard this morning Brooke Cole was killed last night. I would imagine that's why he's here to see Green."

"Who is she? Or, was she?"

"Our Manager of Internal Audit."

"Car accident?"

"No." Nichols stared at Reed. "She was murdered in her home."

"No shit. A domestic issue? Did her husband do it?"

"No idea. They haven't told us."

"How did *you* hear about it?"

"The murder? Darin Gray told me this morning as I came in."

"Who?"

"Darin Gray, he's one of our VP wannabes."

"Oh?"

"He's one of the people who are up for the Assistant VP job opening next month. Brooke was in consideration for the position as well."

"Wow. How did he know about her murder? Do you think *he* killed her?"

"What? No. He's not the type. He didn't say how he knew, but he prides himself at being well-informed. Tries to be everybody's friend. He loves to tell folks things they don't yet know. Darin thinks information equates to intelligence and it will get him somewhere. He's not difficult to manipulate, so he comes in handy sometimes."

"You never know. Those are the ones who do it and get away with it while everyone is looking elsewhere for the killer. What about the other guy who's up for the job?"

"LeBlanc? Maybe. I doubt it."

"LeBlanc." Reed repeated. "It's a great name for a serial killer."

"Give me a break." Nichols sighed as he rocked back in his chair and stared out the glass wall again. "I don't know. The cop being here is enough to make *me* uneasy."

"Why? Did you kill her?"

Nichols looked at Reed. "Hell, no. I was referring to something else." He raised his eyebrows.

"Oh. That."

"Did *you* kill her?" Nichols asked, as a counter attack. "You're a damn site more likely to do it than I am."

"I didn't even know her."

"Does his being here not cause you concern?" Nichols asked.

"Not if he's asking questions about a murder and keeping his nose out of bank business. Besides, I'm just a customer. Remember? I pay interest. You're the one who works here and pulls the strings."

"Nichols leaned forward with elbows on his desk pad. Your hands are as dirty as mine. Dirtier in fact. If I remember right, all this convoluted bullshit was your idea."

"I don't recall you fighting me on it," Reed said. "You jumped on board as soon as I told you it was a way for you to make a buck. You worry too much."

"Yeah. Maybe you don't worry enough. That also concerns me. This cop's presence here is more than sufficient cause for worry."

"Since you're here at the bank everyday doing whatever it is you do, why don't you keep an eye on him and whoever he's talking to. Try to find out anything you can about what he's investigating and where it's taking him. We don't need him stumbling onto anything that might turn his head toward you."

"Or you."

"Yes, or me." Reed said. "You think you can handle this?"

"Screw you."

"No thanks. I get screwed enough already." Reed smiled. "Speaking of getting screwed reminds me. Now that you've put some significant cash in your pocket, are you making any headway on getting your family back together?"

"Not yet." Nichols leaned back in his chair. "I have to be careful with how I explain my new found fortune. I don't need her getting suspicious and spoiling everything."

Reed heard all about Nichols's family issues. One afternoon, while gathering information for his first commercial loan, Nichols spilled his guts on his family conflicts, the failure of his career at the bank and the failure to meet his wife's expectations on maintaining the comfortable lifestyle she was accustomed to while still living at home with her parents.

This was exactly what Reed wanted to hear. The news of Nichols's marital discord opened the door for him to approach Nichols with a plan that would benefit them both substantially. Greed was always a great motivator.

Reed looked at his wristwatch and stood. "I'm going to check back with you later today. I have an appointment with one of my subcontractors in a half hour." He turned back toward Nichols before leaving. "I may need another loan."

"We shouldn't push our luck," Nichols said, "especially with this cop snooping around."

Reed shook his head as he opened the door. "I'll call you."

Chapter 16

Mike sat alone in the small Davidson Savings & Loan conference room reviewing his notes from both his time with Jon Cole last evening and with Brooke Cole's supervisor, bank president, Thomas Green earlier this morning. He was waiting for his next interview when his phone interrupted his thoughts.

"Good morning, Detective."

"Hey, Mike. Do you have a few minutes?" Cris asked.

"Sure. What's up?"

"I checked with Wendy for the name on the grocery receipt and I just left the store where Brooke Cole stopped on her way home yesterday. The manager was helpful. He reviewed his digital video recorder with me. Brooke came into the grocery at 18:20 and left at 18:48. She was alone and the cam facing the parking lot did not show anyone leaving with her or following her."

"Okay."

"And, I ran the Cole's two credit cards and found they didn't use them often."

"Remember," Mike said, "Brooke was a member of the banking

81

community and was described as fastidious by her peers and her husband. I would be surprised to find much use of credit, other than for emergencies. She likely preferred to avoid paying interest."

"Brooke used her cards for occasional clothing purchases and car repairs. Usage went up some at holiday time. But, she paid the balance off each month to, like you said, avoid the interest.

"Jon seldom used his cards. I did find a recent purchase from the Schermerhorn Symphony Center. The record shows six weeks ago he purchased two tickets to a Nashville Symphony performance of Tchaikovsky & Copland. The concert date is still two months away. Why would he do this if he planned to kill her?"

"Maybe he didn't have plans to kill her at the time. Or, maybe he did and he bought these tickets in an attempt to give himself an alibi, to cover himself and his actions. This could help make him look innocent."

"I don't know. So far, he doesn't seem the type to me."

"Don't close any doors," Mike said.

"Doors are all open."

"What did you find out from Verizon?"

"Once I received the signed search warrant, I talked with the carrier. I asked Dean McMurray to help me with the phone's data so we could get access to it sooner." Cris stopped herself. "By the way, Dean's comment was, 'If your killer had also taken the victim's phone, this could all be done even faster by simply chasing down the tower pings and arrest him.'"

"Tell him," Mike said, "his scholarly grasp of the obvious is quite impressive."

"Kinda what I thought," Cris said. "Maybe he should leave the investigating to us."

"I assume the carrier was cooperative?"

"Yes. Dean received the file from Verizon less than an hour ago and, since the volume of data was so small, it took only a few minutes to crunch it and email me a copy."

"What did you get?"

"Over the last thirty days, Brooke's phone showed twenty-three incoming calls from eight different callers, nineteen outgoing calls to seven different numbers, twenty-eight outgoing texts, most to Jon's number, and twenty-three incoming texts, all but two from Jon. She must not get out much since she pinged only nineteen towers in that time and all but five were between the Cole home and the bank."

"Looks like she's sort of a home body. Makes sense, based on what we heard from Jon about her wanting him at home more."

"Correct. I'm not sure about Brooke yet, however Jon doesn't seem to be technologically oriented or else he doesn't take the time. According to Scott, Jon has a considerable fan following, his Facebook page is the only social media effort he's employed. It was actually built and is managed by a guy who's paid by Scott Lindsey. Jon had nothing to do with it. He told me he didn't even know how to sign into his Facebook account.

"As Jon told us, his phone shows him pinging the cell tower near downtown on lower Broad at the range of time covering the approximate time of death, from 18:12 to 02:03."

"At least his cellphone was there. Hard to be sure."

"True. Jon's phone usage revealed a different user profile from Brooke. During the same thirty day period his phone received sixty-eight incoming calls from fourteen different numbers, forty-nine outgoing calls to twelve different numbers, thirty-eight outgoing texts and thirty-three incoming texts. He pinged a bit more towers than Brooke, but most were between their home and downtown and several between those two locations and Scott Lindsey's home in Franklin."

"Did anything unusual float to the surface to grab our attention?"

"We were able to pull names or business names on all the numbers. Not much out of the ordinary. Everyone on Jon's lists, in and out, were tied to his music in some way. Well, except Pizza Hut, Paradise Park and his mom and dad.

"Oh, that reminds me. I spoke with Jon. He called his parents. They have sixty-eight head of beef cattle, a half dozen horses, a small herd of goats and three dogs. They have seven of their cows within days of calving. They'll need to arrange for friends and neighbors to come and take care of their menagerie before they can leave. So, they won't be able to leave for Nashville until sometime Friday.

"By the way, he said his parents have never flown, are afraid to and would be driving up from Tyler."

"My dad wouldn't fly either. It is what it is."

"Okay. Most of the other folks on Jon's contacts were already on my list of players. I was able to get Scott to clarify who they were. Many of the calls were actually to or from Scott or members of Jon's band or support team. I don't think Jon had a life outside music."

"That seems to be part of the Cole's relationship problems."

"Likely. With Brooke's data, most was limited to communication with Jon or her family between the afternoon and around 22:00 each night. But, I found one incoming call received six days ago lasting over an hour from a Charles S. Rosedale. His number was not in her contacts list, so I had it searched and the call originated from Hoover, Alabama. I'd never heard of Hoover, so I asked around and found an officer at the CJC who grew up outside Birmingham, actually in Northport. She said Hoover was sort of like Brentwood. South of town and definitely an upper level income area."

"So, Charles has money? Who is he?"

"Looks that way. He owns a car dealership, actually three of them, in the Birmingham, Tuscaloosa, and Hoover areas."

"How does he know Brooke?"

"I'm getting to that. I found from talking with Jon last night, Brooke went to college at the University of Alabama, so I called them before I called you and had the administration office check their records. Seems he and Brooke graduated the same year, 2008."

"So. Are you thinking he's an old flame who decided to flare up and reconnect, rekindle and possibly reignite?"

"Mike."

"Well?"

"Maybe."

"Maybe?"

"Okay. Yeah. That's what I'm thinking. It's a possibility. However, you're the one handling Brooke's side of this investigation, so I thought you would be the one to drill down and find out the facts."

"Thank you. It sounds like something *you* would love to pursue."

"Gimme a break."

"Just jerking your chain, detective."

"I know. You do it well."

"Thanks. Text me his number and I'll see what I can find out."

"Sure."

"Who are you interviewing next?" Mike asked.

"I'm going to talk with Bill Sands shortly. He's Jon's band leader and long-time friend from Tyler, Texas."

"Good. Hopefully he'll have a helpful perspective. Thanks for running the phone histories. Good work, detective."

"Thanks for saying so—Sergeant. So. Call me when you talk with Rosedale?"

Mike laughed. "I will. I'm about to go into an interview with Brooke's friend here at the bank, Patti Woods. I'll call Mr. Rosedale as soon as I can. It may be this afternoon."

"Good luck."

Mike disconnected the phone and as he leaned over to put his phone in his pocket, the sharp pain in his lower abdomen hit him again.

Chapter 17

Davidson Savings & Loan
Nashville, Tennessee

"Good morning." Mike pushed his chair back from the table and stood. He tried not to allow his pain to show on his face. "I'm Sergeant Mike Neal."

"Hi. I'm Patti, Patti Woods." The young woman had a box of tissues in her hand.

"Please," Mike gestured toward the chair at the end of the long table. "have a seat."

Patti moved slowly toward the chair and sat. Her hair hung straight, cropped just below her ears. A do of convenience for a woman whose social intentions were likely few. Her clothes were simple and modest, corresponding to her hair style and a plump face with little makeup. She did not look to have much in common with Brooke. But, Mike learned long ago to avoid making assumptions, especially about people and their appearance.

Mike stepped to the conference room door and pushed it closed. "I assume you know why I'm here."

She tightened her lips. As she nodded, her brow wrinkled and she pulled two tissues from the box.

"I hear Brooke Cole was your friend. How long did you two work together?"

She dabbed her eyes and her nose. "Brooke came to work here in 2012. I was here almost two years by then."

"What type of work do you do?"

"I'm a Residential Mortgage Loan Officer."

"Did you work closely with Brooke on a regular basis?"

"No. We became friends because we take our lunch at the same time and we were good listeners for each other."

"So, the two of you talked a lot?"

Patti smiled. "Sometimes, we talked so much at lunch, we'd look up at the clock and it would be time to go back to work. We'd barely touched our food. We'd both wrap it up and eat it the next day. If we didn't spend that day talking too." She pulled another tissue from the box. "I'm going to miss her so much." Her voice quivered.

Mike gave her a minute. "Since the two of you shared so much at lunch, did Brooke ever talk about her personal life or about her husband Jon?"

"Oh, yes. She loved Jon."

"What sort of things did she tell you about him or about her home life?"

"Brooke wanted Jon to be happy, but she wanted to be happy, too." Patti hesitated. "Brooke didn't like going home to an empty house. She wanted Jon to be with her more than one or two nights a week. Brooke was torn between being proud of him and having the life she'd dreamed of with him. She was frustrated. I tried to keep her talking about other things so she didn't get depressed about it.

"She'd been confident when they married; Jon would recognize his spousal obligations and step up, as she put it. That he would surrender his futile Nashville musical ambitions and settle into a nice and normal day job. Then, the two of them could come home at night, make dinner, have a glass of wine and chill—together.

"I'll never forget what she said about it, 'Isn't it what young married couples do? But, no. *I* had to fall in love with a damned musician, a musician with *dreams*.'"

"Did she ever talk about divorce?"

"Oh, no. She never brought it up to me, but I can't tell you she never thought about it. She loved him so much, I'm not sure she could ever go through with it."

"What about any mention of affairs outside of marriage?"

"No. She never spoke of anything. I believe she was faithful to Jon."

"Did Brooke discuss with you anything about Jon canceling last year's tour?"

"Yes. She cried a gallon of tears over it. Some of the days around the time the tour was cancelled last year, we took our lunches outside so she wouldn't be embarrassed here inside the bank. She cried the entire lunch hour for several days. She hated asking him to do it, but she couldn't bring herself to handle being alone for so many days and nights. It took a toll on her."

"I take it she didn't consider staying with someone while he was on tour?"

"I doubt it. It would have been a difficult thing for her."

He nodded as he made more notes.

"She also had some panic attacks during this time. Some here and some at home. When she felt one coming on while at work, she would call me to meet her in the ladies room on the fourth floor."

"Did she tell Jon about these episodes?"

"No. She said she didn't. She was afraid it would only make things worse."

"Did you and Brooke talk here at work on this past Tuesday?"

She nodded. "Yes. We had lunch together like always."

"Did she talk about anything unusual? Anything that might have been bothering her or anything out of the ordinary?"

Patti sat quietly for a moment. She looked at the conference room door and leaned forward toward Mike as she placed her forearms on the conference table and spoke softly.

"Brooke was in the middle of another departmental audit. It was her job. She wasn't supposed to talk about the audits with anyone except Mr. Green. This wasn't the first time we'd talked about them, but she knew she could trust me to keep it between us. She said she needed to tell someone."

"I understand."

"Yesterday's lunch was normal. We talked about mostly inconsequential stuff. Later when I was getting ready to leave for the day, I ran into Brooke in the ladies room. I found her bent over one of the sinks with a wad of wet paper towels in her hand. She was holding them against her forehead. I asked if she was sick. She shook her head and said, 'Not in the way you mean.' I thought maybe she was having another panic attack.

"She turned around and leaned her backside against the sink and said, 'When Mr. Green promoted me to Manager of Internal Audit, he told me the job was ideally procedural, hopefully uneventful and occasionally downright boring. He was right—until today.'

"I asked what she was referring to. She explained she'd been auditing the Commercial Loans Department and found some discrepancies."

"Discrepancies?"

"Exactly what I said. She explained there was a parcel of commercially zoned property which was used as collateral on multiple mortgage loans. It wouldn't have been a problem. However, the original property appraisal amount was worth only enough to cover the first loan on the parcel.

"As she looked further, she uncovered loans on other properties supported by questionable documentation. That's when she began to get apprehensive and went to the restroom to try and de-stress.

"She said she knew she had to tell Mr. Green, but she'd decided to do it in the morning since he'd already left for the day; she didn't want to discuss something like this over the phone. She also wanted to sleep on it to prepare the bad news in a more professional manner.

"I'm not convinced her intentions were totally principled. I know Brooke. She knew if she was able to confirm the fraud and point to the culprit, she would surely be in the driver's seat for the Assistant Vice President position coming available next month. This was the opportunity she needed to demonstrate her skills and her value to the bank. She wanted the promotion and wasn't one to let an opportunity like this slip away."

Mike's brow wrinkled. "Who was the borrower? Or borrowers?"

"She didn't say."

"Did she tell you who approved the loans?"

"The loan committee approved the first one. She said the folder for the other loans was missing the committee's approval forms."

"How did the second and subsequent loans make it through approval without adequate collateral?"

"According to Brooke, it appeared to have never made it to the loan committee to start with."

"How can that be?" Mike asked.

"There are only a few people who could do something like that without the loan committee reviewing it."

"Who?"

"Mr. Green or one of our senior managers in Commercial Loans, I guess."

"Who are these managers?"

"Mr. Nichols or Mr. Frederick."

"How well do you know them?"

"Mr. Frederick has a reputation for being demanding and tight with the bank's money. So, I have serious doubts he would consider something like this."

"What about Nichols? How well do you know him?"

"Enough to know I don't care for him," she whispered.

"What do you mean?"

"He is not the most personable individual. He walks around with his nose in the air like he's better than the rest of us. Most folks here see through him. I'll admit, he's had some trying things happen to him in the last year or so. His wife left him and took his boy. That can't be easy to deal with. Maybe he's putting up a front to protect his feelings. But, he's not the only one with an attitude around here."

"Oh?"

"Marc LeBlanc is about as much a jackass as Nichols."

"Isn't he one of the two who were up against Brooke for the Assistant V.P. position?"

"Yes. With Nichols having input on the decision, LeBlanc or Darin Gray had his vote I'm sure. Nichols comes across as an old school male chauvinist. He favors men for management and women for secretarial and clerical positions. With Brooke's fellow candidates both being men, and knowing them like we do, she knew they would likely do their best to eliminate her from consideration. Oh, they smiled in her face and proudly lied that they regarded her their equal and more than qualified for the position. Despite this, she had reliable information confirming what they really thought and what they were willing to do to stop her."

"What kind of information?"

"She told me she found out three weeks ago. A male co-worker here, uninvolved in the promotion process, was in a restroom stall when he overheard LeBlanc and Gray talking as they entered the men's room. They were discussing something they'd uncovered in Brooke's past which would paint her with questionable judgment and a dubious ability to lead. Whatever it was, real or not, it could prevent the executive board from considering her for this, or any, promotion. Depending upon what it was, she was concerned it could even cost her the position she currently held. She was furious. With this claim of questionable credibility, and Nichols already in the men's corner, Brooke was beginning to doubt herself."

Mike did not let Patti know Jon told them about the restroom conversation.

"Have you spoken with Patrick Nichols yet?"

"No. I planned to see him later today."

"You'll be able to spot the things I'm describing. He doesn't hide his prejudices well."

"I'll keep an eye out for it." Mike scribbled some notes. "You said you were in the ladies room when you talked with Brooke? Is it possible someone could have overheard you two talking about the audit? Maybe someone inside one of the stalls?"

"No. We looked in all the stalls. And, we were whispering. Besides, it was late, most folks had already left work."

"Did you tell anyone about Brooke's audit before today?"

She hesitated. "I don't think so."

"Patti. 'I don't think so' is a reluctant way of saying 'yes'."

"Who did you tell and when did you tell them?"

She exhaled a large breath. "After talking with Brooke, I returned to my cubicle to get my purse. While I was shutting down my computer, Darin Gray came by my desk. He'd seen both of us come out of the ladies room and noticed Brooke wiping her eyes. He asked me what was wrong with her. I told him nothing. But, he persisted in his flirting way."

"Do you and Darin have a relationship?"

"We talk. He likes to know everything he can about what goes on at the bank."

"Do you like Darin?"

Patti shrugged. "I guess."

"So, what did you tell him about Brooke and her audit?"

"I—uh. I told him she was in the middle of an audit. He asked who was being audited. I told him." She folded her arms across her chest.

Mike nodded. "Okay." He added to his notes. "Do you know if I can get a look at Brooke's personnel file?"

"You'll probably be able to ask Linda in Human Resources. She can help."

"Linda?"

"Linda Thornton. She's been our Human Resources manager since before I came on board. I can take you to her office when we're through here."

"Is there anything else you feel I need to know?

"I don't know about anything else."

"Okay. If I have any more questions, I'll call you. Okay?"

"Yes. Anything I can do to help Brooke, I'm in." Patti stood and opened the conference room door. "Follow me. Linda's office is on the fourth floor."

She started down the hallway with Mike at her side.

As the elevator doors closed behind them, Mike turned to Patti, "Do you have any thoughts on who may have wanted her gone?"

She spoke softly, "I—I've watched enough television series, news and movies to know how frequently the killer is someone the victim knew. It usually makes sense, at least on those shows, but I can't imagine anyone who knew Brooke would want her dead.

"She had a good spirit. Some folks didn't know her as well as I did, and some may have seen her as unapproachable. Brooke was smart, diligent and focused. But, she was no diplomat."

"I understand." Mike added to his notes.

"I wish I could help you more. I hope you find out who did it and put them away for a long time."

The elevator doors parted.

"Patti. Do you think Jon could have done this?"

She hesitated, then pushed and held the button to close the elevator doors.

"Wow." She faced Mike. "I don't. Based on all the things Brooke has told me over the last couple of years, I can't see it. He doesn't seem the type. I believe he really loved her."

She released the button. The elevator doors opened.

"Did you ever meet Jon?" Mike asked as they stepped into the hallway.

"Oh, yes. A few times. And, from what I could tell, he treated her better than she treated him."

"Really?" Mike scribbled more notes.

"Don't get me wrong. I loved Brooke and I would never criticize her for this. But, she expected Jon to abandon his exciting dreams and follow her into domestic boredom. That's a lot to ask of a handsome young man who already has thousands of adoring fans."

Mike nodded.

"That's my opinion, of course. Personally, I'd love to find a man like Jon." She smiled.

Chapter 18

Criminal Justice Center
Nashville, Tennessee

"Bill, I assume you probably know Jon better than anyone?"

Sands chuckled. "Oh, yeah. Jon and I have known each other since junior high. We met in English class. Mrs. Hull was crazy. She had the most boring monotone voice. She sounded like she was as bored as we were. We called her Mrs. Dull."

He and Cris both laughed.

"We've shared most of our lives. We found out we both owned a guitar and were trying to learn how to play them when we got to know each other. I was a bit farther along in the process than Jon. I had an acoustic guitar and a cheap electric. He had an acoustic his daddy bought him. He'd learned all the most used major chords, but still wasn't able to play any lead riffs or finger pick. I showed him a lot of stuff he hadn't yet got into." Sands leaned back in his chair and smiled as if recalling pleasant memories. "We had so much fun back then. No responsibilities. No problems. Just music. Life was good in Tyler, Texas."

Sands nodded as Cris made notes.

"How would you describe Jon's home environment during those

years? Were you in a position to know?"

"Oh, yeah. I was around his family as much as mine. Jon's mom and dad were farmers. They raised beef cattle and some feed crops. Both were front porch musicians and singers. They used to invite me over on Sunday's after church for dinner. After our meals settled a bit we'd all gather on the porch with our guitars and sing. Jon's mom loved to sing gospel songs, hymns and such. His dad was a big Hank Williams and George Jones fan. Me and Jon, we sneaked in some George Strait and Alan Jackson tunes whenever we could.

"Jon's parents were good God-fearing people. They loved their son and they raised him right. When he wasn't in school, he was feeding cattle or working in the garden or playing his guitar. Life was simple, but happy."

Sands' responses matched up with what Jon told Cris about their past. So far, nothing in his words or body language caused her suspicion.

"It sounds like it. So, what happened to move things forward?"

"Jon was always a singer. And, a good one. I have trouble carrying a tune in a bucket myself. He played good rhythm guitar. I played lead. He and I were asked to play some school assemblies, talent shows and stuff. It built up our confidence. Then we found a bass man and a drummer and we put together a garage band." Sands laughed. "We practiced a set list we could stumble our way through. We thought we were flying high. After several weeks of practicing, we got the chance to play some private parties, a couple of weddings and a grand opening for a freakin' grocery store. I'm telling you. We were the next big thing." He laughed again.

"I remember something Jon said when we were playing the high school homecoming dance in Whitehouse, Texas. The girls were five or six deep asking for his autograph. The rest of us stood off to the side and watched. Hell, we were only sixteen and seventeen years old.

"When the girls got his autograph and some who held his hand or gave him kisses, walked away and kept looking back, he turned to me, laughed and said, 'Is this what it's like to have fans? I could get used to this.'"

"When did things become serious with your music?"

"A few years later, we were playing a country bar in Henderson, Texas one Friday night. This guy in a nice leather jacket and a pair of rattlesnake boots came to our table during a break and told us we sounded real good. He asked Jon a bunch of questions and then handed him a business card and told him to call him if he ever wanted to take his career to the next level. As soon as he left, Jon showed us the card and we all busted out laughing. We were still a bunch of kids having fun. Legal, but still kids."

"Who was he?"

"He was, according to his card anyway, a record producer from Austin, Texas. Assuming, of course, he was not one of those shysters we read about."

"Did Jon ever call him?"

"Not that I know of. I suspect the whole idea scared Jon a bit. We still joke about it and wonder, what if? That guy's discussion with Jon got him thinking seriously about his music and the possibilities. We talked a lot after that night about our chances of doing something meaningful with our music and his songwriting. We talked about moving to Nashville and giving it a chance. It was a dream.

"We were still young and we knew we'd not yet paid our dues, as they say. We decided to work a little longer on polishing up our performance before we jumped into the Music City fray. We'd read stories about several folks who moved too fast, became overly aggressive and the skilled competition swallowed them up. We wanted to learn from all their mistakes and try not to make them ourselves. We wanted our leap toward success to be—successful."

"How long was it before Jon met Scott Lindsey?"

"Five, maybe six years. We played a hell of a lot of gigs between the rattlesnake boot guy's business card and Scott Lindsey's. We had no trouble booking gigs and staying busy in Texas. I know when Jon met Scott and he finally listened to us play, he heard a much improved product over the one in the Henderson bar. That's for sure."

"With all the ladies clinging to Jon, did he ever take advantage?"

Sands chuckled. "Jon was always a good looking guy, even in high school. The women flocked to him like he was the second coming of Elvis. He ate it up. He played their emotions to his advantage, probably much more than *I* know about. But, he never seemed to take any of them seriously, until he met Brooke."

"Why do you think it was different with Brooke?"

"She was easy on the eyes, but she was not like the others. She didn't fawn over him like the rest. She just kinda exposed her charms, her smile and her good looks without all the groupie crap. This was new and interesting to Jon. I could see, soon after she began to come to our shows, Jon was getting hooked. He sat with her and talked during our breaks instead of sitting with the band and our dates like he usually did. We could see what was happening. Honestly, we were concerned about what effect she was having on him, and therefore on us. However Jon went, so also went the band."

"I can imagine. I'm trying to figure out why Brooke became interested in Jon if she didn't like country music or his life as a performer."

Sands moaned. "Yeah. We tried to figure that one out ourselves after he announced their engagement. The whole thing made me nervous. I asked him about it several times. 'Are you sure this is what you want? Is this going to work with your career? Are you sure this won't become a distraction from your goal?' I prodded him to look forward, into the future. He kept telling me she would come around when she saw how successful he would become."

"When did you see her begin the resistance?"

"She didn't begin her push back until a few months after the wedding. After we spent a few late nights playing gigs downtown, some of those nights getting home at two thirty, things didn't sit well with her."

"Did she believe she could pull him away from his music?"

"Who knows what she thought? Jon's music runs deep inside of him. His family instilled it in him like his Texas drawl and his love of this country. In my opinion, she didn't have a prayer of separating him from his music. She didn't realize it." Sands laughed. "Maybe you gotta be from Texas to understand. Pardon me if I seem prejudiced to anything related to Texas. I just am. But, Tennessee is a close number two." He smiled. "You know, T for Texas." He began to sing the old Jimmie Rodgers tune. "T for Tennessee."

Cris smiled. "Believe me. I understand. I'm from Texas too."

"Really?"

"Yes. Houston. I was an officer there, too. I came up here in 2001 to work for the Nashville Police Department."

"Houston's cool," Sands said. "A little flat for me. Love the ocean, but I love my rolling East Texas hills. I guess it's why I like Tennessee. It kinda reminds me of home."

"Tell me about *your* life during those years you and Jon developed your music."

"Well." He hesitated. "My life during our high school years was basically identical to Jon's. Other than the adoring females, of course. We were inseparable as they say."

Sands leaned back in his chair and exhaled. "It was a few years after high school when I made my mistakes."

Chapter 19

Davidson Savings & Loan
Nashville, Tennessee

Patti stopped outside one of the office doors and turned to let Mike know this office was Human Resources.

"Good morning, Linda." Patti remained at the office door and allowed Mike room to enter.

"Hi, Patti."

"Linda Thornton, this is Sergeant Mike Neal with the Nashville Police Department."

"Nice to meet you, Ms. Thornton."

"What can I do for you two this morning?" Spoken tactfully as if she didn't know anything had happened.

"Sergeant Neal would like to ask you a few questions, about Brooke."

"Oh—what a loss." Her smile left her face. "Brooke was such an asset for the bank. I don't know how we'll be able to replace her competence and dedication. Do you know yet what happened?"

"No ma'am," Mike said. "Not yet."

"I'll leave you two to talk. Call me if you need something, Sergeant."

"Thank you Patti," Mike said, "I may want to speak with you again."

"Not a problem." Patti waved as she left the doorway.

"What can I help you with?"

"Patti said I could see you to find out about any performance evaluations, warnings, confrontations or other disciplinary actions, emergency contact information, or benefits provided for Brooke by the bank. I'm sure Mr. Green has approved it."

"Yes, he has. Let me pull her file." She crossed the office to a four-drawer lateral file and opened the top drawer. "Cole. Here it is." She returned to her desk and began to thumb through the file.

"She was so young. How is her husband handling it?"

"He's doing as well as could be expected."

"Okay. It shows here, Brooke's annual evaluations were some of the highest in the bank. It looks like her husband and her father are her emergency contacts. I don't remember any disciplinary issues or confrontations with anyone and I don't see any here in the file." She continued to peruse the file.

She pulled a document from the file and read from it. "Brooke was provided the standard term life insurance coverage for all our middle level managers."

"How much is that?"

"One hundred thousand."

Mike made notes. "Can I assume her husband Jon is listed as the beneficiary?"

"Yes. He is the primary on the company paid policy. The supplementary term coverage, which Brooke added and paid for through payroll deduction, lists Jon as primary and, like the company paid coverage, lists Bonnie Marie Ashton as secondary beneficiary."

Mike looked up at the H.R. Manager and paused to digest what she'd said. "Is that her sister?"

"Yes. Her sister, Bonnie."

Mike leaned back in his chair and gave it some thought.

"How much is the supplementary term policy?"

"Two hundred and fifty thousand."

Mike nodded slowly and wrote the additional amount in his notebook.

"Sergeant, I will need copies of the death certificate in order to request dispersal from our insurance carrier."

"The Davidson County Medical Examiner will provide those once she's completed the autopsy. I'll see you receive one."

"Is there anything else I can help you with?"

"Did you know Brooke well?"

"I'm not sure how to answer. I feel like I knew her. We have shared some enjoyable chats over the last few years. She and Patti were fairly close and she's much more capable of helping you than I am. I do know one thing. Mr. Green was a big fan of Brooke. She did exceptional work for the bank. Brooke was—. She was a good person."

"Do you know of anyone here at the bank or elsewhere who Brooke had trouble getting along with or who may have seen her as something other than a good person?"

"I can't imagine who it could be." She turned her head. "Unless. Well, all I can come up with is the two men she was being considered with for the Assistant V.P. position, LeBlanc and Gray."

"What makes you say this?"

"We try not to foster gossip here, but I've overheard talk. According to the grapevine as they say, these two men seemed to feel Brooke was less qualified than they are."

"Oh?"

"It's what I've heard. Personally, I'd say she was the best of the bunch. When I was asked, I let Mr. Green know my feelings. I guess I'm a little prejudiced. I like seeing women succeed."

"I guess it makes me prejudiced too. My best detective is a lady. Thank you Ms. Thornton, for your time."

"You're welcome. Good luck with your investigation."

"Thank you."

Mike found his way back downstairs and was directed back to Thomas Green's office. Fortunately, Green was walking back to his office as Mike came down the hallway.

"Sergeant. Did you get to speak with Patti?"

"Yes, and Linda Thornton in Human Resources."

"Good."

"I'd like to see Brooke Cole's office now."

"Sure. This way."

Mike followed Green back down the hallway three doors to a closed door on his left. He opened the door and stepped back into the hallway to allow Mike to enter the office. The office looked much like Linda Thornton's office with a wooden desk and a row of black metal file cabinets along one wall. On the desk was a large computer monitor and an empty PC docking station.

Mike looked around the office briefly and turned to Green who was standing at the door.

"Can I assume you have keys to these lateral file cabinets?"

"Yes."

"I'll need you to try and find anything Brooke would have been working on in the last week. Maybe your IT people can tell you what files she'd requested recently.

"I know there is a degree of confidentiality involved, but we are investigating a homicide. If we need a search warrant, we can get one. Try to locate her most recent work."

"I'll do my best."

"I need you to lock her door for now. I've called our locksmith and one of our uniformed officers who will come by the bank this afternoon and secure Brooke's office with a padlock. The office won't be accessible, except through me, until we've completed our investigation. So, if at all possible, try to locate this recent activity before they lock it."

"Okay."

"You and I should talk again," Mike said. "Do you have a few minutes?"

"Certainly. Let's go back to my office."

Green shut his door behind Mike and took his seat behind his desk.

"While talking with Patti, she shared the fact she'd spoken with Brooke in the restroom here before leaving work not long before her death."

"I knew they were friends."

"Yes, but the issue here is what Brooke told her. It seems Brooke was in the process of completing an audit of your Commercial Loans Division. She uncovered what she described to Patti as fraud."

"Are you sure? It's hard to believe."

Mike watched Green's responses to news of the audit. His initial responses appeared to reflect anger.

"I only know what Patti Woods told me. She described Brooke as being in the restroom because she was physically sick as the result of what she'd uncovered. Patti was concerned Brooke was having a panic attack."

"I'll speak to Patrick Nichols and Bob Frederick right away," Green said.

"I must ask you to *not* do that. It could seriously jeopardize our investigation."

"Why?"

"We don't know yet all the variables related to Brooke Cole's murder. We don't know who was involved. Justice for her is currently higher on our priority list than identifying and punishing bank fraud. I must insist you not discuss any of this with *anyone*, not anyone here nor outside the bank, until I let you know otherwise."

"Okay. Whatever you think. Do you feel at this point Brooke's death was connected to this fraud?"

"We have no way of knowing. This is why we can't afford to make assumptions and act before we know the truth. I hope you understand and will help us by maintaining your discretion."

"I understand. The interests of the bank can take a junior position to Brooke's murder investigation. I would ask you to let me know when I can pursue the fraud further."

"I'll have Sergeant Brent Spangler from our Fraud Division contact you as soon as he receives word to begin his investigation. I'm sure you are aware, the FBI will also be called."

"I know." He shook his head. "It's strange. I was reading an email from our corporate office a couple of weeks ago. The topic was fraud in our business. It said, according to certified fraud examiners, an average of five percent of all banking revenue was lost to internal fraud each year in our country. I didn't want to believe it at the time. When it strikes close to home, it becomes reality."

Mike stood and waited for him to walk from behind his desk.

Green handed Mike a sheet of paper. "Here's the list of contacts at the bank I feel Brooke would interact with in her day to day work. It's not a long list. Her work was more or less solitary. She always said she enjoyed working alone."

Green offered Mike his hand and said, "Please let me know if there is anything I can do to help with your investigation. Brooke was—she was special. I don't know of anyone I've worked with in my career who was more dedicated to their work."

"Mr. Green, I assure you we will do our best to determine the truth about what's happened with respect to Brooke's death and, afterward, hopefully the findings of her audit."

"Thank you, Sergeant."

Chapter 20

Criminal Justice Center
Nashville, Tennessee

"What sort of mistakes?" Cris asked Sands.

"I'm not sure what, other than weakness, sent me down the wrong tracks. I'm sure stupidity played a role and lack of focus, another. It may have been my watching Jon's good looks and great voice rally so much attention for himself. It could have done a number on my self-image. I can't be sure. I'm not blaming him. It's all on me. But, for some half-witted reason I got screwed up on drugs and tequila."

"What drugs?"

"You name it, weed, mescaline, peyote, LSD. I even used opiates a few times. Whatever was available and popular at the time." Sands looked down at the table and rubbed his face with his hand. "I had a cousin who was screwed up on the junk. He came to visit from Arkansas and I allowed myself to be influenced by him and his bad decisions."

"How long did this last?"

"A couple of months, or so."

"Was Jon getting high too?"

"Jon? No way. He's too much of a straight-shooter to ever fall into that trap. He's a lot smarter than I am."

"Did you ever get high around Jon?"

"I tried to only get high when I was away from him for a day or so, but it was increasingly difficult. I knew he'd pitch a fit if he knew. Over time, my efforts to hide my sins from him were overtaken by my desire to get stoned. I failed. After seeing me in an altered state a few times and watching my guitar playing suffer, he stopped believing me when I said I'd only been drinking beer. Jon was no fool. He sat me down one day and told me he knew I was using drugs and maybe even becoming an alcoholic."

Cris added to her notes.

"He shamed me pretty bad. He couldn't believe I did it. I felt like such a heel. I'd let down my best friend, the person I cared the most about. I'd jeopardized *my* career and, more importantly, his. I was weak. I knew it. He and I both knew I needed help."

"What happened after your discussion?"

"Fortunately, Jon was more of a friend than I was. He helped me get into a program in Tyler which allowed me to break the hold the drugs and tequila had on me. I stayed there over a month, during which time the band had to cancel our gigs. Man, they were all pissed off at me. But, after a couple of weeks of hearing Jon tell them about my progress, they decided to forgive me. Jon said they began to believe I was going to get past it.

"I was able to leave the facility and rejoin the band. Three more weeks and we were playing booked gigs again. "Jon and I talked a lot after that and frequently too. I know he was keeping me close to be sure I was clean. He kept me on track with my meetings and made sure I wasn't back-sliding."

"We should all have friends like that," she said. "Tell me about how things went when he announced the tour cancellation last year."

Sands was quiet for a moment. He stared down at the table, grunted and then he said, "It was a difficult time. All of us were pumped in anticipation of the tour. We'd begun to see our dreams come alive. Jon had been smiling twenty-four seven." He laughed. "I loved seeing him so thrilled. He showed us some of the promo material with pictures and the tour stop list. Two of us in the band even purchased new guitars for the tour."

He paused.

"Scott called a band meeting at his house. We thought it was another update on the tour and all the variables we would be facing as we moved from town to town on the bus. We went into the meeting laughing and picking on each other about having to live in such close quarters for so long. We thought Jon was late to the meeting. But, he couldn't yet bring himself to face us.

"No. The meeting wasn't about us. The look on Scott's face as he walked into the den told us something was wrong. We waited for him to sit, but he didn't. It got real quiet as everyone began to look from Scott to each other, wondering what was up.

"Scott tried his best to cushion the facts and their effect on the band, but nothing he could have said would have accomplished this. These men had prepared themselves for years. We'd fantasized, like so many others, about becoming part of a successful country act, touring the United States and maybe playing, or receiving an award, at the CMAs. Now the dream was finally coming true. Until Scott's words busted every bubble our dreams and our desires had ever blown. He said, 'Jon has cancelled the tour.'"

"What were their responses? Did anyone get angry?"

"Hell, yeah. It was ugly and loud. Walt Casey was first. He's known for being sorta mouthy anyway. I'll leave out the cursing. He lashed out at Scott, telling him he was supposed to be running the show. With all the work that went into the tour no one, even Jon, should be able to simply pull the plug and cancel it at this point. He said, 'it's a stupid, damned stupid, thing to do.'

"That's when our drummer, Clint Boles spoke up. He spent five minutes telling us what this was going to do to his financial situation, and how the judge was gonna hang him out to dry if he didn't make his alimony payments on time. He said he'd been late several times and the judge already threatened to lock him up once.

"Scott listened to our complaints, but none of them altered the reality he'd shared with us. I asked him to tell us why Jon cancelled the tour. I knew the answer the moment he'd walked in and begun his sermon of bad news, but I wanted the others to hear it from Scott. They wanted to hear it too. Initially, all they'd focused on was the cancellation's effect on themselves.

"Scott began by telling us of the marital turmoil Jon had been experiencing in the last several months. Then he restated what Jon told him. I guess he did it so we saw the bad news as coming from Jon and not from him. Who knows?

"Few of us had any compassion for Brooke at the time. That day, it was all about us and the pain we were going to suffer thanks to her. No one was feeling much empathy for anyone. Maybe a little for Jon. He was the one losing the most, putting up with her and having to, at some point, face us."

"So, Scott was up front about Brooke's pressure on Jon to cancel the tour?"

"Yep. We all knew it was her doings, not Jon's. Jon was as excited about the tour as we were."

Cris scribbled lots of notes. "Okay," she finally said, signaling Sands to continue.

"After the meeting and on the way out to our cars, I knew it was my job to do damage control. I asked the guys to meet me at one of our local burger joints so we could talk and figure some things out."

"Did they all come?"

"All but Clint. He was so upset thinking he would go to jail over all this. He said he was going home and try to figure out which of his possessions he could sell and what he could do to appease the judge and hopefully stay out of jail."

"So, everyone was sufficiently angry with Brooke."

"Safe to say."

"What about Jon?"

"We were able to vent to each other over the next few weeks when we were mad about the tour. Jon didn't have the luxury. When we finally saw him again several days later, I could tell he was pissed off, but he was just as much embarrassed over his wife's behavior. And, he didn't want to hear anyone talk about how much money she was costing everyone."

"Did things get better?"

"Somewhat. We still complained to each other, not to Jon or Scott, of course. We tried to help each other when we could. Scrambling to find other work to support ourselves was not easy when the quality of the competition in this town is first-rate. You need to know someone in addition to being a master musician.

"Scott found us some work as a band, but alone, those few gigs weren't enough. The local gigs downtown, like we were used to playing before the tour was scheduled, were never booked. Other performers snatched up those opportunities since we were supposed to be out of town and unavailable.

"Somehow, we survived. Some of us barely."

"After all the pain from back then, do you see enough animosity remaining for someone on Jon's team to want to end Brooke's life?"

"I think, after several months, everyone who I interact with got over last year's tantrum. Making it financially, somehow meeting our bills and avoiding bankruptcy, helped us."

"What is your personal take on all that's happened?"

"Well." He thought for a moment, then looked at Cris. "Frankly, my opinion, I saw Brooke and her demands as selfish. She wanted what *she* wanted. With her, what Jon worked for all his life took a backseat. I guess what confused me most was how she could profess she loved him and ignore what meant so much to him.

"In the last few months, Jon had become frustrated and was stressed out much of the time over Brooke. It was coming through in his performance. Most folks couldn't tell. His stage presence masked his pain. But, I knew. I've watched him perform for longer than anyone. He's been different.

"He was writing less and the quality of his writing was suffering. He loved her. He loved his music. It was like a ménage à trois. A three-way relationship. He was trying to hold things together with her *and* his music. Both relationships were failing and all three were losing.

"Jon and I talked a lot. More, I'm sure, than with anyone else. I knew Jon loved her too much to leave her. I was watching all three suffer. Him, her *and* his music.

"Jon was so much more tolerant and forgiving than I could have been, but I'm pretty sure he was approaching his limit. There were rumors after the announcement of last year's tour cancellation—Jon came close to losing his recording contract."

Cris stopped writing and looked up from her notes.

"Yeah." Sands nodded his head. "It could have been the last nail in his career's coffin. Jon may have given up after that. I was afraid, at the time, his success may be passing him by. Luckily, Scott worked things out and saved the contract. In turn, he saved Jon."

"And the band."

"Yes, ma'am. And the band. And several others. Losing last year's tour cost the band dearly. It cost a lot of others who fly at a much higher altitude in this business, a lot more. I'm afraid losing the record deal would have ruined everything for everybody."

"What about the upcoming tour this year?"

Sands turned his head and looked Cris in the eye. "You know about it?"

"Scott told us."

Sands hesitated. "Jon told me he'd handle it. He promised Scott and the band. This year's tour would not be cancelled. They were excited to hear it. They all love playing with Jon. But, in reality, a couple of them still weren't convinced."

Chapter 21

Davidson Savings & Loan
Nashville, Tennessee

"Marc LeBlanc?" Mike asked, as LeBlanc entered the conference room.

"Yes."

"I'm Sergeant Mike Neal from the Nashville Police Department."

LeBlanc stepped forward and shook hands with Mike.

"I have a few questions for several folks here at the bank this morning. Have a seat." Mike closed the door.

"Can I assume you've been told, Brooke Cole was murdered last evening in her home."

"I heard a few minutes ago. I was still hoping it wasn't true. What happened?"

"That's what we're investigating. It appears she was killed as she returned home yesterday evening after work."

LeBlanc appeared deflated in his chair. "This is so unbelievable. You see it on the news, but it doesn't register. You feel confident it will never happen to anyone you know."

"Did you interact with Brooke often in your work?"

"Occasionally, not often. She answered to Mr. Green. I spoke with her yesterday afternoon. She was so good at her job. She kept us all between the lines and out of trouble."

"How well did you know Brooke?"

"I only knew her through our work here at the bank. I'm told she'd been here around four years or so. I came on board just short of three years ago from a competitor, Wells Fargo."

"What is your job here?"

"I'm a Senior Commercial Loan Officer."

"So your work didn't interface with Brooke Cole's tasks?"

"Rarely. Brooke, as our Manager of Internal Audit, inspected and analyzed the financial operations of the bank to ensure its compliance with industry and federal guidelines and adherence to established checks and balances. We rarely worked together on anything, which is what most folks here would likely tell you. Brooke's job was more or less policing *our* work, keeping us, and the bank in general, on the straight and narrow."

LeBlanc smiled.

"Tell me about the upcoming Assistant VP vacancy and the candidates being considered for the position."

"Mr. Nichols—."

"Who?" Mike asked, acting as though he didn't know who Nichols was.

"Patrick Nichols, one of our Vice Presidents came to me when he heard about the position coming available. He said he thought the timing was right for me to toss my hat in the ring."

"Why would he come to you with this, instead of one of the other two."

"That's just it. He also went to Darin Gray with the same message. He said he felt we were both qualified and ready."

"Did he also deliver this same information to Brooke Cole?"

LeBlanc hesitated as if his answer might cause concern. "I don't think so."

"Why not?"

"I'm not sure. I saw Brooke in the break room a day or so later. She told me she'd heard about the opening from Mr. Green himself. He recommended her for the job."

"Sounds like that may have been a bit intimidating. Was it?"

"Maybe a little. I've felt throughout the waiting and evaluations, she could have an edge since she's been here longer and enjoyed longer relationships with people like Mr. Green and most of the board members."

"Tell me about the evaluations, the interviews."

"The three of us have interviewed individually with Mr. Green and also with board members in the last few weeks. We've answered what feels like hundreds of questions and provided dozens of documents demonstrating our past performance. I'm confident all three of us presented ourselves as the bank's best option." LeBlanc smiled.

"Are you aware of anything to do with the other two candidates' interviews? Or, are you merely speculating."

"I guess I'm speculating based on my recent experience in the process."

Mike nodded as he made notes in his notebook.

"I'm told one of Mrs. Cole's fellow workers overheard you and the other candidate, Mr. Gray, talking about something involved in a plan to discredit Mrs. Cole. What can you share with me about that?"

"It's a huge misunderstanding." LeBlanc shook his head.

"Oh? Explain it for me." Mike was confident LeBlanc and Gray had more than enough time to conjure up a plausible explanation to absolve themselves of their restroom condemnation of Brooke Cole.

"Well, you see, Darin and I were talking about a client of mine who was pursuing a considerable business loan in an attempt to expand her trucking business. Through a mutual acquaintance, who's also in the freight business, I discovered she had some less than honorable dealings with one of our competitors also here in town.

"As we walked into the restroom, I was in the middle of explaining the situation to Darin and how this latest discovery would take her out of consideration for the loan from us. You see? It was all a misunderstanding." LeBlanc smiled a used car salesman smile that screamed, 'You must buy what I'm selling.'

Mike spent a portion of the last twenty years studying and practicing his skills in kinesics, better known as body language, during his interviews and interrogations. Many of the interviews were with people who committed crimes and were convinced they were much smarter than him and were sure to get away with their illegal acts.

This executive wannabe reminded him of several poor liars Mike had locked up over the years. LeBlanc's mouth was selling one story and his body, especially his eyes and the muscles around them, were exposing a different one. The worst part for LeBlanc and his over-confident approach was, he had no clue his attempt at deception was so obvious.

"Tell me," Mike said. "Why did your toilet talk come to such an abrupt halt once you realized someone was occupying one of the stalls?"

LeBlanc did not appear to have a prepared answer for this question. After stumbling over an expelled breath, he said, "When Darin turned back to me with his index finger at his lips I, like him at the time, was afraid it could be Mr. Green in the stall. He doesn't like us gossiping about our clients. It was merely a self-preservation response."

As Mike focused on LeBlanc and his apparently conjured explanation, he remembered his visit earlier to Mr. Green's office where he recalled seeing the door to a private restroom off the President's office. It's doubtful Mr. Green would ever use the public restroom when he had one of his own.

Mike added to his notes. "Tell me about your thoughts on the viability of Darin Gray as a candidate for Assistant Vice President."

"Hmm. Darin's a good guy. I don't like saying anything critical about him, but—. He's not the kind of leader we need in our upper management group. He has trouble maintaining a level head when things begin to fall apart."

"What makes you say that?"

"I've only worked with Darin for about two years, but I've seen him more than once in situations where he was, without much thought, addressing his team about an issue he found embarrassing. He showed little concern for his people's feelings, their self-image, or the fact ears outside his team could hear his disparaging remarks. I believe him to be short on experience, and he has a short fuse."

"I see. Has he been reprimanded by management for this?"

"I don't suspect they are as aware of it as I am."

"Can I assume you'll be sharing this information with them prior to the Assistant VP decision?"

"I haven't decided. It's a difficult topic with us competing for the position."

"So, no one in his group has addressed this issue with his chain of command either?"

"I don't know."

Mike scribbled several more notes and looked up at LeBlanc. "That should do it for now. I may want to talk with you again as we move into the investigation."

"No problem."

Both men stood.

Mike was confident all he'd heard from LeBlanc was not the truth.

Chapter 22

Jon Cole's Apartment
Nashville, Tennessee

Valerie Webb had been involved in much of Jon Cole's evolution into a popular country music performer and songwriter. Val was Gabe Hanson's assistant and over the last half dozen years, helped him develop and handle several new country artists for their record label. Part of Val's job was to get the new artists trained in professionalism and proficiency on stage as well as any time they were in the public eye. Doing this exercise with Jon Cole was like teaching Alan Jackson to sing a country song.

From the start, she and Gabe had both noticed it. There was something unusual and unexpected about Jon Cole. Many of the required skills which normally had to be taught to nervous, clumsy, new performing artists over several weeks were second nature to Jon. As Gabe once said to Val, 'Jon makes Blake Shelton seem shy'. He was born to perform.

There wasn't anything timid about him, and when he flashed his smile, you smiled too.

His natural ability to use one of his songs to touch the emotions of an audience reminded Val of the late Keith Whitley.

The more she was around Jon, the more she found reasons to be around him. His charisma was irresistible, both professionally and personally.

Val saw in Jon numerous things she'd begun to love. His handsome chiseled face, his trim physique in those tight jeans, his Texas country boy personality and his poetic genius all hooked her and had her thinking long term thoughts. The probability of significant future earnings did not get in the way.

Val herself was a catch. Five foot eight and a buck twenty, green-eyed brunette, she had a shape that was hard to ignore. Val didn't hesitate to try and use her collection of curves to grab and hold Jon's interest.

She saw Jon regularly during the first year of his work with the label and she was confident things were moving along the way she'd hoped. And, then Jon went to a party with two of his bandmates and met Brooke.

Val noticed the difference in Jon immediately. She wasn't sure what it was, but something took his eye from her. Her normal suggestions, and requests to share his free time, were met with excuses about band practice to learn a new song or time he needed alone to finish a new tune he was working on.

She decided to confront him about the changes on a day he was home working on a new tune. She went to his apartment and found no one home. She called his cell and could immediately tell by the background noise. He was in a restaurant.

After the uncomfortable exchanges on who, where, and why, Jon agreed to see her the next day and talk.

Once Jon became enamored by the flaxen-haired female, Val was forced to sit back and watch as Jon's attentions were hijacked by the one Val called 'The Skinny Blonde'. She'd hoped Brooke's attempt to sink her talons into Jon wouldn't work, but unfortunately—it did.

As time passed, Val was forced to accept it. Jon was lost to her. Yet sometimes, fate has a plan of its own, offering up second chances on romance, thought to be lost.

Val felt sincere sympathy for Jon following Brooke's death. She hated that he was hurting like this. No one deserved this kind of suffering. He was a good man who deserved a second chance. She was going to help him secure his second chance, both at his music career and also with her. He shouldn't be required to suffer through this alone.

"Just a minute,"

She heard Jon shout in response to her pressure on the apartment's doorbell button. "Coming."

She saw the peep hole darken, and then saw light through it again. The door opened and Jon stood there shirtless.

"Well, hello."

"Hi." Val smiled. She was glad to see him. She was even more glad to see his bare chest. She'd forgotten about his tattoo of a Jack Daniel's label on his upper left arm. "How are you?" She couldn't help but stare. Her once scarred emotions swelled.

"I'm—. I'm okay." He crossed his arms over his chest when he realized she was surveying his body. "How did you know where I was staying?"

"Gabe told me. Uh, can I come in?"

"Oh, sure. Sorry." Jon stepped back to allow Val into the small apartment Scott rented for him while he transitioned through the trauma of losing his wife. The Nashville Police Department had not yet released his home from crime scene status. Jon still wasn't sure he could be comfortable staying in the house where his wife was murdered only hours ago.

"Thanks."

Jon closed the door. "Have a seat. I'll grab a shirt."

"You don't need to put on a shirt on my account." She smiled.

Jon acted as though he didn't hear her and continued down the hallway toward his bedroom.

"What brings you to this side of town?" He shouted from his bathroom where he was about to shave when he heard the doorbell. As he pulled the Nashville Predators T-shirt over his head, he heard her answer, but not from the living room. She was standing in front of him at the door to his bathroom.

"I came to see you, Jon."

"Oh." He looked at Val and gave her a tight-lipped smile. "Thanks. But, I'll be okay."

"Jon. You're important to us, all of us. We're all concerned about you and what's best for you." She paused. "But, not just for business." She stepped toward Jon and began to stroke his forearm.

"I know. I appreciate all you guys do for me. I really do." He looked down. "It's not easy."

"I understand. It can't be easy. I want to be here for you. I can help you through this, Jon."

He nodded. "I know, but I need some time alone to grieve and kinda sort things out. It's an awful lot to handle all at once."

"I'm sure it is." She looked into his eyes. "I've told you before how I feel about you. It hasn't changed."

He didn't seem sure of how best to respond. "I know. I'm in a difficult place right now. You do understand, don't you?" Jon began to walk back toward the front door.

"I do." Val nodded. "It's difficult, but I do understand."

"Help me by giving me some time. Okay?"

"Okay." She smiled. "I'll try to be patient, but I want you to promise me something."

"What?"

She took his hand. "You have my number. Promise me you'll call me if you need something—anything." She smiled as she backed through the doorway.

"I will. Thank you." Jon raised his hand in a wave and closed the door.

Val pulled in a deep breath and sighed as she walked back to her car. "I'm not going to give up on you Jon," she whispered to herself.

You were taken from me once. It won't happen again.

Chapter 23

Davidson Savings & Loan
Nashville, Tennessee

Mike was reviewing his notes from his discussion with Patti Woods when a shadow came across the conference room table.

"Are you Sergeant Neal?"

Mike stood. "I am." He offered his hand. "And you are?"

"Patrick Nichols."

"Have a seat." Mike closed the door, gestured toward the chair at the table's end and quickly covered his notes.

Nichols appeared to be a bit older than Mike suspected. Brown salt and pepper hair. Mostly salt around the temples. Likely early fifties. Five foot eight, one seventy.

His inexpensive suit had seen several days of wear since its last cleaning and pressing. His tie matched the suit, but the tips of his shirt collar reflected the level of wear past the point when Mike's shirts would be cleaned and dropped at Goodwill.

"Mr. Nichols, tell me about your role here at the bank."

"I'm a Vice President, Commercial Loans."

"I guess it's sort of self-explanatory isn't it?" Mike asked.

"Yes. About thirty percent of our loans are to commercial clients."

"I gather you are aware of the reason I'm here today?"

"I heard this morning about Brooke. She was so young. She didn't even have any kids yet. I guess that was a blessing."

"Do you have kids?"

"A boy. Ben. He's eleven."

"Is he a soccer nut like all the kids these days?"

"Oh, yes. He's a Midfielder, but wants to be a Forward. I don't get to see all his games."

"Oh?"

"My wife and I are separated right now."

"I understand." Thanks to Patti, Mike didn't need to ask more questions about it.

"Mr. Nichols, tell me about your normal interactions with Brooke Cole."

"We didn't see each other much. Brooke's work kept her busy in a secluded environment. She did most of her work alone or working with Tom. Sorry, Mr. Green. She answered to him."

"Right." Mike made some notes. "Tell me about the Assistant VP position Brooke Cole was being considered for."

"The position is more or less a transition job into upper management of the bank. The person in this job will work with each of the bank's Vice Presidents for a period of time and seek out the areas where their skills can best serve the leadership of the organization."

"And, I'm told there were two others in consideration?"

"Yes. Darin Gray and Marc LeBlanc."

"I understand you recommended both these men?"

"Yes."

"Who recommended Brooke Cole?"

"Mr. Green."

"You said she reported to him?"

"Yes."

"Can I assume you also report to him?"

"Yes."

"Did either of these men report to you?"

"Darin Gray works with me quite a bit, but also has other responsibilities."

"So, you know these two men well." Mike said.

"I've worked with them both from time to time over the last couple of years. I don't know them outside of work."

"Have you seen anything in your dealings with either of them to cause you to suspect one of them might be willing to hurt Brooke in order to advance their careers?"

"Oh, no. Neither of them has shown any such traits. They both saw Brooke as equally deserving of consideration."

"Did you see Brooke as deserving of consideration for this step up into upper management?"

"Sure. I don't have the experience with her work that Tom has, but I'm sure he saw her as capable or he wouldn't have recommended her." He paused, appearing to be about to speak again.

"I personally feel upper management is best occupied by men. All the issues women bring into the workplace can more easily be dealt with in the clerical areas."

"Such as?"

"Well, you know, the monthly thing, sick kids and pregnancies. There's always something. They have more issues and have to be away from work more, sometimes without warning. They miss planned meetings and events. It seems to put their work in a second place ranking for them. Men are more able to dedicate themselves to the job. It's much more important in an upper management position."

"I see. Did any of these issues you mentioned create a problem for Brooke Cole in the performance of her job as Manager of Internal Audit?"

"I have no way of knowing, since she reported to Mr. Green."

"If they did," Mike said, "he didn't mention them to me when we spoke earlier."

It looked as if Patti Woods's description of Nichols was spot on.

"Is there anything you can tell me about Brooke Cole that could help point us toward someone who might want her dead?"

"I had such limited experience with her, I can't think of anything that might be of help."

"Okay, Mr. Nichols. I appreciate your time." Mike stood. "I may have reason to speak with you again."

Nichols stood and left the conference room.

Mike went over his notes, adding his thoughts. With this guy's attitude about women, Mike wasn't surprised the man was estranged from his wife.

Nichols may have been resistant to Brooke's consideration for the new job, but he didn't show any obvious signs of being willing to take action against it.

Chapter 24

N-Town Publishing
Nashville, Tennessee

"Good morning. How may I help you?" The young lady at the front desk asked.

Cris offered her card. "Hi, I'm Detective Cris Vega with the Nashville Police Department. I'd like to see Mr. Gabriel Hanson."

"Is he expecting you?"

"I doubt it."

"Let me check to see if he's available." She picked up the handset from the desk phone and pushed one button.

Cris wandered away from the desk in case the girl felt she needed privacy. She heard the sound of the handset being returned to the phone's cradle and turned.

"Mr. Hanson will be right out."

"Thank you."

"I don't mean to be nosey, but is this about Brooke Cole?"

"Yes."

"I hate this for Jon. He is such a great guy."

"Do you know him well?"

"He's one of our most popular young clients. He has such

charisma. The public, ladies and guys alike, can't get enough of him. He's a natural performer."

Cris wondered if the young lady's failure to answer her question might be significant.

"Detective?" A thirty-something man dressed in business casual khakis and a Polo entered the lobby area and approached Cris with his right hand extended.

"Mr. Hanson? Cris Vega with the Nashville Police Department. I'd like to ask you a few questions, if I could?"

"No problem. Follow me. Val, hold my calls please."

"Yes sir." She smiled at Cris as she passed the desk.

Hanson stopped inside the door to a moderate-sized office and extended his arm toward a small conference table. "Have a seat."

Cris pulled the chair beneath her and sat. "Mr. Hanson, help me understand what you do for Jon Cole." She flipped her note pad pages until she located an empty one.

"Call me Gabe."

"Okay, Gabe." She looked at him, waiting for the answer.

"So, when songwriters publish their tunes, they sign a contract transferring ownership of the copyright in the musical composition or group of compositions to the publisher. In exchange for this, the publisher agrees to handle the business and pay royalties to the writer from the song's proceeds. The better a song does in sales or the bigger the star who chooses to record it, the more money it makes for all involved parties. I represent our publishing company and work with Jon and Scott to get Jon's work recorded and heard."

"What about Scott Lindsey?"

"Scott advises Jon in his relations with us because he knows the business. Scott's been around a while. What's in Jon's best interest is frequently in Scott's as well."

"What's interesting is it's not the same here in Nashville as in New York or Los Angeles. Even though there are several folks who've moved here now from the east and west coasts, the culture is still different. It's just as tough to succeed as it ever was. However, when your ass gets kicked here in Music City, they do it with a smile on their face, a wink and a 'Bless your heart'."

Cris laughed. "Tell me about how things went when Jon cancelled his tour last year."

Hanson grunted. "Things were not good then. Jon Cole, to this day, doesn't realize how close he came to losing everything. I'm sure Scott knows. Every one of us who supported him and have beaucoup cash and time invested in him and his endeavors were ready to toss in the towel. Some of us had seen family interference like this before and we were suspicious this was going to be another roadblock."

"Why didn't you call it quits?"

"Scott Lindsey."

"Oh?"

"Jon Cole has a lot going for him. More than most. But nothing he brings to the table is as significant for his success as Scott Lindsey."

"That's quite a testimony."

"Scott Lindsey is a pro. He has made other people into stars. He has a proven track record. If I could have anyone managing all our artists, it would be him. He's willing to do whatever it takes for his clients. Then, in turn, they feel the same loyalty and are willing to go all out for him. It works."

Cris continued making her notes.

"Scott called us all together the evening after he announced the bad news, Jon's leadership team that is. He explained his position on what was happening. He told us how much he'd invested in Jon so we didn't feel alone. He convinced us this cancelled tour was only a bump in the road for Jon's career and he was confident he could turn it around and use it to all our advantages." Hanson laughed.

"What?"

"I was thinking how everyone always talks about Jon Cole's performance skills, his charisma with his fans. Val calls him a 'Salesman on Stage'. After his shows downtown, CD sales always spike. Scott Lindsey has the same skills. But, he uses them on Jon and us. He is a star maker and I will always want to be on his team."

"Impressive." Cris added to her notes. "We spoke to Scott early this morning at Jon's home. He did seem to know his way around this business."

"Absolutely."

"What about the members of Jon's band? Do you normally interact with any of them?"

"No. I've met them at one time or another, usually during recording sessions and such, but that's about it. I doubt if I'd recognize them on the street."

"How well did you know Brooke Cole?"

"I didn't."

"Clarify."

"I was never introduced to her."

Cris nodded and noted.

"What do you know, if anything, about her and Jon's relationship?"

"I can't say I *know* anything. Every time I saw her, she appeared to have no interest in Jon's music or his career.

"His decision to allow her to pressure him into canceling last year's tour was remarkably stupid. It cost him, Scott Lindsey and several of us a considerable amount of money. I told Jon in private this could not be tolerated again.

"We have other artists who want and deserve our help to take them and their careers where they want to go. He knows this will be the only mistake he will be allowed with our company.

"I told Scott, the boy has significant talent, but if he's going to let his wife run his show, he's destined for failure.

"In this business, like any other, you seize opportunity where and when you find it. He may have lost the opportunity when he cancelled last year's tour.

"He's not as popular with the young CD buying populace as he was last year. He lost some favor and he's going to need to fight his way back up. He's doing a fairly good job of it, so far. We'll see.

"The music buying public is fickle and unpredictable. The ordeal here with his wife's passing could help him or it could sink him. He has to decide which he's going to allow to happen.

"It's unfortunate and it's sad, but it can be turned to his advantage if he responds properly. We can help him do it. Jon is talented. He can make himself and the rest of us successful if he'll listen to those of us who have traveled this road before and reached our intended destination."

"I assume you're aware of the plan to launch another tour this year?" Cris asked.

"Yes. Quite aware. We're hoping to get Jon back on track and help him become what he has the potential to be."

"Were you concerned about a replay from his wife?"

"I had no idea who'd been told about the new tour. I'd hoped Jon took care of that with his wife. But," he held up his hands, "who knows. Jon wouldn't be the first up and coming performer to have his career shipwrecked by love." He sighed. "It's just fodder for another sad country song."

Chapter 25

Davidson Savings & Loan
Nashville, Tennessee

"Are you Mr. Gray?" Mike offered his hand.

"Yes. Darin Gray." He shook Mike's hand.

"Have a seat. I'm Sergeant Mike Neal with the Nashville Police Department. I'm here to speak with a few folks at the bank today. I assume you are aware of why I'm here?"

"I heard about Brooke this morning." He seemed hesitant and spoke softly.

"Where were you last evening between six o'clock and eight thirty?"

Gray seemed unsettled by Mike's question.

"I, uh. After work, I picked up my things at the dry cleaners and dropped them at home. I was there long enough to change into some casual clothes. On the way downtown, I filled up my car and I got to the Benchmark around six thirty or so. Marc LeBlanc arrived not long afterward. We talked. We drank beer, ate wings and fries, and watched the Predators."

"What time did you leave the bank?"

"I left the bank around five thirty."

"What time did you leave the bar?"

"The game was over a little before ten and we left shortly afterward, so I'd say close to ten o'clock."

Mike finished his notes. "I've already spoken with Mr. Green about Brooke Cole's consideration for the upcoming promotion to Assistant Vice President here at the bank. I heard you and Marc LeBlanc were also in consideration for this promotion?"

"Yes."

"What is it you do for the bank?

"I am the Senior Commercial Credit Analyst."

"And whom do you report to?"

"Patrick Nichols. He's a Vice President."

Mike added notes.

"Tell me a bit about yourself and your experience both here at the bank and where you worked before." Mike watched for Gray's body language and his speech patterns. His level of discomfort was apparent.

"I am single. I started in banking fresh out of college in 2007. My degree is in Accounting and I have a minor in Finance from the University of Memphis. My first position was as Bank Management Trainee at the Bluff City Bank in Memphis. After four years there, I pursued and was offered my current position here at Davidson. I've been here since then."

"Tell me about who you interact with on a normal day here and what the interaction entails."

"I work, mostly, with the folks in the mortgage groups. I work with Patrick Nichols on special projects."

"Did you ever work with Brooke Cole?"

"No. Her work was mostly centered on auditing. She rarely worked with anyone else, other than Mr. Green, of course."

"Did you associate with her outside your normal responsibilities?"

"Like socially?"

"Or otherwise. During breaks, after work?"

"No. Our paths rarely crossed. When they did, it was just to speak in the hallway or break room getting coffee. That sort of thing."

"I see. What about Marc Leblanc? Did his work provide the opportunity for him to interact with her?"

"It would be best to ask him. I'm not sure."

"Speaking of Marc Leblanc, I understand you and he were

involved in an effort to discredit Brooke Cole by attempting to acquire some dirt from her past." Mike hoped to blindside Gray, catch him off guard and get the truth from him before he had time to think.

"Wait a minute." Gray's tone sharpened as he sat forward and leaned over the table. "That was his thing. I had nothing to do with it." Gray began waving his hands as he spoke, attempting to sell his innocence. "He came to me with what he'd learned about her use of drugs over the last few years. I listened. Okay. I wasn't exactly sad about what was uncovered, but I had nothing to do with hiring the investigator. It was all Marc's idea."

"So, you were not a part of hiring him, but you were supportive of using the investigator's discovery to try and discredit Brooke Cole and prevent her from receiving consideration for the promotion. Is that correct?"

Gray grunted. "If she was using drugs, she had no business getting promoted. If it was *me* using, I would have lost the promotion and my current job. What's the difference?"

Mike continued making his notes without comment.

"Has your area been audited since you've been here at Davidson?"

Gray sat back. "I have no idea. We're not always aware of the audits when they're happening. I would assume yes, but I've not been made aware of it. Let's put it that way. I would suspect if we were audited and something out of the ordinary was found, I would have heard about it, post haste. I guess no news is good news."

Mike nodded. "I see. Are you aware of what Brooke Cole was working on yesterday or possibly the last few days prior to yesterday?"

"No. Mr. Green and Brooke were not in the habit of sharing anything of this nature with the rest of us, and rightly so. Her work called for discretion."

"But, there are other ways of hearing about things like audits, right?"

"What do you mean?" Gray's eyes darted down and back up to Mike's enough times to convince Mike he was pushing the right buttons.

"Every workplace has a certain amount of inside information that travels through the troops. You know, the grapevine, chit-chat, office gossip."

"I guess."

"Have you heard anything lately about Brooke or her audits?"

Gray rubbed his face and then pushed his hands back and forth across his thighs.

"Not that I recall."

"You don't recall Patti Woods telling you last evening Brooke Cole was in the middle of an audit? An audit of the Commercial Loans Department? A department you are involved with?"

Gray was blinking more. His eyes looked as if he was searching the room looking for something to help him.

"Oh, yes. I remember now. It was casual talk as we were leaving. I didn't think much about it."

"Really? You just told me you didn't know what Brooke was working on lately. You said her work called for discretion. Isn't that what you said?"

"I guess it is. I'd forgotten about what Patti said. It didn't seem important at the time. Just idle chit chat, as you called it."

Mike made several notes before speaking again. He could see in his peripheral vision, Gray was fidgeting in his seat.

"Do you know of anyone here or outside the bank Brooke Cole may have had a confrontation with?"

"No. I've not heard of anything," Gray said, with an irrefutable tone.

"Do you know of anyone who may have reason to cause her death? Anyone here or outside the bank?"

"I don't." He paused. "I will say I've heard rumors about her, her husband and his career. I'm not sure she was happy with his being away so much. But, I can't imagine it elevating to this kind of passionate event."

Gray seemed anxious to throw the discussion in another direction.

"So, you were aware of her frequent nights spent at home alone?"

"Well." He sat up straight in his chair and seemed to realize the impact of what he'd said and where Mike was going to take it. "I knew about it because I heard some of the women talking in the break room when she wasn't there. You know how women are."

"No. Tell me. What do you mean?" Mike tried to appear clueless to see what Gray would tell him.

"Hey. Women like to talk, okay. It's in their nature. They talk about men, or other women, especially when the other women are having troubles. They just talk. They don't seem so concerned about being tactful. I can't help but overhear them when they talk across their cubicles."

"Has the talk you've heard about Brooke been all about her relationship with her husband?"

"Mostly."

"What else?"

"I don't know. Some have talked about her being considered for the Assistant VP job coming up."

"Criticism or support?"

"From the women? You're kidding, right? Support. They stick together."

"So they gossip about other women's private lives when they're not around, but support each other professionally, regardless?"

"Yeah. That's it. Hey, it's what they do."

"Do you interact with many women here in your job duties with the bank?"

"A few."

"Do you have any trouble getting along with the women, or the men?"

"I get along with everybody. It's just—." He waved his hand as if it could finish his thought.

Mike stopped his note taking and looked at Gray as if to say 'What?'.

"Sometimes, the women get a bit out over their skis."

Mike leaned back and offered Gray his full attention. "How's that?"

"If any of them are allowed to move up the corporate ladder, they get all big-headed and start looking down on some of the little folks. I had a female manager when I was working my way through school. It was all I could stand. Surely you've seen it in your work world."

"I'm out in the field more and rarely in the office." Mike was determined not to make Gray think he was in agreement.

"Oh, it's there. It's their feminist nature. They take up for each other."

"I see. I guess I'd better watch things a little closer when I'm in the office?"

"I would."

It was easy to see why Darin Gray was recommended by Patrick Nichols. Mike was beginning to think Gray was his clone.

Chapter 26

Davidson Savings & Loan
Nashville, Tennessee

Mike completed a half dozen interviews at the Davidson Savings & Loan. LeBlanc's multiple denials of the restroom event had been adamant, but Gray's admission and attempt at self-absolution came without hesitation. His willingness to throw LeBlanc under the bus and save himself exposed his propensity toward self-preservation at all costs. His degrading critique of women in the workplace caused Mike to wonder if Patti Woods knew how he really felt.

Mike smiled to himself. He was glad Darin Gray hadn't been one of Cris Vega's interviews. It may not have ended as well.

It was now 14:30 and Mike was back in his car, ready to leave. He was generally pleased with his collection of information from the bank people and felt hopeful it could help the investigation.

He decided to call Charles Rosedale in Hoover, Alabama before leaving the bank parking lot. He knew the odds may be slim this type of investigative lead would be fruitful, but he also knew better than to discount any lead.

There had to be a reason why a man at this level of substance would contact a young woman who lived two hundred miles away and talk to her for more than an hour. They had to know each other. If nothing else, Mike wanted to know why the call was made and what could be the significance of the timing in relation to her death.

"Hello."

"Charles Rosedale, please."

"Speaking."

"Mr. Rosedale, this is Sergeant Mike Neal. I'm with the Nashville Tennessee Police Department. Do you have time to speak with me for a few minutes, sir?"

"Sure. What can I do for you, Sergeant?"

"Do you know a young woman by the name of Brooke Ashton Cole?"

"Yes. I do. We were in the same class at Bama."

"Sir, Mrs. Cole was murdered in her Nashville home last evening."

"Oh, my God. No. That's impossible."

Mike gave him a minute.

"What happened?"

"That's what we're investigating. When was the last time you spoke with Mrs. Cole?"

"I don't think I've spoken with Brooke since graduation in May of 2008. I can't believe this. Alex is going to be heart-broken."

"Alex?" Mike said, mirroring Rosedale.

"Alex is my fiancé. She and Brooke were sorority sisters and good friends."

"I see."

"If you don't mind me asking," Rosedale said, "I'm curious. What prompted your call?"

"The search of Mrs. Cole's cell phone history reflects a call from your cell number six days ago that lasted well over an hour. Do you remember making this call to Mrs. Cole?"

"No. I didn't call her. My fiancé did. Alex spent most of the day calling sorority sisters and close friends from college to tell them of our engagement and wedding date. In the middle of one call her cell phone battery died and she asked for mine. Before she was done she'd burned more than half of my phone's battery."

"I see." Mike added to his notes.

"Alex and Brooke hadn't talked in a while, so I guess they seized the chance to catch up."

"What is your fiancé's last name and cell number, so I can identify it in the contacts list on Mrs. Cole's phone? We may need to talk with your fiancé, but I can't be certain yet."

Rosedale gave Mike the information. "I'll let her know you may call."

"I'd appreciate it."

"One other thing you may want to know," Rosedale said.

"Oh?"

"Your research may uncover it, so I'll go ahead and save you some time. Brooke and I dated for close to a year when we were seniors in 2007 and 2008. We thought we were in love, but things fell apart over time. Brooke started getting possessive and controlling. She had a problem whenever I was around other women. It became uncomfortable for me, even embarrassing at times. When this began to happen, I realized quickly we weren't such a great match after all."

"Noted. Thanks."

"Alex and I didn't date in college. We didn't start seeing each other until late last year when we unexpectedly crossed paths in Birmingham. Sergeant Neal, Alex called Brooke to ask her to be one of her bridesmaids. Brooke accepted."

Mike could hear Rosedale's deep breathing.

"Alex is going to be devastated."

"I'm sure you'll handle it well."

"This may not be any of my business, but as an investigator into Brooke's death, I think you'll want to know this. Alex told me Brooke was not completely happy in her marriage. Much of that hour on the phone was Brooke sharing with Alex. Later, Alex shared her concerns with me."

"Thank you."

"I don't suppose you know about—the arrangements?"

"You'll have to contact her husband Jon or the *Nashville Tennessean* newspaper for the information. The medical examiner has the body for now. Mr. Rosedale, please tell your wife, I'm sorry for her loss."

"Thanks. I dread having to tell Alex."

"Good luck. It's never easy."

"Thanks for calling, Sergeant Neal."

Chapter 27

N-Town Publishing
Nashville, Tennessee

When Cris completed her questions for Gabe Hanson, she took a few minutes to finalize her notes. She stepped into the hallway and let Val know she was ready for her in the conference room when she could step away from her duties.

As the only female listed by Scott Lindsey as involved in Jon's business, Cris was most interested in Valerie Webb's perspective on Jon and on Brooke Cole's murder.

"I let Gabe know to catch the phone for me." Val closed the door and sat across from Cris.

"Thanks for talking with me. Tell me about Jon Cole."

"I've known Jon since Gabe signed him to a recording deal."

"I hear he's done well. Better than most?"

"Much better. Jon Cole is one of the most talented and worthy individuals Nashville has seen in decades. His songwriting comes from his heart. His ability as a storyteller is comparable to Kristofferson and his performance skills on stage rival Garth or Chesney. He owns the stage. I'm telling you, this guy is the real deal. I can't believe all the crap he's having to handle in his personal life. But, he's resilient. He will bounce back. If he was a stock, I'd buy it." She smiled.

"You're selling him to me as if he was the next Entertainer of the Year."

"It's easy to get excited about a client who's meant for this Music City chaos. And yes, I'm sure you've heard, Jon and I were seeing each other when—when he met Brooke."

"Were you two sharing a serious relationship or were you casually dating?"

Val took a deep breath. "We'd been dating off and on for months when she entered the picture."

Entered the picture? That says a lot. Cris thought as she made notes in her pad.

"At the time, I felt things were getting serious." She paused. "It didn't appear, once she showed up, Jon was as committed to *us* as I'd hoped."

"Did you two continue dating after they met?"

"No. Not even once," Val said, followed by tight lips. "She sorta moved in and took over his heart." Val looked down as she shook her head.

"That couldn't be pleasant."

"It wasn't. I was hurt. He knew it. I told him. We talked. He apologized. But—." She looked up at Cris with glassy eyes. She held her hands out, palms up and shrugged. "It still hurts."

"So, tell me about Brooke. Did you know her or get to know her at all?"

"No," she said, with a curt tone as if to add 'no way'. "The only thing I knew about her was the pain she caused me and, after they'd been married a while, the pain she was causing him and all those who were trying to help with Jon's career.

"Look. I don't mean to speak ill of the dead, but woman to woman," she pointed at herself and then Cris, "she was a needy and demanding bitch."

"Did Jon feel this way?"

"I doubt it. That was *my* impression, and that of a few others who knew enough to know the truth."

"Can you explain?"

"As I said before, Jon and I saw each other frequently before they met. We shared a mutual concern for each other, a mutual concern for his music and his career. We were also friends. After they were married, I had the occasion to listen when he needed a sensitive ear. I tried to help, but honestly, I had trouble helping him to understand her. Hell, as a woman, I couldn't figure her out either. She and I were different, I guess. She wanted him to give up his dreams and find a day job so he could be home with her at night. To me, it's freakin' selfish."

"Wanting her husband at home with her isn't exactly unusual expectations for a wife," Cris said.

"I understand, but she knew about his music before she fell for him. I think she believed she could get him to throw it all away for her. If she'd bothered getting to know him, she'd have realized how much his career meant to him. Jon has been singing and playing music his entire life. Music *is* his life."

"Tell me about the people who were hurt most by her insistence for Jon to cancel last year's tour."

Val hesitated as she gazed at the floor. "The ones hurt most, I'd say, were Jon and Scott. They lost the most invested money and potential money, both immediately and long term. The band lost a year's income, too. Gabe Hanson, my boss, and our record company lost considerable CD sales since Jon was releasing an album before the tour. Without the tour, sales for the album were maybe twenty five to thirty percent what they would have been.

"It's common knowledge, performance tours sell albums. People see the artist in concert and then, if they don't already have it, they buy their album. It's one reason CDs and shirts are sold at the venues. Emotions are high. Frequently, the fans are too." She smiled. "You strike while the iron is hot. It is simply music business law.

"We still have thousands of CDs sitting in a warehouse. They should have been sold by now and another run manufactured to meet demand. It's sad, all that was lost because of her."

"Do you know of anyone else, other than those you've mentioned, who were hurt by the tour cancellation or even who might have benefited in some way from her death?"

Val looked up at Cris with enlarged eyes. "When you asked about who was hurt by last year's cancelled tour, I didn't mean to say those people could—. They wouldn't. These people love Jon. None of them are the type to want to harm her for what she did."

"I understand. We ask these questions in order to uncover the facts surrounding the victim, their friends and families. It's standard procedure. It helps us to draw a picture, it's called Victimology. It helps us to know what was going on in the affected peoples' lives at the time of the murder. You're being quite helpful. I'm sure Jon would be most grateful for your assistance. I'm sure he wants her killer caught as much as we do, most likely even more. Okay?" Cris smiled, then nodded.

"Okay. I wasn't trying to throw anyone under the bus. I have no idea who might have wanted her—you know."

"I know. So, do you know who might benefit from her passing?"

Val was obviously stressing over Cris's questions. "I overheard the guys in the band back when the tour was pulled. They were talking amongst themselves about her and what she was doing to Jon's career, and for that matter, theirs. Their words weren't kind. But what can you expect? She cost these guys a full year's pay with bonuses. They were pissed off. They had to pursue local session work where they could in order to pay the rent. His bass player took a job working in a local warehouse in the daytime and then took a gig with another band at night. People have to eat.

"Three of the band members ended up moving in with each other in order to get by. They were hurt in a lot of ways and were not in a position to let it show to Jon. I know how they felt. They'll benefit because this upcoming tour—won't be at risk of being cancelled." She stopped. "Can I assume you know about the new tour?"

Cris looked up from her note taking. "Yes, Scott told us."

"Good. I guess, as tacky as it sounds, everyone involved with Jon's career will benefit." She stopped and stared down at the table before looking up at Cris.

"I'm sorry. It may sound hateful. I don't mean it to be. But, I hope I benefit from her passing as well."

Chapter 28

Criminal Justice Center
Nashville, Tennessee

Notified of his guest's arrival by the guards at the CJC, Mike readied his desk and started for the lobby. Before he cleared his office doorway, he was stopped by the tones from his cell phone. He looked at the screen and accepted the call.

"Hi, Jennifer."

"Mike. Are you where you can talk for a minute?"

"Sure. What's up?"

"I just received a call from St. Thomas Hospital. They admitted Mr. Hinkle today and he has listed us as his emergency contacts."

"Oh no." Mike had frequently wondered how long it would be before his eighty something friend and neighbor would succumb to ill health. "Did they say what's wrong?"

"The lady who called said they'd found cancer in his pancreas."

"Oh, no. That's a death sentence for a man his age." He paused. "I have an interview right now with the father of a homicide victim. He's waiting in the lobby. I'm not sure how long this will take. Let me call you when I'm finished and we'll make some decisions. Okay?"

"Sure. I'll wait to hear from you. Mike, I know Carol is out of town. Can I make your dinner this evening? You can eat with Mason."

"I wish I could. Let me take a raincheck. We'll do it soon. I promise. Right now, I'm helping Cris since her partner is on two weeks vacation. Thanks, Jennifer. I appreciate the offer."

"Your welcome. Let me know if I can do anything to help."

"Thanks. I'll call you a little later."

Mike leaned against the wall outside his office. He sighed and thought about his elderly neighbor. He was into his mid-eighties, but Mike was unsure how far into them.

Jennifer was Jennifer Holliman, Mike's tenant in the upstairs apartment in his house. Jennifer and her son Mason moved in shortly after the apartment remodel was complete. They'd lived there since, becoming valued neighbors for both Mike and Mr. Hinkle.

Mike and Jennifer looked after Mr. Hinkle for years, watching as his age became the enemy of his health.

According to him, he had no one else. Mr. Hinkle hadn't shared much about his health. When it was time to see his doctor, he called medical transport. He wouldn't let Mike or Jennifer go with him. Mike had witnessed the outward signs of his declining health over the last couple of years.

We should all make it into our eighties.

He couldn't help but consider his own recurring pain and his uncertainty about what was causing it.

Mike made his trek to the lobby and after rounding the back of the staircase, he saw Mr. Ashton waiting.

"You again," the elderly gentleman offered a turned up nose when he saw Mike. He made no effort to stand. Likely, his way of displaying his disrespect.

Ashton was the same well-dressed, but supremely frustrated old man Mike encountered years ago when his wife decided she'd had all the pain and drugs she wanted. Mike realized why Brooke's maiden name rang a bell when Jon mentioned it, and why the framed photo in their bedroom was familiar.

Thirteen years ago he and Norm Wallace, his detective partner at the time, worked the homicide of a middle-aged female in the Woodmont area. This death investigation turned out to be a suicide, but the lady's family could not accept it. They insisted she was murdered, and nothing Mike or the D.A. told them could cause them to change their minds.

"Mr. Ashton," Mike offered as a greeting. He knew, for now at least, a handshake was out of the question.

"Why you?" He glared at Mike. "Are you the only detective Nashville has left, or am I just that damn lucky? Well, if you ask me, they're scraping the bottom of the barrel. I want another detective. I can't trust what you're gonna say about my little girl."

Ashton's voice quivered and he began to cry. "I've already lost my Doris—to a murderer you can't find, won't find, and you say she killed herself. How disgusting. You should be ashamed of yourself. And the Nashville Police Department should be ashamed of you and the Herman Munster look alike you called your partner." Ashton pulled his handkerchief from his pants pocket and blew his nose.

Mike looked around the lobby to see if his guest was creating a scene. Fortunately, they were alone.

It was a rare occasion when Mike encountered someone so dissatisfied with one of his investigations, much less an entire family who felt this way. The finding of suicide in Mrs. Ashton's case was not only Mike's and Norm's determination. The criminalists from the MNPD Crime Scene Unit, the Medical Examiner, Mike's Supervisor at the time, Lieutenant D.W. Burris and even the Davidson County District Attorney all reviewed the case multiple times before confidently declaring it a suicide. When the family responded so vehemently, the law enforcement professionals revisited the decision in an attempt to cushion the impact for the Ashton family.

There was simply no evidence to indicate a murder, no suspects, no physical evidence, no trace, no motive and no one with opportunity outside the Ashton family.

Even the existence of her one million dollar life insurance policy didn't generate a suspect in the death of Mrs. Ashton. However, it did cause Mike to wonder about her family's intentions with regard to their insistence her death was murder. Mike had seen many cases where the dispute over money had a more negative influence on families than their loss of a loved one.

Mike knew from his years of experience, the impact of death in a surviving family released emotions no other event could awaken. He also knew part of his job was to deal with the emotions death delivered, regardless of the effects on him.

Ashton wiped his eyes and his nose before wadding up his handkerchief and tucking it inside his rear pants pocket. "So, what are you here to tell me? More bad news?"

"Let's move to a more private place where we can talk." Mike extended his arm in the direction of the elevator.

The short walk to the elevator and ride to the second floor included no words between the men.

As they arrived at his office, Mike stopped and indicated for Mr. Ashton to enter. He adjusted the chair where he wanted Ashton to sit and then took the seat next to and facing him rather than sitting behind his desk.

"I'd like to discuss whatever you can tell me about your daughter's life in hopes we can determine who may have reason to want her dead."

"So, you agree it was murder?"

"We have not completed our investigation, but the evidence we've collected so far points to murder. Yes."

"Who do you suspect?"

"Sir, we're not there yet. I'm sorry, but it's too early. There are several people yet to be interviewed and alibi's to be verified. Do you know of anyone who had reason to do harm to your daughter?"

"How the hell would I know? Outside the bank where she worked, I don't know who she encountered on a daily basis or who may have reason to do her harm. Have you talked to Jon about this? He's her husband. He ought to know who she knew, unless of course he's spending more time with his *hobby* than with his wife."

"Yes. We've talked with Jon at length and will talk more later today."

"What did he say?"

"He told us about conversations he and Brooke shared involving folks at the bank and customers she worked with."

"And?"

"And we're not at a point in the collection of evidence and information where we're ready to speculate as to what happened, who was involved and why. We're still collecting information we hope will point us where we need to go in order to do this. Some of these people are still being interviewed. Some will be interviewed more than once."

"When are you people going to know something? Isn't there a forty-eight hour rule or something you people have to catch the killer?"

"It's best if we're able to narrow things down within the first couple of days, but not all cases are tied up so quickly, especially when they involve so many people outside the family such as this one."

Ashton gave a weak nod.

"How often did you see Brooke in the last couple of years?"

"I saw her more often in the time right after her mother passed."

"You live here in town, right?"

"Yes. Well, I live on the north side of Franklin. After Doris passed, Brooke and her sister tried to see after me like I was an invalid or something. Don't get me wrong. I enjoyed seeing them and I appreciated their concerns, but they acted like I couldn't even fix my own dinner."

"I understand. Often, it's what the ladies do to help them deal with the pain."

Ashton sighed and nodded.

"When you spoke about Jon it sounded as though you believe his efforts toward his musical career were possibly a problem in their marriage."

"I believe a man is supposed to be with his family and support his family both with his money and his time. I'm not so sure Jon has been doing this. He doesn't seem to be profiting from all his musical fun. Most importantly, he's rarely at home with his wife when she needs him. That bothers me since his wife is my—." Ashton pulled out his handkerchief again and began to cry.

Mike sat patiently, allowing Ashton to deal with the emotions he'd conjured up with his thoughts of his daughter and her less than perfect marital situation.

"She wasn't happy with their detached paths toward their separate careers. She felt Jon should be home at night with her. The path he'd chosen appeared to allow anything but that. Needless to say, they were having trouble with it."

"Were they fighting about it? Or, were they just having trouble with the physical separation?"

"Brooke's sister, Bonnie, my youngest daughter, told me she and Brooke talked on several occasions when Brooke opened up about it to her."

"Brooke told her they were fighting?"

"Yes. Brooke told her she discovered an email that, despite her steadfast opposition, gave her reason to believe Jon's team was planning another tour for later this year. She already caused him to cancel a tour last year, but I'm sure you already know this."

"Yes sir. Jon told us about it."

"Well, Bonnie told me Brooke was irate because Jon told her nothing about this new tour yet. She was afraid he planned to spring it on her at the last minute and tell her it was too late and he couldn't cancel it."

"I see. When was it Brooke discovered the email?"

"I'm not sure, but Bonnie told me about it Sunday night."

"So, three days ago?"

"Yes. I don't know for sure. You can ask Bonnie what she knows and see how it matches up with Jon's story."

"She's on my list."

Chapter 29

Mike and Cris were sharing information from their interview notes when the tone from Mike's cell phone announced an incoming call.

"Mike Neal."

"Mike. It's Elaine Jamison. Do you have a minute?"

"Sure, Doc. What's up?"

"I'm calling to apologize."

"Oh? For what?" Mike put the Medical Examiner on speaker phone so Cris could also hear the discussion.

"For failing to contact you or Cris earlier. I had to move up the Cole autopsy and I failed to tell you in time for one of you to be here to view it. I had to postpone two other exams and I moved this one into their place. I hope this doesn't jeopardize your investigation. I was in a rush and I simply forgot."

"That's fine."

"The report is ready and I was about to send it to your email when I realized I'd failed to inform you of the schedule change so you could attend."

"I don't see a huge problem." He looked at Cris. He knew this was okay with Cris since attending autopsies was the least favorite part of her job. "Were there any unusual discoveries?"

"Not really. The toxicology report has been ordered. I should have it back within a day or two. I can run through the report with you if you'd like. You should have it in your email by now."

"Let me pull it up on my laptop so we can follow along." Mike selected his email icon and waited for it to load. He turned the screen so Cris could also see.

"Let me know when you're ready," Jamison said.

"Okay. Hang on a minute." Mike watched as a list of new emails filled his screen. He clicked on the Medical Examiner's incoming email and attachment and watched as it populated his monitor. "Got it. It's opening. We're ready."

"The body is that of a normally developed ectomorphic white female measuring sixty-six inches, weighing one hundred and five pounds and appearing generally consistent with the stated age of twenty-nine years. The body is clad in a gray business suit over a white silk blouse. Beneath the outer clothing is a white lace camisole, bra and matching underwear. Underclothes appear to be undisturbed and genitalia reflect no evidence of injury. However, a rape kit is being used and submitted for testing.

"The decedent's hair is medium blonde with artificial lighter blonde highlights, wavy and approximately twenty-two inches in length at its longest point. Some of the hair at the rear of the decedent's head is pulled out, but remains within the bulk of the hair.

"The decedent's hands were bagged prior to arrival at the morgue and after examination, fingernails are false, medium length and nail beds are bluish in color due to cyanosis. Nail scrapings have been submitted for DNA testing along with the facial swabs requested.

"The third finger of the left hand shows signs of normal ring impression, but there is no ring. The decedents ears are pierced, but no earrings are present. No other jewelry was found.

"Lividity is fixed in the dorsal portions of the body. Multiple abrasions and contusions are present on and around the area of the head and neck. There is evidence of blunt force injury to the left malar area of the face. Several contusions, some superficial, are found in the pelvic region, as well as the infra scapular regions of the lower back. Both #11 and #12 vertebral ribs on the left side are fractured.

"Petechial hemorrhaging is present in the conjunctival surfaces of the eyes as well as the periorbital region and upper gingiva.

"Closer examination of the cervical region of the spine reveals a broken hyoid bone. The thyroid, as well as the cricoid cartilages are both fractured.

"Most internal organs are found to be well within size-weight ranges and unremarkable.

"The exterior rear of the decedent's scalp reflects evidence of recent blunt force trauma in the form of contusion and minor laceration. On examination, the perimeter surface of the brain reveals evidence of the primary intracranial brain injury along with beginning signs of secondary injury, but the expected cerebral edema and resulting intracranial pressure were halted by the interruption of coronary function.

"It is my opinion, based upon currently available information and autopsy data, Mrs. Brooke Ashton Cole died as the result of asphyxiation due to manual strangulation. The manner of death is best classified as homicide."

"None of this is all that surprising, based upon our investigation to date. Would you agree?" Mike asked as he looked at Cris.

"Sounds like a relatively typical strangulation," Cris said. "I assume the rape kit, toxicology and DNA reports are scheduled to come to us?"

"That's correct, Cris," Jamison said. "To me and copied to the two of you."

"Anything else of significance from the autopsy?" Mike asked.

"You say it as if you are expecting something. How did you know I was saving the best for last?"

"I don't know, Doc," Mike said. "Maybe—working with you for thirteen years gave me a hint?"

Dr. Jamison chuckled. "I found more of the approximately six centimeter hairs you said you found at the crime scene on the decedent's blouse. They were found on her gray skirt and also inside the cadaver bag."

"Good," Mike said. "Every bit helps."

"Also—," Doctor Jamison interrupted.

"How did I know there would be more?" Mike whispered to Cris.

"I discovered a piece of Nitrile approximately 2.5 centimeters in diameter hiding between her right jaw and gum."

"Really?" Cris shook her head and turned an ear toward the phone as if afraid to miss anything Dr. Jamison might say.

"Yes. I can't be certain which finger, but the material has a light treaded texture like you find near the finger tips on some gloves."

"Good work. I don't suppose you were able to pull a nice fingerprint from the Nitrile." Mike laughed.

"Are you ever satisfied?"

"Amazed Doc, but never satisfied. I'm always happy with your work. But, you know, we never have enough evidence."

"Understood and agreed."

"Cris," Mike said, "can you call Wendy? Let her know the odds just went up on locating a print inside the Cole home. She may think about making another visit there before we release the residence."

"I'll let her know."

"Thanks, Doc. We really do appreciate your work."

"You're welcome. Good luck to both of you with the investigation."

Chapter 30

Criminal Justice Center
Nashville, Tennessee

"Mike Neal," he said, in response to the tone and vibration of his cell phone.

"I love you."

"Hey, I love you, too. How are you?"

"I'm good. Tired, but good. I miss you very much."

"I miss you too. Is the baby keeping late hours?"

"Some nights. She thinks she's a rock star and has to scream when she sings for her desires. But, she's a good baby. I'm enjoying caring for her and I'm learning a lot, getting ready for a few of my own."

"A few? I'm sorry. You must have the wrong number."

"No more than a half-dozen or so."

"Oh. Well, of course. At least enough for a basketball team." Mike realized the time with her niece had ramped up Carol's desire to be a mother.

She laughed. "So. How are *you* doing?"

"I'm better when you're in Nashville. But, I'm okay."

"I hope so, but you better be good when I'm not there." Carol chuckled.

Mike laughed. "So, what does your brother-in-law say about all this?"

"He's grateful I came to help. With his work schedule, he couldn't have done this without using the Family Medical Leave Act and devastated their savings. The jury is still out about his abilities as an infant caregiver."

"I understand. I take it you're not within his earshot at the moment."

"No. I'm out running errands."

"Us hairy-legged boys aren't as good at some things as girls are. So, how is the relationship and their efforts to deal with the PPD?"

"Better. Not ideal in my opinion, but much better than it was. Bryan seems to understand now how his help with the baby when he's home can improve Marie's ability to deal with the depression."

"It's an improvement. Any idea yet on when you can turn all this over to them and get back to Nashville and take care of *me*? I'm easier than a baby to care for and I don't scream quite as much at night. Unless of course there's a full moon."

Carol laughed. "After all this work, I was hoping someone could start taking care of me."

"Oh, I can definitely take care of you. I'd love to have that job."

"You're hired," Carol said. "How's your workload?"

"Same as always. More than we can get done."

"Is Jerry back from vacation?"

"No. They're out there for two weeks."

"Must be nice."

"Hey. You've been gone for *more* than two weeks."

"In case you haven't noticed, I'm not in California. I'm in Topeka freakin' Kansas. The ocean here is made of wheat and the beaches are black dirt. Fun experiences here include waiting to see what color my niece's latest poop is going to be and whether or not I need a SWAT Team gas mask to clean her up. The water park here is me getting soaked bathing her in the kitchen sink. It's a lot like sunny California."

"You get to have all the fun," Mike said.

"Don't I? Oh. Before I forget to tell you. We all go see the psychologist next week, so keep your fingers crossed. I may get to come home soon if he thinks Marie and Bryan are improving. I hate to think about leaving the baby, but I know I have to at some point. I should get back to Nashville and get started working on having my own."

"Pardon me. We got engaged less than a month ago. We're not married yet. We're not supposed to do the deed until we're wed."

"Hello? We've been doing *the deed,* as you put it, for years."

"Yeah, but that was when we were lovers. That's different."

"And we're no longer lovers? Carol asked. "I have obviously allowed you to be by yourself for entirely too long. Your mind has begun to leave you."

"I knew something was different back here in Music City. *You've* not been here. That's it."

"If I was there, I'd punch you."

Mike laughed. "Oh, if you were here, you'd have to punch me to stop me from kissing your beautiful face."

"I miss kissing your face, too."

"Let me know what the psycho says. I mean the psychologist."

"You're the psycho."

"No argument. I'm *psycho* for you."

"Stay safe."

"Copy that."

Mike ended the call. He decided not to mention his recurring pain. He knew all it would do is cause Carol to worry about him for the rest of her visit.

As hard as he tried to eat healthy and work out several times each week, it must be something minor. The pain was beginning to make him think it could be another kidney stone.

The last stone was over a year ago and the pain was more in his back, but the doctor told him sometimes the pain radiates to the lower abdomen and groin. The pain had begun to come in waves and fluctuate in intensity.

Mike couldn't help but feel the time in Kansas caring for her niece ramped up Carol's desire and anticipation for motherhood.

She's going to make such a great mom.

Chapter 31

Jon Cole's Apartment
Nashville, Tennessee

"Hi, Jon."

"Detective Vega. Come in." Jon stood back and extended a welcoming arm.

"I hope I'm not intruding."

"No way. Please, come in. Do you have anything new on the investigation?"

"We're still interviewing all the people you and Scott gave us as well as the people Brooke worked with and her friends. It takes time."

"I understand."

"I wanted to drop by and see how things were going for you. I know how draining this ordeal can be. I've not lost a spouse, but I did lose my brother, my only sibling."

"I'm sorry to hear it." He gestured toward the sofa. "Have a seat."

"It's been several years, but as you can imagine, you never stop missing them and wishing you could sit and talk one more time. Maybe, to say goodbye."

"I keep trying to imagine a time when the grief won't occupy the entire day."

"It will come, but it'll take a while. It's understandable. Losing a loved one is our most traumatic pain in this life. Time doesn't heal it all, but that's okay. It does help you to better deal with it."

"I haven't been able to think about my music."

Cris sat patiently without comment.

"All I can focus on is the sight of Brooke on the kitchen floor—." His voice broke.

"I loved her. She became my inspiration. She wanted me home at night. But, I wanted my music. The son of a bitch not only murdered my wife," he looked up at Cris, "he killed my music."

"Jon. This is a temporary issue. It's normal. It will take some time to adjust. Just give it a chance. Brooke would not have wanted you to give up."

"No. This is exactly what she wanted. But, I couldn't do it. It's what would have made her happiest and prevented all this." He put his head in his hands and sobbed.

"I was cursed with two loves and neither had any compassion for the other."

Cris watched him, hoping she could come up with something to say, something that would help.

"Jon, your talent is yours. It's a gift. It can't be taken away by something or someone else."

He looked up at her.

"A God-given talent like yours is rare, and not something to be discarded. It will reveal itself to you again in time. That's when you'll realize it never left you.

"I wasn't going to tell you this, but I've read the lyrics to some of your songs."

"You have?"

"Yes. I asked Scott for them. He sent me an email."

"Why?"

"I thought they might give me a window into your personality, maybe even your soul."

Jon chuckled. "Uh oh."

"I can see you are a poet. They're great. Much too good for you to think the source from which they came is dead. And, too good for you to give up. Use this time. Step away from songwriting for a short period if you think it's best. No one gets over these things quickly. No one expects *you* to, either."

Jon nodded.

"Wouldn't Brooke want you to be happy?"

"I guess so."

"Let's assume Brooke, and I'm sure your fans, want you to use this time to reflect on your life with her and all the good that came from it. Then, look forward. You're a young man. Look to the future and the opportunities that lie ahead of you.

"I was told by Scott, your fans are thriving on your work, your songs and your stage performances. Your songs are meaningful. They're reaching their hearts and their lives. Isn't that what music does? We connect with music because it has meaning in our lives. It triggers memories. Mostly memories of time we spent with people we love or have loved."

"Yes. You're right."

"So. Why would you choose to deprive all your loyal fans of those emotions and the pleasure your words and music stir in them?"

Jon smiled.

"I would say, before long, Brooke may once again become your inspiration."

Jon sat thinking for a moment. He began to nod. "I hope you're right."

"Me too." She stood. "I'm glad I got to see you. Hang in there. We'll keep you posted."

"Thanks, and thanks for the advice."

"You're welcome." Cris smiled.

Chapter 32

Criminal Justice Center
Nashville, Tennessee

"For the life of me, I can't understand why you cops can't see what's right in front of you. Brooke was in Jon's way, preventing him from reaching his goal, becoming some kind of country music star. So, he killed her. Why isn't this clear to you, Sergeant?"

Bonnie Ashton, older unmarried sister of Brooke Cole, was animated and determined in her attempt to convince Mike of Jon's involvement in Brooke's death. He knew the look on her face was merely the warning shot for the coming barrage.

"We don't have sufficient evidence at this point in the investigation to arrest *anyone* for your sister's murder," Mike said. "Besides, Jon has a solid alibi."

Mike and Brooke's sister had been talking in his office for almost an hour. She was standing her ground, convinced Jon was guilty. She appeared equally convinced the detectives investigating Brooke's murder were failing to do their jobs.

"Just because he can prove he was somewhere else at the time of her death doesn't mean he didn't have it done. He wouldn't have dirtied his little guitar strumming hands anyway.

"If you talk to the people who know him, who truly know what's important to him, and who know how he treated her, you'll see it can't be anyone else. He had the most to gain from her death."

"Such as?"

"Isn't his freedom motivation enough? Isn't a clear path to what he truly loved enough? All he wanted was to be free to pursue his music and all those adoring young girls."

"He could have achieved this with a divorce, or even a legal separation. It doesn't seem plausible for him to kill her. We've talked with several people who knew both of them. They spoke openly about him and about her. No one, other than you, has painted Jon as this insensitive, selfish individual. Do you have any idea why we're getting this from only you?"

"Maybe because I was her sister and the only one she felt she could open up to. Did you ever think of this?"

Mike wasn't convinced he should believe her, but *she* appeared to believe in her critique of her brother-in-law.

"What exactly did Brooke open up to you about?"

Ashton exhaled her disgust. "All Brooke wanted was a normal life. A normal marriage. You know, work in the daytime, enjoy each other's company in the evening. A traditional, normal arrangement." She stopped talking and stared at the floor. "I can't tell you how many times she called me late at night crying because she was at home alone and he was out somewhere with his friends playing music. She felt—abandoned. As a man, you may not be able to relate to this."

Mike had learned some personal critiques from interviewees should be ignored.

"Did Brooke ever mention anything about seeking attention from other men? Any mention of an affair?"

"How dare you? Brooke would never do something like that. It's ridiculous."

"Tell me. What part of Jon's career and love of playing music did Brooke not understand prior to their marriage? Was this not what he was doing when they met as well as during their dating and engagement?" Mike decided a counter attack was called for, since Ashton's salvo of accusations was dominating their discussion.

"Yes," she admitted, and then took some time to answer. "Brooke loved him. She was convinced his experience would turn out like most of the other Music City hopefuls and he would realize his efforts were pointless. Once he realized the facts, she felt he would come to his senses and get a real job."

Mike nodded. "Did she not see he was talented and had a good chance at success here in Music City?"

"Brooke was not what you would call a country music fan. She was more a fan of classical music."

"Most folks would be ecstatic to discover their loved one was becoming a success at their chosen profession, regardless of the genre. Any idea why Brooke didn't see it this way?"

"She wanted Jon to love her and be her husband first, and whatever else he wanted should come afterward."

"Oh." *Sounds selfish to me.* "Jon didn't come across as the type of person who fits the description you're portraying of him. His reactions during our interviews have been consistent with those expected from a husband who loved, and suddenly lost, his wife. He was traumatized. He answered all our questions without hesitation and provided all the information we've requested."

"So?" She leaned toward Mike. "Jon's acting skills carried over from his stage performance to your interviews. You need to drill a little deeper, Sergeant. He has you all fooled. Hell, he had *me* fooled for quite a while. I thought my sister finally found her soul mate. But, I was wrong. So was she. We found out he loved himself and his adoring fans more than his wife."

"I get what you're saying, but we'll be required to secure supporting evidence before we can act on it. So far, I've seen none."

"You do whatever the hell you want to," she stood, "but you'd better lock his ass up before he makes a bigger fool of you and your detective friends than he already has. And, so you'll know," she pointed her finger at Mike, "my father and I are not going to accept a shoddy investigation like the one you and your big brother did on my mother's murder.

"You know, if you were a good detective, you'd already know Brooke had a significant life insurance policy at the bank with Jon as her sole beneficiary. Doesn't that seem like motivation to you?"

"Hmm." Mike hesitated nodding his head. "And, I guess if I was a *really* good detective, I'd already know Jon is *not* the sole beneficiary and that *you* are in fact listed as the secondary beneficiary who could collect the three hundred and fifty thousand dollars only if Jon Cole was dead or serving time in prison for killing his wife."

Bonnie looked down and away from Mike, more or less admitting she was already aware of what he'd said.

"If someone thought enough of me," Mike said, "to list me as a beneficiary on their life insurance policy, I think I'd remember it."

"You don't know," Ashton shouted. "Your sister may have you listed as her beneficiary and you don't know it."

Mike paused in order to try and remain professional for his forthcoming response. "My only sister—was raped and brutally murdered twenty-two years ago when she was seventeen years old. She didn't have a life insurance policy." Mike's tone elevated, no longer as professional as he'd prefer. "She didn't even get to have a *life*."

Bonnie Ashton obviously didn't know what to say, so she wisely kept her mouth shut.

"Please understand," Mike calmed his voice and began to speak slowly. "I'm trying to discover who murdered *your* sister so they can be punished and so you and your father, as well as Jon and all those who cared about Brooke, can glean some kind of understanding or, for lack of a better term, closure. This is why it's so important we know as much of the truth as we can determine. Because, without facts, we have little else to direct our investigation.

"Which reminds me, since we're discussing the life insurance as provocation, where were *you* the night Brooke was killed?"

Ashton gasped, her brow wrinkled and her eyes bulged as she looked into Mike's eyes. She appeared to be at a loss for words. She jerked her body into a turn and stormed out of his office without further comment, at least any comment he could comprehend.

Mike knew his chances of getting Bonnie Ashton to agree to the possibility of Jon's innocence was no more likely than getting her to accept her mother's suicide. She had once again made up her mind and, regardless of the facts in evidence, decided what really happened. And, in her sister's murder, who was guilty.

Mike reviewed his notes and replayed from his memory Bonnie Ashton's verbal judgment of Jon Cole. He couldn't imagine what was driving this much disdain for Jon. Maybe her conversations with her sister fueled her belief in the criticism she was spouting. Or, maybe it was the temptation of the life insurance money.

Chapter 33

MNPD Crime Lab
Madison, Tennessee

"Well, hello there. Welcome."

"Hi, Wendy. How's it going?" Cris asked.

"Sergeant Mike Neal and Detective Cris Vega," Wendy said, as the two detectives stepped into the crime lab, "I'd like you to meet Lisa McConnell. Lisa is a Forensics Department intern from Middle Tennessee State University working with us here in the crime lab for her final senior semester."

The young woman removed her gloves and safety glasses, and pulled down her respirator so she could speak.

"Nice to meet you, Lisa." Mike offered her his hand and a smile.

"Thank you. It's my pleasure."

"Same here. You're in good hands with Wendy," Cris said. "She does a great job for us at our scenes and in the lab. What's your major?"

"I double-majored in Forensics and Chemistry with a minor in Criminology."

"Wow." Cris looked at Wendy, who was smiling. "That sounds great. Maybe after graduation the chief will make you an offer."

"It would be nice," Lisa said, smiling.

"We could sure use the help," Wendy added.

"I consider it an honor to be here and work with you guys. I've only been here for a couple of weeks and already I've learned a lot from the lab and crime scene folks and hope to learn a lot more. I hope to be able to apply some of the Chemistry and Forensic methodologies I've learned in my four years at MTSU."

"I'm sure you will," Mike said. "And, I'm pretty sure Wendy has already told you, don't be bashful if you feel you can add something to our efforts to more thoroughly analyze crime scene evidence and work toward finding the truth. That's our goal. We're all on the same team."

"I'll do my best."

"Great. Wendy, what can you tell us about the evidence you were able to collect at the Cole home?" Mike asked.

"Okay, let's move over here." Wendy led them all to a lab work table where she'd positioned evidence she and the CSU team obtained from the Cole home.

"The first report here is from our hair sample analysis. The tested samples were provided by each of the people on the list I received from you Cris. We were able to visit with each of these folks and secure both buccal swabs, hair samples and prints.

"None of the hair samples matched the hairs found on the victim's body by Mike, the CSU Team and Dr. Jamison. The unidentified prints from the Cole residence also do not match any of those from your list. The buccal swabs have been sent out for analysis. As is normal, we're waiting.

"The next data is considerably more interesting and, we hope, more helpful. On the night of the murder, we brought back to the lab the victim's purse and briefcase from the kitchen floor and a jewelry box from the master bedroom. We were able to fume these items under the hood using Cyanoacrylate and pull some nice quality partials.

"With the news from you about Dr. Jamison's discovery of the piece of Nitrile from a glove finger in the victim's mouth, we returned to the Cole home. We reviewed the locations where we'd found latent prints the night of the homicide. On our return trip we found another partial on the lower corner of a nightstand drawer.

"We were able to eliminate all our readable full prints as

matching either Jon Cole, the Coles' maid or the victim. Our four partial prints did not match any of these three persons. As always, we found numerous smeared prints from several areas of the home.

"We submitted the partials to the MNPD database and to IAFIS. No matches were found in our local database. However, IAFIS returned three twelve point matches on the four partial prints, as you can see here in the blown up photos."

"Edgar Aaron Fletcher," Mike read the name at the top of the page and scanned for his physical description. "Six foot two, one hundred seventy pounds. No scars, tattoos or body piercings. Doesn't sound like the big man the neighbor spotted."

Mike held the enlarged partial fingerprints so Cris could see as well. Matching points were marked. Six bifurcations, three ridge endings, two islands and one enclosure all match the print on file at the FBI's Integrated Automated Fingerprint Identification System for Fletcher's right index finger.

"What's his record look like?"

Wendy handed Mike the report from IAFIS.

He and Cris both keyed on the small grainy slim-faced photograph on the first page.

"He has some drug arrests, an armed robbery and an attempted murder conviction. Last known address is in Saint Louis, Missouri."

"When did he last show up in Missouri's system?" Mike read and answered his own question. "A 2010 arrest, it says here. A 2013 release from Missouri's prison system. Nothing after that."

"I wonder how old the photo is?" Cris asked. "And, where has he been?"

"I'm not sure where he's been, but I know he was in the Cole home Tuesday. And, we have to find him."

"Mike," Wendy said, "Lisa and I have an idea we'd like to tell you about. It won't take long and it may help you locate Fletcher."

"Oh?"

"I'd prefer Lisa explained," Wendy said with a smile.

"Good," Mike said, turning his attention to the intern.

"Early last semester in my Forensic Analytical Chemistry Lab we were tasked with the analysis of over one hundred head hair samples. We were instructed to check them for drugs, legal and prescription as well as illegal drugs, all of which were listed in the instructions. At first we felt a bit overwhelmed. But, there were fifteen of us in the lab so each of us took at least seven samples. Five of us took eight.

"The hair samples were identified with numbers only and each sample, we were told, contained at least fifty hairs. There was considerable speculation on the origin of the samples. But, at no time were we made aware of the donors' identity."

"Might I ask if there was a consensus speculation on the donors?" Mike asked.

"I'm not sure I'd call it a consensus. However, several students were comfortable presuming the sources of the samples were all of the university's scholarship athletes. I had doubts the school leadership would task us for such a consequential assignment."

"I agree," Mike said. "I didn't mean to interrupt."

"No problem. One thing I might add which could have skewed opinions on the scholarship athlete speculation," Lisa said. "The printed instructions we were given specified the list of drugs we were searching for. It included cocaine, amphetamines, cannabinoids, opiates, bronchodilators, ketamine, phencyclidine and a number of anabolic steroids."

"Interesting," Cris said.

Mike nodded. "I can see how the list could push suspicions toward the athletes."

"It was quite the topic of conversation," Lisa said. "But, there was never any proof."

"Okay," Wendy said. "Back to the facts."

"On average, the hair samples we were given were five to eight centimeters in length and approximately two hundred and forty milligrams in weight. Our samples, like those you guys recovered from the Cole crime scene, were not pulled out so we had no follicles. But fortunately, follicles aren't required for the drug screening."

"In order to cut to the chase, as they say, I made a recommendation to Wendy. Since your investigation revealed a witness claiming a large muscular man was seen near the crime scene at the approximate time of the murder, I asked if we could perform a similar analysis on the hair you found on the victim. She agreed and we did.

"Following removal of the sample from the hair using liquid-liquid extraction, our drug-screening employed liquid chromatography coupled to tandem mass spectrometric analysis using the dynamic multiple reaction monitoring method."

"Time out," Mike said. "Give me the net-net, in English."

Wendy and Cris traded smiles.

"The report revealed the hair's donor was a long term user of Trenbolone acetate, an anabolic steroid used in veterinary medicine to increase muscle growth and appetite in livestock right before transport to market."

"The guy's an animal alright," Cris said. "Anything else?"

"Cannabis and a lower level reading for Dianabol, an oral anabolic steroid."

"So, it appears the man the Cole's neighbor saw on the street *is* likely our suspect." Mike said, "and he's a juicer."

"Juicer?" Lisa asked.

"Only one of the many monikers for users which have grown out of the abuse of steroids. Our photo there must have been taken before he began his relationship with steroids."

"He may have picked up the bodybuilding and steroid habit while in prison. It's one of the favorite inmate pastimes, Cris added."

"Good work Lisa," Mike said.

"Thank you, Sergeant."

"Yes. Really good work, Lisa." Cris patted the intern on the back.

"Ladies, have a great day." Mike turned toward the door.

"You too, Mike."

"See you later." Cris waved.

"Some good news, huh?"

"Yes," Cris said, "and it gives me an idea."

Chapter 34

Tony's Cafe
Nashville, Tennessee

Mike and Cris were at Tony's Cafe enjoying coffee and waiting for Officer Mark Bolger. Bolger was an officer who normally worked out of the North Precinct on 26th Avenue off Clarksville Highway when on patrol duty. He also assisted the department's Narcotics Section when they were investigating the sale and distribution of steroids and related issues anywhere in Music City.

Bolger was not a typical MNPD officer. Mike was about to discover why.

"Here he is," Cris said, as she and Mike stood.

"Good morning," Bolger offered his hand to Cris. "I'm a little nervous about shaking her hand," he said to Mike.

Mike smiled knowing well what he meant. But, coming from a man who looked like The Incredible Hulk in an MNPD uniform, it sounded strange. The man's neck resembled a tree trunk and his arms looked like legs coming out of his shirt. Mike found it hard to look away from his swollen muscles.

"Sergeant Mike Neal, this is Officer Mark Bolger."

"Mark, good to meet you."

"Same here, Sergeant. I've heard a lot about you."

"It's all lies." Mike smiled.

"Have a seat, Mark," Cris gestured to a chair as she sat.

He smiled at Cris and turned to Mike. "Has she told you how we met?"

"I don't believe so." Mike cut his eyes toward Cris.

"I was running at the department gym one morning and I hear this plea from the other side of the building. It sounded like an Army Drill Instructor. 'Officer!' I could tell it was a female voice. And as usual, I'm always up for helping the females of the world."

"Always," Cris said.

"You're not married?" Mike asked.

"No sir."

"So, I stopped and made sure it was me who was being summoned. She waved for me to come over. I saw ten, maybe twelve, ladies looking super nice in colorful tight workout clothes, so naturally I was willing to get closer."

"Naturally." Cris shook her head.

"When I got there, they're all smiling, so I'm a happy guy. Cris told me she needs help with her class. I'm focused on a dozen nice looking ladies and more than willing to help."

"Just a helpful guy," Cris smiled.

"That's me. Anyway, she asked me to attack her from behind. I'm like, are you sure? She said, 'Yes, Come at me from behind and grab me as if you were about to assault me.' So, I said 'How do you want me to grab you?' I was afraid to hurt her."

Mike snickered.

"Little did I know," Bolger said.

"She said, 'Grab me like you mean it.'" He shrugged. "So, I heard earlier in the week during roll call about a guy who grabbed a lady in the parking lot at Rivergate Mall last weekend. He snatched her hair from behind, so I thought I'd try it." He shook his head.

"Bad mistake?" Mike was way ahead of him.

"You know it." He looked at Cris out of the corner of his eye. "I tried to be gentle about it, but it wasn't appreciated. She interlaced her fingers and clamped both her hands on top of my hand, pulled it tight against her head. Then she quickly turned to face me as she gained control of my hand, turning my wrist upside down. Her move forced me into an extremely uncomfortable position and opened me to a kick to the groin and another to my solar plexus, which landed me on my ass in front of the ladies."

Mike looked at Cris. "You didn't."

"I pulled both kicks," she pleaded. "I wouldn't do it full force. He'd be out of work for days."

"Gee, thanks. If those kicks were pulled, I'd hate to be on the receiving end of the full force ones."

"Yes. You would," she said, laughing.

"You are dangerous." Bolger pointed to her.

"Coming from you," Cris grabbed his index finger, "that's a compliment."

All three cops laughed.

"Mark," Mike said, "the reason we wanted to talk with you today, we have a homicide where a young woman was surprised and strangled in her home. The next door neighbor was outside with his pup around the same time and saw a man, a large muscular man, leaving the area.

"We found several hairs on the victim's body which match each other, but not the victim. In fact they didn't match anyone in the victim's frequent or recent contacts. The fact we found a significant number of these hairs causes us to ask why several hairs and not only a couple.

"Also, these hairs were not pulled out. There's no follicle attached. They had to have fallen out, or at least been ready to fall out, and the struggle with the victim finished the job. We believe the hair loss and the spotting of the large man on the street could be related and directing us toward a person of interest who's using steroids."

Bolger nodded. "It's feasible. Some anabolic steroids do speed up hair loss in men, especially those who are already prone to hereditary hair loss."

"Can you tell us about the steroids being used around the city today?"

"The steroids of choice here, at least lately, have been Dianabol, which is the first anabolic steroid developed and mass produced for distribution. Winstrol and Trenbolone are also quite popular. Trenbolone or Tren, for instance, is known for accelerating hair loss and promoting Roid Rage."

"Roid Rage?"

"Increased aggression."

"Interesting you mentioned Trenbolone," Cris said. "The toxicology report confirmed the multiple hairs we collected showed Tren in their analysis."

"I'm not surprised. It is believed to be the most effective of the popular steroids. However, it is the harshest when it comes to side effects. If used for any length of time, it's been known to cause serious liver and heart damage."

"Don't these goofballs have any concern for side effects?" Cris asked.

"They aren't as concerned about side effects as they are building muscle. Increasing muscle mass and losing fat are current events. In their way of thinking, heart and liver damage are down the road and can be dealt with later."

"Did you ever take the stuff yourself?"

"Unfortunately, yes. But, I realized early what it was doing to me and I stopped. I was retaining massive amounts of water. My cholesterol went sky high. I gave it up.

"Now I focus on a high protein diet and natural dietary supplements. I have to work much harder now to maintain my physique, but at least I'm not killing myself to get there."

"I can't help but notice your uniforms don't seem tailored the same as others," Cris said.

"I buy larger uniforms and take them for alterations in order for them to fit. It's not as bad now. I'm smaller than I used to be."

"You're what?" Mike raised his eyebrows in disbelief. "You were larger than this?"

Bolger smiled. "I've dropped over twenty pounds and several inches. My old uniforms are much too big now." Cris looked at Mike and laughed.

"I'm guessing," Cris said, "but I'd say you don't get a lot of pushback when you make an arrest?"

"Not usually. Most folks seem to equate the muscles to a needlessness to resist."

"Let's talk about the Nashville body builders who use steroids and which gyms in the city they frequent," Mike said.

"Actually, the majority of steroids are consumed, not by body builders, but by young 25 to 35 year-olds. Most folks don't realize it, but the typical steroid user is well-educated, and earns an above average income in a white collar job. They don't plan to use steroids long term, but instead have specific goals to reduce body fat, increase muscle mass and make themselves more attractive to the opposite sex.

Mike shook his head.

"The over-built narcissistic long time users we see posing in front of the gym's mirrored walls are not in the majority. Many of them are the Mr. Universe wannabes who too often end up with the life-threatening or life-ending side effects from their drug usage.

"These walking advertisements for muscle are the ones who frequently supply the younger men with their drugs. Stopping the sale of steroids to these young guys is our primary focus.

"Most of the users in Nashville frequent one of two gyms. Either Hard Corps or Heavy Metal. Most go to Hard Corps. I'd say seventy-five or eighty percent. Both have large quantities of free weights, so few people are required to break their rhythm to wait for equipment. And, most importantly, the wall along the free weight area at both gyms is floor to ceiling mirrors to accommodate all the narcissists, and they're *all* narcissists."

"Where do you work out?" Mike asked.

"I usually go to a small gym near my home when I'm not using the equipment at the MNPD gym. They allow me to workout there as much as twice each week without charge, to have a law enforcement presence. The manager knows what I do for a living. He doesn't share it with the staff and I don't wear my uniform when I visit. I can't afford to visit the more popular gyms, in case I'm called to do undercover work."

"So," Mike said, "according to the elderly neighbor who saw him the night of the murder, the guy we're looking for is large and muscular. Height was estimated at six foot to six three. Dark medium length hair with a full beard. Broad shoulders, big arms. He said he thought he may weigh two fifty or more."

"Much of the description, not only fits me, but more than half the users who workout at the gyms I told you about."

"I figured as much," Mike said.

"If your suspect is cutting up with Tren and using a public gym to build his physique, and possibly even selling steroids, the odds are high you'll find him at Hard Corps."

Chapter 35

Her arms were full of file folders and legal pads. The strap of her flexible leather briefcase was straining her neck as it weighed down her right side causing her to walk with a noticeable tilt.

"Do you need some help with those?" a uniformed officer asked, as he passed her in the hallway.

"No. I got it. Thanks, anyway."

Cris tapped the open door with the toe of her shoe and continued into Mike's office. It was the only method of knocking she had available.

He looked up from the accumulation of papers spread across his desk. "Hey. Come on in."

By the time he'd acknowledged her, she'd dropped the paperwork into one of the chairs facing his desk and her briefcase slipped off her shoulder and onto the floor. She deposited herself into the other chair, leaned back and sighed.

"I'd like a Jack and Coke, please."

"Sorry. My bottle is at the house. What about just a Coke?"

"No. Thanks. All I wanted was the Jack anyway."

"You look like you've had a day full."

"You know it. Had a day full and I'm approaching a brain full. I'm ready for my second wind to kick in."

"Okay. Let's put both of our brains together, and determine where we are with the Cole investigation."

Mike stood and turned to the whiteboard behind his desk where he'd listed all the names of people the two of them planned to interview.

"Are we in agreement Fletcher is likely our killer? And, it is also likely he was hired by someone to kill Brooke Cole?"

"Yes. I don't see any evidence pointing in another direction," Cris said.

"We'll run with it for now. Who on your list had the most to gain from Brooke Cole's death?" He picked up a marker.

"Jon, the most I think, because of the insurance money and possibly the loss of resistance to his career."

"But, the insurance payout is in today's money," Mike said. "With Jon Cole, there is a lot more future money than today money. Significantly more."

"True. For him and *all* his minions. Everyone involved with Jon's career gained because of no further pushback from Brooke."

"By the way," Cris said, "I don't mean to change the subject but, I received the search warrant for the Hard Corps gym's membership list. I spoke with the manager earlier. He's emailing me the list of active and inactive members. I'm going to run searches for the names of all Jon's and Brooke's personal contacts and all others related to our investigation."

"Including Fletcher, for the hell of it?"

"Including Fletcher."

"When do you expect to have this?"

"Today. I'll copy you on his match list, assuming we have one, if you'd like."

"That's fine. Then you can call me, so we can discuss it."

"Can I assume you've covered our need for discretion with the gym manager and appropriately described the troublesome consequences for him should he fail to remain mute on this topic?"

"He has been thoroughly counseled on the unpleasant repercussions if he should decide to speak to anyone, but me, about our discussions or our efforts."

"Good. So, is there anyone on our list of Jon's players you

haven't interviewed yet?"

"No. Everyone at least once. Some, I may talk with again. I've already spoken with Jon again since you and I talked with him at the scene." She scanned the white board once more. "What about Brooke's list?"

"Same here. I don't feel like I'm finished with a couple of them. I'm not satisfied I've asked all the questions or possess all the answers I need. We should both know more about which folks deserve another look after we see the gym membership list."

"Agreed."

"We didn't get to talk much after the Crime Lab visit. What have you learned since we talked last on the phone?"

Cris pulled out one of her legal pads. "I was able to speak with both Gabe Hanson and Val Webb at N-Town, Jon's record publisher. Have I told you about them?"

"No."

"Both were helpful. Not much concern about Gabe. He's a businessman focused on making money. With Jon or with someone else. It didn't seem to make much difference who. He's been around long enough to see scenarios like this one before where artists' personal relationships torpedoed their careers.

"Val is another story. She told me she and Jon were once an item. Well, in *her* eyes, they were, until Brooke sank her claws into Jon. Then, everything changed. No love lost there. She felt sorry for Jon, but seemed to see the net of it all as a second chance for her."

"Should we put her on the POI list?" Mike asked.

"I can't justify leaving her off. She had motive, not necessarily to *kill* Brooke, but to want her gone. Hell hath no fury—."

"Agreed." Mike looked at his notes. "As one of the contenders for the bank job along side Brooke, Darin Gray has to remain on our list. He said nothing to convince me to absolve him. Actually, I'm still trying to figure if he has photos of someone at the bank in a weak and lust-filled moment. He isn't that sharp."

Cris smiled.

"Brooke's dad came here to talk with me. He is the same man I recognized. If you remember, we saw the photo in their bedroom the night Brooke was killed?"

Cris nodded.

"Norm and I investigated Mrs. Ashton's death in 2010 and, like the CSU and the District Attorney, found it to be a suicide. Mr. Ashton and his daughters were convinced it was murder. No evidence whatsoever to support it. Turns out she had a considerable life insurance policy which did not pay off." Mike shrugged.

"When I finished at the bank, I made the call to the number you gave me in Hoover, Alabama. Turns out, Mr. Charles Rosedale was a former beau of Brooke Ashton when they were students at The University of Alabama.

"If I remember correctly, you were thinking he was likely calling to rekindle the old flame."

"I simply suggested it could be the basis for his call."

"Okay." Mike smiled. "Mr. Rosedale did not even make the call. His fiancé did. She was a friend and sorority sister of Brooke Ashton. She'd called Brooke to ask her to be a bridesmaid in her wedding. She was marrying Brooke's old boyfriend." Mike took a deep breath. "Sad, huh."

"Very."

"By the way. Brooke accepted."

"Wow."

Both detectives sat for a brief moment in thought.

"I was thinking today and I have a suggestion to run by you on how we can set ourselves up to locate and hopefully arrest our man Fletcher. It should work assuming he is still in Nashville and, as Officer Bolger suggested, if he's using Hard Corps Gym."

"He could have left the city if he feared being discovered," Mike said.

"True, but I'm not convinced he fears being found. I think he may feel he's covered his tracks sufficiently and altered his appearance well enough so he doesn't have any fears of discovery. If he looks like the man the neighbor described, he is not still the man in the photo we saw. He has become a different person.

"Besides, as we discovered from the IAFIS report, he hasn't crossed paths with the law in a while. Like so many others, he may have selected Nashville as his new home. Maybe he's comfortable, relaxed. Until now, he's kept himself clean, except for his steroid abuse."

"I'm all ears, detective."

Mike was a by the book kind of boss, but he'd always been willing to listen to Cris's ideas even when they'd seemed a bit risky or outside the MNPD playbook. She never felt she wouldn't be allowed to think on her feet and consider an innovative approach. She and Jerry Rains had proven their skills often and were still Mike's team with the best case clearance record.

She explained her thoughts on trapping Fletcher and was pleased to hear Mike's approval.

"I like it. Set it up and then give me the details."

"10-4."

Chapter 36

Davidson Savings & Loan
Nashville, Tennessee

"Got a minute?" Darin Gray said, as he barged inside the door to Patrick Nichols's office and grabbed the door knob, ready to secure their privacy.

"Not really. I've got to finish this project report for Mr. Green before the end of the day." He checked the digital clock on his desk. "Make it quick." Nichols leaned back in his chair.

"This won't take long," Gray pushed the door until it latched.

Nichols rolled his eyes and slowly shook his head as Gray took a seat in one of the chairs facing the desk.

"I wanted to let you know, I think I've discovered who the Cole bitch caught with her audit."

"Oh? I didn't realize her audits and their results had become common knowledge at the bank."

"It's common knowledge she was in the middle of an audit when she turned up dead."

"Common knowledge? I feel left out, for some reason. Do you have an access channel with the police, or maybe with Mr. Green that I don't have or know about?"

"No. But I do have access to Cole's friends."

"And they have an open channel with the police?"

"No, but they talked with Cole before she left work."

"Okay. I'll bite. What do *they* know?"

"One of them knows who is perpetrating the fraud Cole uncovered."

"Oh? So, Brooke told this friend who was the subject of her audit? This would be a violation of her confidentiality agreement. This truly doesn't sound like Brooke."

"I don't think she's concerned anymore about confidentiality or things she signed while alive."

"We shouldn't be disrespectful of the dead," Nichols said.

Gray held up both hands, open palms. This was the closest he would come to an apology.

"So who was it Brooke supposedly told her friend was involved in her audit?"

"You."

Nichols laughed as if he'd heard a new and hilarious joke. "Seriously?"

"Yeah. Seriously."

"You've got to be kidding." Nichols lost his laughter and continued his act of confusion. "She knows better. What makes *you* consider this has merit?"

"She was auditing commercial loans, according to Patti Woods."

"And you know this how?"

"I have Patti Woods wrapped around my finger." He smiled with raised eyebrows.

"I'm sorry." Nichols held up a hand. "What does Patti Woods know about commercial loans or audits of commercial loans? She's in residential mortgage."

"She's Cole's friend. *Was* Cole's friend."

"This puts her in the know on Brooke Cole's auditing? I don't get it."

"The day she died Cole told Patti she was auditing commercial loans and found a disturbing violation of bank policy which appeared to qualify as fraud."

"Fraud? Okay. What was the disturbing violation?"

"She didn't say."

"Oh. So, this is enough information for you to come in here and accuse me of some wrongdoing? This is pretty bold of you, Darin. Don't you think?"

"I'm telling you what I heard."

"Sounds to me like you're telling me what you think, not what you heard. You heard a comment about Brooke's audit, factual or not, and little else from a person uninvolved with the audit. You took this and massaged it into some dramatic bullshit your imagination conjured up for you. This doesn't sound like the kind of level-headed thinking Mr. Green needs in the members of his management team."

Gray sat, still staring at Nichols as though he'd caught him with his hand in the cookie jar.

"I thought we always supported each other. What happened?"

Gray shrugged.

"You expect me to speak up for you in your quest for the Assistant VP position when this is an example of your fact gathering and analytical thinking? Darin, you're disappointing me.

"I don't know what inaccuracy Brooke thought she'd found, but I can assure you, it was nothing to do with my loans. I've been doing this work for sixteen years. I intend to continue for at least another sixteen."

Gray began to nod and grin as if to say I hear you, but I don't believe you.

"Is this all you have to cause you to condemn me for some act you can't even identify? Come on. Is this Patti Woods's thinking as well? Is she as confused about this as you are? We've taught you folks better than this."

"Okay. I didn't expect you would own up to it."

"To what? Own up to what? I haven't done anything wrong. We have standards in my department, procedures to follow. If, for some reason, we fail to conform to these standards, the result would be apparent immediately and not only to Brooke Cole. It would not take an audit to uncover the misstep."

Gray pushed himself out of the chair and stood. "I realize I've not been with the bank as long as you or some others. However, this doesn't mean I'm incapable of critical thinking. I'll admit, it's possible I could be wrong about this."

"Damn straight. But that fact," Nichols interrupted, "and my support of you over the last couple of years, didn't cause you pause when you decided to barge into my office and accuse me of a crime? Don't let me find out you mentioned this preposterous idea to anyone else at the bank, even Woods. My reputation is strong, but I don't need this kind of unfounded criticism from anyone."

Nichols's fear of what discovery could mean to him was being displayed as anger.

Gray stepped to the door, grabbed the knob and turned back toward Nichols. "If, for some reason, you decide I'm right," he said with a confident tone, "consider the Assistant VP position as compensation for my silence." He pulled the door full open and said, "Have a good afternoon."

Nichols fell back in his chair contemplating the seriousness of Gray's bold allegations. He couldn't believe the man's new found demeanor. Gray moved rapidly from willing to do anything for Nichols to gain his support for the promotion, to threatening him in order to win it.

Ruthlessness didn't look good on him. Gray's sudden willingness to threaten him was nauseating.

Nichols scrolled the lengthy contact list on his cell phone and made a call.

"Hello."

"Jared."

"Yeah."

"We need to talk."

Chapter 37

Hard Corps Gym
Nashville, Tennessee

Cris called Mike twice, but received his voicemail both times. She decided to leave a message.

"Mike, I've finished with the membership list. I found only two matches. Both are bank people. One active, Marc Leblanc; and one inactive member whose membership was allowed to expire last year, Patrick Nichols.

"I'm about to make my entrance at Hard Corps Gym and begin my investigation. I'll call you later."

From the time she began her training in Judo at twelve years old, and then in Brazilian Jiu-Jitsu at fifteen, Cris spent considerable time in dojos and gyms of all types and sizes, mostly across Texas and Louisiana. Her developing skills and competitive wins created a reputation which preceded her throughout her high school days. She was convinced this same reputation had a negative effect on her dating life. She was told by other girls, 'Most boys are afraid of you.'

Not long after she became a recruit for the Houston Texas Police Department at 24, fresh out of University of Houston

Downtown, she began to teach her fellow officers some of the moves, throws, fighting and defensive techniques she'd practiced for the last twelve years. As the department increased the number of female officers on duty, Cris's classes grew in size and became a favorite of the HPD ladies.

Cris dialed the number for the gym.

"Hard Corps Gym," the young female voice said.

"Hi. I'm new in town and I'm looking for a new gym. I was thinking maybe I could come by and get a look at your place. If I do, could you show me around?"

"You bet, honey. When do you want to come over?"

"What about now? According to your address on the Web, I'm like five minutes away." Cris had driven by the gym for a look and parked a half dozen blocks away before making her call.

"Works for me. See you shortly."

"Thanks."

The gym parking lot was large and appeared to be almost full. This early evening time of day appeared to be one of their busiest.

"Hello and welcome." A slender perky twenty-something with her hair in a bouncing blonde ponytail greeted Cris inside the entrance.

"Hi. I guess we spoke on the phone?"

"Yep. I'm Morgan." She tapped her name tag. "And you are?"

"Cris."

"Okay, Cris. Let's look around and see if we have what you're looking for."

Morgan walked Cris through rows of machines while explaining each of their uses. Cris was familiar with most all the machines, which in some cases were parked mere inches apart. She'd used most of them at one time or another over the years.

She followed Morgan, nodding as her hostess went into detail on equipment used mostly by the ladies. When her guide wasn't looking, Cris took the opportunity to study the big men. More than half sported facial hair in some quantity. Several had full beards. Some appeared wholly focused on themselves, their workout and were unaware of her presence. A few others, she felt, were groping her with their eyes.

"Let me ask you a question," Cris said, as she scanned the fifteen or so men who were lifting free weights.

"Sure, honey."

"This area over here with the free weights and the mirrored wall and all the uh—testosterone. Is this the time of day those guys are usually here?"

Morgan laughed. "The real body builders and the wannabes come and go all throughout the day, but this is about the time when the biggest group of larger men are here. A lot of them are friends and they spot each other when they lift heavy." She stepped closer to Cris. "They also enjoy looking at themselves in the mirror as they lift. Narcissists honey, all of them."

"I like to look at them, too."

Both women laughed.

"Some of them look damn fine to me too," Morgan said. "But, they look better when they act like gentlemen. There are a couple of real jackasses in the group. You come here for long, you'll find out."

"Those guys are everywhere," Cris said. "I know how to deal with them."

"You go, girl." Morgan laughed again.

"Okay. I guess I'm good. You said I could workout now?"

"You bet. Enjoy everything, ladies showers are through there and to the left, beyond the Zumba room. Let me know what you think and if you'd like to join us. We'd love to have you."

"I will and thanks for the tour, Morgan."

"Have fun." She headed back to the front desk.

Cris was wearing skin tight workout clothes and a tiny pair of polyester gym shorts under a loose-fitting sweat suit for her initial visit to the gym. She walked to an area near the end of the mirror wall, took off her jacket and sweat pants and draped them over the handlebars of a recumbent bike, not currently in use.

She chose this spot so she could enjoy her workout and further observe the brawny patrons as they checked her out. When last measured, Cris's body fat percentage was 15%. Less than the average male. She was, indeed, a hard-bodied lady.

She tried to appear focused on her routine as she watched most of the men who were watching her. They shared their whispered thoughts as they stared and smiled. Her movements caught the eyes of several. That was her plan.

When she did her Brazilian Jiu-Jitsu flexibility stretches, she heard one of them groan. She ignored the animal-like sound effects. Others turned and reacted verbally to each other. They didn't seem to be concerned with her overhearing them.

When she finished, she stepped to the weight rack and picked up two twenty pound dumbbells. She sat, then laid back on a padded bench and began two ten-rep sets of flyes, designed to work the upper body.

The men's smiles turned to widened eyes and shared looks as she lifted the weights with relative ease. She knew they could tell she was no stranger to the weight room.

When she returned the dumbbells to the rack, she turned and noticed one of the muscular guys standing behind her.

"I see you know your way around a gym."

"I've worked out a few times."

"I can tell." He looked her over and smiled like a fox who'd just entered the hen house.

Cris ignored his flirt.

"Are you new in the city or are you gym shopping."

"Recently moved down from Clarksville."

"Done with your duty?" He was assuming she'd recently been discharged from the Army.

"You could say that," Cris lied.

"I was with the 101st Airborne myself in a former life."

"Cool." She kept her responses brief.

Others began to collect around them while they talked.

Cris watched as one big guy approached her from the back. She waited for him to step out and in front of her, closer to the others. He didn't. She knew he was still there. She watched his shadow on the floor with her peripheral vision as she talked with the others. He moved closer, but remained behind her. She could see his shadow as he bent forward. Then, she felt it.

She turned her head to her left side and delivered an unruffled response. "You want to remove your hand from my ass?"

"Not really," he said, then laughed as he squeezed her muscled left buttock.

The rest of the men fell silent, no doubt waiting to see what she'd do.

Cris knew, based on his shadow and what she could see over her shoulder, the man's arm size could prevent her planned defensive move from working as well as it normally did in her training class. It would depend on the degree of surprise.

While the jackass was enjoying her disadvantage, Cris thrust out her left hand and snatched the man's muscular paw from her rear. She rotated her body toward him and met her left hand instantly with her right and used both to put his right arm into a wrist lock. She rotated his thick wrist into an awkward and painful position. This forced from his throat a loud groan as she took the hulk to his knees and then over onto his side. He tried to resist the rotation of his wrist, but Cris was using his thick thumb and fingers as levers. Even with his dominant size, he was now the one at the disadvantage.

The other men remained silent, appearing fascinated by her skill.

Four seconds after she'd removed his hand, Cris was standing over the man, her feet shoulder width apart, her knees flexed and her hands with the big man's wrist secured in an unnatural position. He uttered more vulgar terms than she'd heard in weeks on the street.

Cris maintained control, even with him reaching for her leg with his other hand. Each time he reached, she tightened the twist and he pulled back, emitting a loud groan.

"Okay," she said. "What say we start over? I need to know if you are going to be able to keep your hands off my ass, as well as any other parts that seem interesting to you."

There was no reply, other than grunts, from the squirming heap on the floor. The men standing about and watching were now trying and failing to contain their laughter.

Cris twisted the wrist lock another painful millimeter or two. "So, tell me."

"Okay! Yes," he said, then after a moment added, "bitch."

Cris had begun to release the hold, but stopped. She retightened it.

"Damn you," he said.

"I'm sorry," she said. "I didn't catch your response."

"Shit!" he shouted, wincing in pain. "Let me go."

"You know, it sounded as though you called me a bitch. But, I know you wouldn't have done this with me standing here in control of half your future ability to play with yourself. Sometimes," she looked up at the other men, "fingers are dislocated during the wrist lock maneuver."

The group of pain voyeurs were now doubled over with laughter.

"Shut up," he shouted at the group.

"Tell me again. Are you going to keep your hands off my ass, or do I need to dislocate some fingers?"

"Okay! I'll leave you the hell alone."

"Better."

She released his wrist and backed away using large steps in case he decided to attempt some form of retaliation.

He stared at Cris shaking his head. "I'm gonna—."

"You're not gonna do anything." The big man who initially began the conversation with Cris stepped between her and the jerk on the floor. "Get up, hit the shower and consider it a learning experience." As he turned toward her, his smile told Cris she was receiving his support.

Fortunately, the jerk on the floor used his brain and decided he'd received enough embarrassment for one day. He started rubbing his wrist and fingers as he used a weight bench to pull himself into a sitting position.

"Bitch," he mumbled, so only a few could hear.

"Hey. Can you show me how to do that?" One of the other men asked.

Cris didn't respond to his question. "Is this how you guys welcome newcomers? I may have chosen the wrong gym."

"He's sorry. His brain is under the influence. What's left of it, anyway."

"Where did you learn how to do that?" Another one asked.

"Were you in the army? Show me how you did it."

"I can't. If I tell you, I'll have to kill you." Cris held a solemn face then finally broke a smile. The men all laughed. She began to explain the wrist lock move and how it worked even on big guys with thick arms.

"Hey, do it on me. I promise *I* won't cry," one man said.

The others laughed. Several of the big guys remained huddled around her demonstration, captivated the move was so effective.

Cris scanned the gym, looking between the men as she gave her demonstration. The ass-grabber was nowhere in sight. She spotted Morgan, standing near the front counter. She appeared to have been watching the entire episode. When Cris's eyes met hers, Morgan gave her thumbs up and a smile.

Chapter 38

South Nashville

Darin Gray laughed out loud as he drove home from the bank, taking all his normal short cuts through the industrial area off Nolensville Road.

"I can't believe how gullible that damn Nichols is." Gray slapped the arch of the leather wrapped steering wheel of his 2012 Certified Preowned Acura TL as he drove. He'd added all of sixty-two miles to the odometer's thirty-eight thousand since he signed the purchase documents last week.

"The idiot is careless enough to trigger an audit with Cole, and then he's mindless enough to allow me to use it to negotiate my way into the Assistant VP position. I love it. I must be better at this than I thought."

Gray enjoyed stroking his ego. "Obviously, I *am* management material after all. I wonder, if I play my cards right, I bet I could—."

As he slowed for a stop sign, his car shook as if he'd struck something in the roadway.

"What the—?" The bright light in his side mirror was blinding. "Son of a bitch."

He'd been rear-ended.

Gray shoved the transmission into park, pushed his door open and jumped out onto the darkened street. He stepped toward the rear of his car to see an early two thousand model Ford pickup with its front bumper occupying part of the same space as the rear bumper of his formerly flawless TL.

Where are the freakin' cops when you need one?

"What the hell, man? Are you blind?" he said, as he stepped to the driver's side door of the truck.

As it opened, a man wearing horned rim glasses, a large coat and a dark baseball cap climbed out at a snail's pace.

"Wow. Sorry about that." He stepped forward to see the damage. I thought you were pulling away from the stop sign. Are you sure your brake lights are working properly?"

"Sorry? Sorry! Look what you've done. I just bought this car last week. What the hell were you thinking? Of course my brake lights are working. This car was in mint condition. Now look at it."

"Hey. It was an accident, man. It's minor. I've got insurance."

"It may be minor to you. I haven't had this car two weeks yet. I gotta call the police. My insurance is gonna want a police report."

"Okay," the man said, "let's share drivers licenses and proof of insurance." The man reached for his wallet.

Gray opened the back door of the Acura to collect his wallet from the inside breast pocket of his jacket, hanging on the backseat hook above the window. "I am not believing this."

As Gray backed away from the car and opened his wallet, he heard a click, but thought nothing of it. He stood straight and turned to hand over his license. The man was now standing closer than before.

Gray saw a blurred movement on his right which appeared to be the man extending his hand. He felt the sharp pain in his throat. Left side, then right.

He dropped his wallet. The sight of the substantial flow of blood drenching his white shirt and tie brought him to a level of fear he'd not known. He immediately grabbed his throat with both hands in an attempt to halt the surge. His effort was useless as the blood gushed from between his fingers.

As he tried to breath in, he inhaled his own blood and started to cough in an attempt to clear his lungs. He was drowning.

Weakening rapidly. He fell back against his car and slipped

down its side. Gray collapsed onto his knees and then onto his side amidst the rapidly pooling blood on the asphalt.

In the fog of his vision, he couldn't see anything. But, he could hear screaming tires accelerating away, leaving him to die on the street next to his car.

Chapter 39

An Apartment Complex
Antioch, Tennessee

Richard Emerson and Walt Casey lived in the same small apartment complex overlooking busy Interstate 24 in the part of southeast Nashville known as Antioch. Richard played the steel guitar and dobro in Jon Cole's band. Walt played rhythm guitar and occasionally the mandolin.

Their two studio apartments were in buildings next door to each other. Walt liked to kid about his apartment. He told people his flat was in building B so his address was B flat. Richard claimed his place, next door in Building C was, in his opinion, much more attractively decorated so he called it C sharp. The truth was, both studio apartments were virtually identical. One large room with a kitchenette and a small bath. The only furniture in either space was a davenport sleeper sofa, a single club chair and a makeshift bookcase for a TV, stereo and each man's most treasured country CD collection.

They spent the majority of their free time together in one apartment or the other drinking beer and writing songs. They enjoyed writing together and had even penned a few songs which were currently being reviewed for consideration by the leadership group at Jon's record label. None of their current tunes were the caliber of Jon Cole's writings, but Scott, Jon and the band agreed to perform one of their compositions each night in a late set.

Richard lit a cigarette as Walt handed him one of the two long necks he'd taken from his refrigerator.

"Have you talked with the Latina detective lady yet? She's pretty good lookin'," Walt said.

"Yeah. I talked to her."

"Two freakin' hours, she talked. I forgot how hot lookin' she was. She kept askin' me the same damn questions over and over like she wasn't listening the first time or she thought my answers were gonna change. What the hell was that about?"

"She was trying to see if you were going to be consistent with your answers or lie to her. By the way, did you hear what our genius drummer did during his interview with her?"

"There ain't no tellin' about Clint." Walt strummed chords on his acoustic guitar and adjusted the tuning as they talked.

"He wore that damn gun on his hip during the interview with the detective."

"Do what?" Walt leaned forward in his chair. "No way."

"He told me. Yep. Said he forgot about it. She saw it, frisked him, made him take it off his belt. She emptied it and laid it on the table while they talked. He told her, 'I have a permit.'"

"I have a permit," Walt mocked Clint's admission.

Both men erupted in laughter.

Walt spilled his beer. "Maybe I should have told her *I* was packin' too, so I could get frisked. What a dumb ass. Who would do somethin' so lame?"

"Only Clint. Yeah. It's always a good idea to go armed during a homicide interview with a cop who's looking for someone to blame the murder on."

"Leaves a great first impression. I'm sure," Walt said, still laughing.

"And, it's a real good way to get your ass shot."

"No shit. I'm sure it helps to move you up on their suspect list too."

Both men turned up their bottles for a long draw.

"Did she ask you about Jon and his wife?" Richard asked.

Walt looked over at Richard and nodded. "Yeah." The laughter subsided.

"What did you tell her?"

"I told her I didn't kill her. Told her I'd never seen Jon and his wife fight and I didn't think Jon was the type who would, or could, do something like that. And, I said I didn't have any idea who might have killed her. Basically, I took up for the boy and told the detective I didn't know nothin' 'bout nothin'."

"That's pretty much what I said. But, I did admit to her, when his wife made him cancel the tour last year, there was a quite a herd of us who wanted to kick her in the ass for what she did to our bank accounts."

"Ain't that the truth. I guess I was kinda careful 'bout what I said. Tried to be, anyway. I didn't want her gettin' any ideas, thinkin' I could do something like that. Hell, I didn't like his wife. Too bossy for me. But, there's a lot of folks out there I could do without. Don't mean I'd like to kill 'em."

"Not all of 'em anyway," Richard added.

"Amen."

Both men laughed and clinked their bottles in agreement.

"Do you think Jon could have done it?" Walt asked.

Richard thought for a moment. "No. I don't. It doesn't seem possible. I've never seen him when I thought he was capable of violence."

"I'm not sure," Walt combed back his longish salt and pepper hair with the fingers of his right hand.

"Why not?"

"I've always believed any man can do about anything at the right time and with the proper inspiration."

"Hmm. Maybe so."

"And with the proper amount of alcohol, of course." Walt laughed as he raised his bottle.

"I don't know. Jon never crossed me as the type to lose control. He's so focused."

Walt nodded. "I overheard him and Scott a couple of weeks ago before the gig at Dusty's. I was puttin' new strings on my Les Paul at the time and wasn't payin' much attention to them. It sounded like they were talking about the new tour. Scott asked Jon if he'd talked to his wife about it yet. Jon told him no, but he was going to do it soon. Scott asked him how he was gonna handle it if she pitched a fit again and demanded he cancel the tour. Jon didn't say anything for a minute, then he finally told him, 'I can't let her kill my chance at success again. I can't. I won't.'"

"Hmm. Interesting," Richard said. "I heard Jon talking to Sands during a break at practice last week. I didn't think anything about it at the time. Jon told him something to the effect of, 'Sometimes, I swear, I don't know what I was thinking, getting married. I love her, but I have a hard time liking her sometimes. She's so set on rearranging my life to suit her needs and her expectations. I guess I pictured marriage differently.'"

"That's why I ain't married," Walt said as he strummed a G chord.

"Hell, man. None of this means he did it."

"I know. But, it has to make you wonder—at least a little. It sounds like the boy was gettin' awfully frustrated."

"Oh, bullshit. The man ain't the type. What else did the cop ask you."

"She asked me if *I'd* ever been arrested."

"Yeah? She asked me too."

"I knew as soon as she said it, I could see it in her eyes. She already knew the answer."

"Cops and lawyers. That's what they do. They want to know if you're gonna lie to them, so they ask you a lot of crap they already know. What did you say?"

"I told her the truth. Told her I was arrested in 2009 for public drunkenness and domestic assault."

"I bet she perked up when she heard that."

"Yeah. I told her my girlfriend at the time and I got drunk together and got into a fight. She called me an inconsiderate rottin' son-of-a-bitch. I told the detective it pissed me off and I punched her in the face. Hey, she knew I was drunk and unable to control my anger. And, she knew better than to push it. But, she did anyway."

"What was the fight about?"

Walt emptied his beer, burped loud enough to rattle the blinds and said, "She wanted to watch The Hallmark Channel. I'd already told her, Thursday Night football was on. She used to do that crap just to piss me off. She knew, whenever I didn't have a gig, Monday Nights, Thursday Nights and Sundays all day from August 'til February were for NFL football."

"Sounds like maybe I should limit your intake of longnecks."

Richard laughed.

"Oh, hell. I ain't gonna hit you. Unless of course, you decide to turn on the Hallmark Channel."

Both men laughed.

"That woman was incapable of understanding men. Don't ever hook up with a woman who don't like football. It'll make your life hell."

"I heard dat." Richard stood. "You up for another one?"

"Man, that sounds like the title to a Country Music song."

Walt strummed his guitar through some chord changes and began to sing with a southern twang. *"She said honey, are you up —for another one."*

Chapter 40

Crime Scene
South Nashville

In the midst of flashing blue and red strobes, Norm Wallace was on his knee aiming his focus and his high lumen LED flashlight, held in his mouth, at the bumper of the victim's Acura TL. Parallel cracks in the paint indicated the car was struck from behind or had possibly backed into something.

It took Norm considerable effort to kneel his six foot four inch, two hundred and seventy pound frame. Straightening his sixty-three year old body into a standing position was a bit tougher still.

Wendy pulled her face mask down and shouted, "Hey, Norm."

"Yeah." He said, as he examined the odd colored paint chips he'd retrieved from the pavement beneath the car's bumper.

"You may want to call Cris or Mike about your victim here."

"Why's that? Don't they have enough to worry about tonight?"

She held something up with her gloved hand. "This guy's work ID says he works at the same bank as their female victim from their case last night."

"Oh? Interesting." *We don't need a damned serial killer.* "What's this guy's name?"

"Gray, Darin Gray."

"Thanks."

Norm secured the paint chips in an evidence envelope and finished the notes he'd begun during his initial exam of the bumper. He stepped away from the car to make his call.

"Mike Neal."

"Hey, partner."

"Norm. What's up?"

"You got a minute?"

"For you, two minutes."

"We got a call from a citizen who found a body lying next to a car in South Nashville near Radnor Yard. It was thought to be a car-jacking or a drug deal gone bad, but according to Wendy, it may turn out to be something a bit different."

"Oh, how's that?"

"Wendy suggested I call you or Cris. Seems this victim worked with your female victim from last night."

"Brooke Cole?"

"I think so. Did she work at a bank?"

"Yeah. Davidson Savings & Loan."

"Wendy found this guy's work ID in his car. She said his name is Darin Gray."

"Oh, no. Can you determine cause of death yet?"

"Based on the wide horizontal gash running from ear to ear, his severed carotid and trachea, and the volume of blood down the front of his shirt, I'd say he drowned in his own blood. What about your lady victim?"

"She was strangled in her kitchen."

"Was it the husband?"

"He wasn't there, so he says."

"Of course. I guess I was expecting a similar method," Norm said.

"Yeah. This complicates things," Mike said. "Darin Gray was one of our persons of interest. He may still be. Looks like we may have two killers."

"I love it when things start working well in one direction," Norm said, "pieces begin to fall together and then it all makes a sharp turn and takes off in another direction. It's one of those things that makes our work so much fun." Norm loved his sarcasm.

"If you say so," Mike said.

"Do we need to get together when I finish this scene and compare notes?"

"Yeah. Or, maybe before you finish," Mike said, as he contemplated the best move.

"Say when, partner. What are you thinking?"

"Actually, I'm gonna wrap up what I'm working on right now." Mike thought for a moment. "Text me your location and I should be there in about a half hour. I'd like to see what you have there. Looking at these two crimes together might help."

"Good deal. We're just getting started, so we're gonna be here a while. There's enough work for all of us."

"I'm sure. See ya shortly."

Norm sent Mike his location and put his phone away. He scanned the area for Wendy, then shouted. "Hey, Wendy."

"Yep?"

He heard her, but couldn't see her. Then she stood.

"Mike's on his way, in case you want to know."

"Why? Does he suspect the two homicides are related?"

"Not sure, but he's got something on his mind," Norm said.

"Two homicides from the same workplace in twenty-four hours kinda causes one to suspect there could be related issues."

"Yes," Wendy said. "I'm thinking I heard Mike say Tuesday night's lady and some others were up for the same forthcoming promotion at the bank."

"Really? Hmm. I guess it doesn't always pay to be ambitious."

Norm shined his light toward the body of Darin Gray. "I wonder if this vanquished soul was up for the job bump? And, who else was in consideration for the apparently desirable position?"

"I don't know," Wendy said. "But, I'd say he, she or maybe even they, will soon be on Mike's shit list."

"No doubt," Norm said. "Let's see if we can help that happen."

Chapter 41

Crime Scene
South Nashville

Mike struggled to insert this latest jagged piece into the expanding jigsaw puzzle surrounding the Davidson Savings & Loan and Brooke Cole's still unexplained murder.

As he drove toward the most recent crime scene, he searched his mental notes for even a remote association, other than just the bank, which could have connected Brooke Cole and Darin Gray. What could have made them both targets for murder?

Was Gray the subject of Brooke's most recent confidential audit? Who benefited from both Brooke Cole's and Gray's deaths? Could Brooke and Gray be connected in some odd way I haven't seen? Did Brooke Cole and Darin Gray simply know something they shouldn't? Was the killer someone who was caught up in Brooke's audit and was now attempting damage control? Could there be someone new the investigation has not yet uncovered? Or, are the two murders actually unrelated?

Mike continued to propose questions and search for answers as he drove, in hopes that some as yet unrealized detail might push the investigation in a fruitful direction.

According to Patti Woods, only she, Brooke and Darin Gray knew about the audit prior to Brooke's murder. Could one of them have shared this information with someone else? He thought he may need to talk with Patti again.

With the death of Darin Gray, Marc LeBlanc was moving up Mike's list of persons of interest. If these two homicides were found to be related, he's the one with the most to gain. But, who could believe that anyone would be willing to kill, even once, for a low level job promotion? It made no sense.

I need to see LeBlanc again tomorrow.

Mike parked as close as he could to the intersection. He stepped from his car still engulfed in his efforts to glue facts together. He spotted Norm towering over the rest of the first responders.

Mike was approaching Norm and was about to ask a question of his former partner when pain stole his focus, redirecting his thoughts and causing him to stop. He leaned against a marked MNPD cruiser and put his hand to his lower abdomen.

"What's wrong? Norm asked. "Are you sick?"

"I've been having this irritating pain. I originally thought it might be a pulled muscle, but the pain is too sharp. It's beginning to resemble another kidney stone."

"Oh, man. I had one. It was like trying to push a bowling ball through a garden hose. Some of the worst pain ever, except for my heart attack. It was worse. Have you seen the doctor?"

"No. But I'm thinking I'm going to. My annual physical is coming up next month. I think I'm going to move it up. I can't handle this another month. If it's a stone, they need to blast it with ultrasound and break it up. I've got to have some relief."

"I don't blame you, partner. Are you sure you feel up to being here? We can handle this you know."

"I know. I'll try and tolerate it." Mike's hand was still holding his abdomen. "I'm hoping something from this scene might help us with the Cole case. Tell me what you guys have discovered."

"Wendy spotted the victim's work badge and told me his employer was the same as your victim from last night. That's when I called. Are you familiar with this guy here, Gray?"

As the crime scene photographer stepped into the area for his close-up shots of the body, Mike and Norm stepped away from the area around the victim and his car.

"I interviewed him, along with several others at the bank, to see if they knew anything about Brooke Cole and who might have wanted her dead. They were both in consideration for the same upcoming promotion at the bank, so when you called, all my senses went on high alert."

"I can imagine. Was anyone else up for the job?"

"One other guy."

"Can I assume he's now been promoted to *top suspect* in both homicides?"

"For the moment, maybe. But, I'm not totally convinced."

"As you can see, there was a considerable amount of passion involved in this carnage. Wendy told me yours was a strangulation?"

"Yes. Inside the home. No blood. Appeared to be a lay-in-wait. The injuries and the scene confirmed the female victim was overpowered. A few items of value were taken, likely after the murder. And a large unknown individual was spotted leaving the area by a neighbor around the time of death."

"Not like all this mess, huh?" Norm gestured toward the victim.

"No."

"So, you were hoping for some degree of commonality in hopes of being able to narrow your field of suspects?"

"It would have been nice. The guilty have been slow about floating to the top. Now this." Mike shook his head. "Cris and I are still trying to add to and subtract from our crowded field of potential suspects in the Cole murder. Actually, Darin Gray was one of our suspects."

"Well," Norm said, "subtract one more."

Chapter 42

Criminal Justice Center
Nashville, Tennessee

"Thank you for agreeing to see me on short notice, Sergeant. I wanted to talk with you before I went to work."

"What can I do for you, Mr. Nichols?"

"I—uh. I need to tell you—about something."

"Okay. Shoot." Mike leaned back in his desk chair and gave Nichols his full attention.

"It's not easy." He hesitated, taking several large breaths.

"Take your time."

It was not exactly commonplace for people to request an early morning visit with a detective in a homicide investigation. With two of his co-workers now dead, Mike was anxious to hear what Patrick Nichols had on his mind.

"I saw the story this morning on the news. It said Darin Gray was murdered last night."

"Yes. I was at the crime scene."

Nichols face was turning red. He looked from Mike to the floor and back to Mike.

"I believe I know who killed him."

"Oh? Who's that?"

"I'm pretty sure Jared Reed killed him. Reed is one of my customers." He looked away.

"Jared Reed? What makes you think so?"

"He knew Darin was blackmailing me in order to get the Assistant VP job at the bank. The job Mr. Green was considering for Brooke."

"Why would it be reason enough for *him* to kill Gray? It sounds more like motivation for *you* to want to stop him."

Nichols pulled in a chest full of air and sighed. "Darin figured out—Reed and I were embezzling from the bank. Reed was afraid Darin would go to the police and expose everything."

"Once again, Mr. Nichols, this paints you as suspect as much as Reed."

"I know. But, I didn't kill Darin."

Mike watched him. "So, you were the ones Brooke Cole uncovered with her audit."

Nichols looked away and nodded. "Yes."

"Did Reed also kill Brooke?"

"It's not likely. Neither he, nor I, knew about the audit until after she'd been killed."

"Haven't you been with the bank for several years?

"Yes."

"How did you get involved in all this?"

Nichols pulled his feet together on the floor, sat up straight and wrapped his arms around himself in a defensive posture. "My wife and I are separated. She has our son. He's eleven. I get to see him every other weekend. She left me because—" he stopped for a moment. "Because in her eyes, I've failed as a husband and father to provide for my family in the manner *she* expected." Nichols paused. "She grew up with money. Her father is a lawyer. Owns his own law firm. She thought I should provide for her in a similar manner. As only a vice president of the bank, she considers me to be a failure."

"Hmm. That's tough."

"Yes. It is." Nichols interlocked his fingers and placed them in his lap. "She somehow expected me to be rolling in the dough by now." He shook his head. "So, when Reed came in and made me an offer that would net me several thousand dollars, all I could see was Ben and me back together throwing the football again in the backyard.

"Reed told me, 'If you'll do what I tell you, I'll set you up so you can impress your wife, get Ben back, and retire from this dungeon in two years or less.'"

Nichols closed his eyes briefly and then looked up at Mike. "It seemed worth the risk at the time. I can't believe I let him drag me into this."

"How did you hope to explain your newfound fortune?"

"I do some day trading on my lunch hour, after I get home and at other times. I've made some decent returns. I'd planned to use it as my explanation. My wife wouldn't know any better."

"Tell me about what it is Jared Reed did to suck you into all this deceit."

"Reed held himself out as a successful businessman from the beginning. He was confident and impressive. He is very much a salesman.

"He provided me his personal financial statement, income tax returns for him and three of his companies, several property appraisals, a stack of deeds of trust for several commercial developments both in Tennessee and North Carolina, tenant lease agreements and rent rolls, cash flow statements, asset and liability reports, credit reports. His portfolio was one of the most impressive I'd ever seen. He had his act together and appeared to be exactly as he purported himself to be. I was impressed."

"I have to ask," Mike said. "Did you not attempt to verify some of his smoke and mirrors?"

"I did. I sent out letters to two banks in North Carolina he offered as former lenders."

"And?"

"Reed came back to the bank only a couple of days after I'd sent the letters. He was excited about an opportunity that came up. He said he needed to act quickly in order to take advantage of it. It was a small strip mall in Dickson, Tennessee which was going to be auctioned off the following Saturday. He found out about it on the Tuesday before and came straight to DS&L. He said the terms stated the payment, cash or local bank check, must be made the day of the sale so he had to go prepared.

"He asked if I could work quickly enough for him to get the money and make the deal, assuming the property didn't go for more than he thought it was worth. I told him I would do my best. He said if he was able to get the property he would make it worth my while. I told him we weren't allowed to accept any type of incentive. He said it wasn't an incentive. It would be a gift to a friend. Nothing more.

"He offered another of his local properties as collateral for the loan. He gave me all the supporting documents. I looked them over and made the loan. This is how it all started."

"He took you out of your element and baited you with a taste of his greed."

"More or less." Nichols nodded. "I've learned a lot since he first came in. I'd read articles and email in the past from various credible sources on the topic of loan fraud, but I'd never envisioned myself as caught up in it.

"Had you envisioned losing your family before it happened to you?"

"No. Reed's use of my weakness, my family, to achieve his ends was deceitful, but effective. He found what he needed to manipulate me in order to get what he wanted."

"At what point did you realize you were being played?"

"On one of Reed's visits to the bank, he came in and pushed what appeared to be a credit card beneath my computer keyboard. I asked him what it was. He said it was the gift he'd talked about when he bought the auctioned property in Dickson. I didn't pursue the topic. I guess I was afraid of what I'd learn.

"Later that same week, I asked Reed about some of the documents he'd supplied when we first talked about doing business. I think he realized I'd begun to question some of the figures from those documents.

"The fact I'd accepted his *gift* opened a door for him to expose some of his secrets."

"How much was the gift card?"

"A thousand dollars."

"Hmm. A down payment for your complicity?"

"I guess." Nichols looked away.

"So, tell me. How was Reed able to maintain his charade?"

"His ability to find a person's vulnerability as well as his salesmanship and his silver tongue drew me to him. His personality was the lubricant that allowed him to manipulate me into becoming his minion. I was weak. I had a need. He used it.

"After he opened up to me and began sharing some of his methods, I discovered he'd falsified documents from the beginning.

These bogus docs outlined the fake assets and liabilities of his businesses. By altering his bookkeeping, he'd inflated his income by approximately $600,000 on his first DS&L loan application.

"He falsified rent rolls and prepared fake leases which he then provided to me in support of his application for fairly large loans secured by a fictitious commercial building in Memphis."

Mike sat staring at Nichols and absorbing the creative methods of a financial criminal.

"I searched for articles on the Internet explaining the fraudulent practices Reed described to me. I found that dishonest owners of distressed commercial properties obtain financing by creating bogus leases and using them to exaggerate the building's profitability, thus inflating their appraisal value using the income method approach. These false leases and appraisals trick lenders into extending loans to the owner. By the time the commercial loans are in default, the lender is oftentimes left with dilapidated, unusable or difficult-to-rent commercial property. This is what Reed did.

"Did you not at some point begin to feel a modicum of remorse for your long term employer?"

"Yes. But, I was looking past it to what was coming to me and my family."

Sad.

"Reed suggested, not long ago, we could make even more money by recruiting straw buyers with cash back incentives. He said we could inflate the property values using false income documents, falsified credit reports and income tax returns and other documents to qualify the straw buyers.

"Subsequent to the property's closing, the straw buyer would collect his cash back incentive, then sign the property over to Reed's company with a quitclaim deed relinquishing all rights to the property. Reed's company would lease the property units without making any monthly payments on the mortgage until finally foreclosure took place several months later, after he's pocketed several thousands of rent dollars."

"Unbelievable. Did you participate in a scenario like this?"

"No. Fortunately, it never got to that point." Nichols sighed. "Everything was happening so fast, before I realized it, I was neck deep in the same greed that has pulled so many other people down.

I can't believe I fell for it. But, I did."

"How long has this been going on with Reed?"

"Only a few months."

"Did you ever hear back from those two Carolina banks?"

"No. I guess the further he and I got into this charade, the less the truth mattered. He and I were accumulating considerable amounts of money and it seemed to be all that mattered."

Mike nodded. "Have you seen or heard from Reed since Gray was murdered?"

"No. But, my guess is he'll call me soon to let me know he's heard Darin had an accident last night." He paused as if trying to decide whether or not to continue.

"There is one other thing you should know about."

"Okay."

"Reed came to me yesterday asking for an additional short term loan. He wanted me to falsify the documents, use one of the bank's largest customer's accounts as collateral for a loan and show, on our documents, the proceeds going to them. He said it didn't matter which customer I used. It just needed to be one who seldom, if ever, accessed the account I used to secure the loan. He said he'd done this kind of thing before with another bank, out of state. He said it was easy and he'd pay it back within a month, possibly sooner, and no one would be the wiser."

"How much did he want?"

"A half million dollars."

"For what? Another piece of real estate?"

"No. When he couldn't give me an address for a property, I told him without some form of surety from him I wouldn't do it. He finally admitted to me. He'd been offered an opportunity to partner with another guy and buy some drugs for a quick resale. As he put it, 'It's all about the money'. He said he wouldn't touch the junk. He was only the investor."

"Seriously? That was bold."

"Yes. I told him no. I told him flatly, I didn't want to get involved. What we were doing already was risk enough. He talked about the explosive market for opioid pain killers in a way to pitch his plan. He sounded like a TV commercial. He finally told me, once it was resold it would net me, personally, one hundred thousand dollars."

"Hmm. What did you tell him?"

"The amount caught me off guard. I told him I needed some time to think in order to make something this big happen without drawing unwanted attention. He said I had forty eight hours. Then, he would need to do something else to find the cash or lose the opportunity."

"Were you tempted?"

"At first." He rubbed his forehead. "Again, I saw my family back together, Ben and me on the lake fishing. Father and son things again. For some reason, I stopped. The fact I was actually thinking about doing it scared the hell out of me.

"When I thought more about it, I couldn't focus on the money. Instead of seeing Ben and me together, I saw all the people the drugs would hurt and I knew I would be part of the reason for their addiction, their overdose or maybe even their death. I—I couldn't do it.

"I've been buying time with him since yesterday. I decided it would be best to talk to you and let you deal with him. He's quite an intimidating individual."

"You're making the right decision. However, you know the embezzlement is going to get ugly for you?"

"It's already ugly. At least one of our bank employees is dead because of my weakness and my stupidity. For all I know, this could be tied to Brooke's death too. It's over. It has to be." He hesitated. "Reed told me this was small potatoes and no one would even notice. I can't believe I was so stupid to believe him.

"My frustration with my situation at home caused me to make a huge mistake. At this point, I'd like to stop the damage and do whatever I should in order to wrap all this up and settle my debt."

Mike believed Nichols was serious. "There's a way you can help us and help yourself as well as put an end to all this."

"Tell me what I should do."

"Call Reed." Mike looked at his wristwatch. "Tell him you were able to get him his loan. Tell him you have a cashier's check and he'll need to come get it at ten o'clock this morning."

"What if he asks me to bring it to him?"

"Tell him Mr. Green is out of the office and you can't leave the bank. Remind him the cashier's check is the same as cash and, for security purposes, you're required to hand it to only him."

"What happens when he gets there?"

"That's our part. You get him to the bank."

"What else?"

"Once he's in custody, we'll set a meeting with the D.A.. I'll let him know you came to me and exposed all this as well as helped us make Reed's arrest. It'll help your case."

"Will I go to prison?"

"I have no way of knowing for sure. But, I'd plan on it if I were you. Your help should reduce the likelihood or at least the length of time."

Nichols nodded.

"Don't talk with anyone about anything. *Nothing*. Go to the bank like normal and call Reed." Mike handed Nichols his card. "Call me if anything changes."

"Okay," Nichols agreed as he stood."

"Good. Try to be calm when you talk with him and not cause any suspicion."

"I'll do my best."

Mike watched Nichols leave. He knew, at some point, he would have to call in the FBI since the crime against the bank was in Federal jurisdiction. However, the investigations of Brooke Cole's and Darin Gray's homicides belonged to the MNPD. Until they were resolved, the FBI would remain in a junior position. Like it or not.

Mike pushed the appropriate speed dial button on his cell phone, held it to his mouth and leaned back in his desk chair.

"Wallace."

"Norm, I need you to try and clear your calendar for the rest of today."

"Why? What's up?"

"We need to pick up your gift."

"Gift? What gift? Where?"

"Davidson Savings & Loan."

"Sounds like my kind of gift."

"Oh, this gift is even better than money."

"No way. There's something better than money? What is it? Food? Is it cake?"

"Geez, partner."

Norm chuckled.

"You haven't solved your Darin Gray case have you?"

"You know I haven't."
"Meet me at the CJC at 09:15."

Chapter 43

Davidson Savings & Loan
Nashville, Tennessee

Mike and Norm stood on either side of the lobby doors as Jared Reed left his Lincoln and approached the entrance of the Davidson Savings & Loan. Mike was on his cellphone with Patrick Nichols who was watching Reed's arrival from his office window.

"It's him," Nichols said.

"Okay, we got him," Mike said.

Reed pushed open the glass door and entered the lobby. He nodded an unwitting greeting to the two detectives, expecting to walk past them.

Norm stepped in front of Reed, held up his large hand and said, "Hang on."

Reed stopped and looked back and forth from one detective to the other.

"Can I help you?"

Both men showed Reed their badges.

"Mr. Reed, we'd like you to come with us," Mike said. "We need to talk."

"About what?" Reed appeared prepared to demonstrate his bold self-confidence.

"We'll explain it all when we get to the Criminal Justice Center," Norm said, as he pushed open the lobby's exterior door.

Reed's reluctant acceptance of the detective's offer was obvious as he shook his head from side to side.

* * *

Reed followed Mike into the Criminal Justice Center. Norm trailed the two of them through the halls until Mike stopped at a door labeled Interview Room #3 and looked inside.

"Let's talk in here."

Once Reed and Norm were inside and the door was closed, Mike said, "Mr. Reed, in the interest of justice and fairness to you, you should know our discussion today will be recorded, both audio and video. And, before we begin, I'd like to share with you your rights under the law." Mike extended his arm. "Have a seat."

Reed looked back and forth from Mike to Norm with a lowered brow as if he had no idea why he was there.

Mike read the Miranda warning. When he finished, Reed spoke up, "Yes, I understand my rights and I have a lawyer if he's needed. But, what I don't understand is why you said we were just talking if you feel the need to read me the Miranda."

Mike and Norm both stopped, stood still and looked down at Reed.

"Are you requesting your lawyer, Mr. Reed?" Mike asked.

"I want to explain to you that I have done nothing wrong and nothing illegal. My lawyer can't tell you this. *I* have to do it. So no, I don't feel like I need my lawyer. Besides, all he'll tell me to do is stop talking to you. That won't get us anywhere."

"You're absolutely right," Mike agreed. "And, we share the Miranda so it's clear to folks what their rights are and record our conversations so none of us are at the mercy of our memories."

Reed nodded.

"You can be certain, you'll be given the opportunity to explain anything you want us to know. But first, I'd like to learn a little more about you." Mike pulled out a chair and sat. "Tell me about your business."

"Okay. Well, I am a commercial real estate investor. Mostly, I buy depressed commercial properties. I refurbish and upgrade.

Then, I either lease and hold or resell once the property is reconditioned. I enjoy turning depressed properties around, but I must make a good profit. Successful real estate investing is all about the money."

"So, you're sorta like a flipper, only with commercial property?" Norm pulled a chair out from the table, plopped his size eighteen shoe in the seat and leaned toward Reed with his most intimidating pose.

"Somewhat. Yeah."

"What about your family?" Mike asked. "Are you married? Kids?"

"Was. Divorced. No kids."

"What happened?"

"What happened? Frankly, I liked making money more than I liked her." He smiled.

"How did you and Patrick Nichols become business associates?"

"I walked into the bank one day and asked to speak with the person who does commercial loans. We talked. He did his thing. He told me what he needed. I told him what I needed. I gave him documentation showing my assets and we came to terms on the property I wanted to buy. He agreed to loan me the money. It's that simple."

Reed's overconfidence filled the small room from the moment they'd entered.

"I assume since you were waiting for me at the bank you are under the impression I've done something wrong having to do with the bank. I can assure you, if anything criminal was done involving the bank, it was done by Nichols or possibly another of their staff. I have no control over the bank, their employees nor what they do with their assets. All I did was ask Nichols for a commercial loan secured by both a property I own here in Nashville along with the distressed property to be purchased."

"You attempted to secure the loan with a property of inadequate value. Is this correct?" Mike looked up from his notes.

"No. It's not correct. My property is easily worth twice what the dumb ass appraiser put on his paperwork. These part time, partially trained appraisers know much too little about real estate and virtually nothing about commercial real estate.

"After I explained to Nichols why my property was worth much more, he concurred and agreed to make the loan. Nichols wasn't required to loan me the money nor accept my properties as adequate surety for the loan. I didn't coerce him or threaten him. I told him I was looking for a bank where I could secure loans when I need them, and that most would be short-term pay back. I also told him I was looking for a long-term relationship. Then, I simply asked him to loan me the money."

Reed held his self-assured gaze on Mike.

"I did suggest how he could make the loan without anyone or anything getting in his way, or for that matter, anyone getting hurt financially. I don't believe a creative suggestion to a banker has become a crime. Has it? And frankly, I didn't get the impression Nichols had much experience with creative financing."

"That could depend on how creative you're trying to be," Mike said. "You paid Nichols, for lack of a better term, a commission, a fee as encouragement to grant you the loan. Is this correct?"

Reed recoiled as if shocked by the accusation. "No. Absolutely not," he barked as he leaned forward and began tapping his finger on the table to make his point. "I paid the bank all the fees they required as listed on their disclosure statement, but I paid Nichols no such thing."

"He stated you offered him a monetary incentive to make the loan."

"What? No. I did not. He is undoubtedly confused." Reed squinted. "Are you asking if I did this, or are you accusing me of it?"

Mike looked at him without answering.

"As I stated earlier, I paid him nothing. *Nothing*. Why would I do this? The bank makes its money from the interest I pay, and believe me, it's enough."

Mike knew Norm's lack of involvement with Patrick Nichols left him at a bit of a disadvantage. He appeared visibly puzzled by some of Reed's answers.

"What were your plans for the loan money?" Norm asked.

"Purchase another commercial property," Reed said, as he held up his open palms as if to say isn't that clear already? "It's what I do. It's a somewhat distressed property which also acts as secondary surety for the loan. It's rough on the surface, but it'll be nice when I get it remodeled. That's what I told Nichols. And, for the record, that's what I did. Do I need to produce for you a copy of the deed to the property I bought? I can do this, or Nichols can do it. The bank does hold the deed to the retail space I purchased using their loan."

"We'll ask Mr. Nichols for it." Mike scanned his notes. "We were told you recently requested a new short-term loan in the amount of five hundred thousand dollars."

"What? No." He shook his head. Reed glared at Mike and then at Norm. "What are you talking about?"

"Patrick Nichols told us you requested a half million dollars and proposed it be illegally secured by another bank customer's assets. The loan was to buy drugs for resale."

Reed began to laugh. "You are kidding, right? Drugs? What the hell would I do with a half million in drugs? I'm a commercial real estate developer, not a pusher."

Abruptly, Reed wrinkled his brow at Mike as his demeanor changed.

"Did Nichols tell you this? This guy is living in a dream world." Reed shook his head. "He told me his wife left him because he wasn't making enough money and he hasn't been the same since. You should check him out a bit closer. It sounds like he was planning to use the money himself, turn the drugs into cash and blame it on me if he got caught. "I can't say I'd be surprised. He does seem quite inventive."

"Tell me," Mike began, "if there was no loan request for the half million, why did you respond to Mr. Nichols's phone call and come in to the bank this morning?"

"Nichols called me and left a voicemail message on my phone. He said my check was ready and I needed to come in to pick it up since it was a cashier's check. He and I had already spoken about possibly getting new appraisals and being able to borrow even more against my properties than I'd initially requested. I told him weeks ago there was another small three unit retail strip available in Donelson I'd like to buy, but I didn't have the funds. I assumed this was what he was talking about and he'd obtained the new appraisals and approval's he needed to get me the money. Obviously, not."

"Mr. Reed, do you know Darin Gray?"

"I'm sorry. Who?"

"Darin Gray." Mike enunciated the name a second time. He worked at the bank, sometimes with Patrick Nichols.

Reed moved his head from side to side. "I don't recall the name. Did I meet him while I was working with Nichols or Green?"

"I don't know."

"I don't remember him." Reed looked from Mike to Norm and back with raised eyebrows and shrugged innocence.

"Why would you ask me about him?"

"He was brutally murdered last night in an industrial area off Nolensville Road."

Reed lowered his brow and recoiled in response.

"It appears the killer tried to make it look like a carjacking gone bad."

"Mmm." Reed grunted and sat forward over the table. "Are you thinking I had something to do with this too?" He looked from Mike to Norm and back. "What is this?"

"Mike glanced at Norm and then to his wristwatch. Mr. Reed, can we get you a bottle of water or maybe a soda?"

"Yes," Reed said, sounding disgusted as he sat back in his chair. "I would like a bottle of water. I would also like to know what game we're playing here."

Mike stood and, with Norm watching, tilted his head slightly toward the door. It was a 'Let's talk' signal the former partners shared numerous times over the years.

Norm made sure the interview room door latched behind him and he followed Mike down the hallway before they began speaking.

"My senses are all screaming liar," Norm said, "but, if he is lyin', he's damn good at it and I'd guess experienced too."

"I need to get rid of some coffee," Mike said. "I'll be right back. Can you grab the waters for us?"

"Sure."

When Mike re-entered the hallway from the restroom, Norm was waiting with three sweating plastic bottles of water each wrapped in a paper towel. He walked up and stopped a couple of feet away from Norm before he spoke.

"This guy is no rookie. He seems to have all his options planned out in case of discovery, so we're gonna need some hard evidence in order to take the upper hand and move this thing forward. I don't see him confessing."

"Doubtful. Not the type."

"We need an affidavit for a search warrant. Can you handle it?"

"I can."

"Based on what we know about him, you might check with the

DMV and see if he has more than one car. If so, list all of them on the affidavit. And, once we're under the warrant, let's get CSU to check all the bumpers for damage."

"He may have more than one residential property," Norm said. "I'll check it and add them to the warrant as well."

"Good idea. Add all personal property as part of the search. Show the judge we're seeking blood evidence or other bodily parts or fluids from the murder victim Darin Gray. Try to get it expedited if you can."

"You bet." Mike checked his wristwatch and Norm did the same.

"Come back inside when the affidavit is on its way to the judge. I'll see what I can get out of him until you get back."

"10-4."

When Mike reentered the interview room and handed Reed his water, he saw a look of cool confidence on Reed's face he rarely saw on faces inside these rooms. The look projected considerably more composure than was due someone in his current position.

"Where were you last night between six o'clock and nine?" Mike pushed in on his abdomen in an obscure way to try and alleviate a sudden jolt of pain.

"Let me see." Reed caressed his chin and looked up.

"You actually need to think about where you were less than twenty-four hours ago?" Mike raised his voice. "Damn, man. We're only talking about last night."

Reed appeared to be taken aback by Mike's elevated tone. Mike didn't normally raise his voice in interviews or interrogations. He was confident the pain was eroding his patience.

"I drove by the commercial property I told you about, to get another look."

"Did you stop or encounter anyone during your drive who could corroborate your statement?"

He squinted and once again appeared to contemplate the question. His dramatics were wasted. Mike had seen it all before.

"To be honest, I don't recall seeing or talking with anyone."

There's that phrase. Mike thought. *'To be honest.'* The thing it proved most often was anything but the speaker's honesty.

"What about cameras in the area where you were that could confirm your presence?"

"I don't notice things like that. I have nothing to hide. But I'm fairly certain since the tenants in these units have all vacated, the cameras, if there are any, are off."

Mike nodded. "Mr. Reed, it is imperative we determine and verify your whereabouts during the time when Darin Gray was murdered. If you have an alibi during this time period, I need to know who or what it is. It's in *your* best interest. You must understand, if we cannot establish an alibi, you will remain a suspect."

"I don't get it. Why am I a suspect? I don't even know this—this Gray character. I haven't killed anyone, and I don't like the way you're talking. You appear to be trying to solve your list of problems by accusing me of things I haven't done. I think I'd like to consult with my attorney now."

"Okay. If it's what you want." Mike checked the time. Norm should be back soon.

"I'll be back."

Mike stepped from the interview room into the hallway. His pain was becoming harder to ignore. It was taking a toll on his ability to concentrate. He located a chair and sat, waiting for Norm.

"Everything okay?" Norm asked, as he entered the hallway several minutes later.

"Yeah. What about the affidavit?"

"Done."

"Good. Reed asked for his attorney."

"Nothing to hide, huh?"

"Yeah. I think he felt I was getting a little accusatory with respect to Gray's murder. When I challenged his flimsy alibi, he pushed back."

"Sounds normal."

"Take him to a phone where he can call his attorney, then bring him back here. When the lawyer gets here, we'll tell them both about the warrant."

Mike pulled out his cell phone and called the Crime Scene Unit.

"Is Wendy in?"

"Sure. Hang on."

"Wendy Egan."

"Are you busy?" Mike laughed to himself, knowing what a silly question he'd asked.

She recognized his voice. "Thanks to you guys, I've never not been busy since I took this job."

"No doubt. Hey, listen. Concerning the Darin Gray investigation—."

"That's Norm's carjacking with the victim who worked with Brooke Cole?" Wendy asked.

"Yeah. We have a new secondary crime scene, possibly more than one."

"Oh, for joy," Wendy said, her mouth full of the caustic wit she'd learned from working with the department's officers and detectives.

Mike ignored her vent. "Yeah. We have a warrant on its way to the judge now. We need to get a look at our suspect's cars, residence and personal property. We're hoping for some biological or other evidence tying this suspect to Darin Gray's murder."

"Cool. Text me the address when you get it? I'll keep working here in the lab until I hear from you."

"Norm will notify you as soon as he gets the call, and then meet you there. Thanks, Wendy."

"No problem."

"Call me when you find something."

"*When* we find something? Not *if*?"

"When."

Chapter 44

"Marc, thanks for coming down." Mike shook hands with LeBlanc. The look on the young man's face resembled many Mike had seen before on the faces of folks called to the Criminal Justice Center for the first time.

"Sure. Whatever I can uh, do to help."

"I assume you know about Darin Gray?"

"Yes sir. I heard from Patrick Nichols."

"Come with me. We'll talk in here."

Mike crossed the lobby and entered the hallway leading to the interview rooms. He stood by the door labeled #1 as he gestured for LeBlanc to have a seat.

Mike was hesitant, but forced to consider LeBlanc a person of interest in both murders. If he was innocent Mike still felt the chances were good LeBlanc could know something, possibly something he didn't even realize he knew, which could help both investigations.

"I guess it didn't register when we spoke at the bank. You're a big guy. What are you, six foot two, six three?"

"Six two."

"Two twenty, two twenty-five?"

"About that."

"Obviously, you work out? Where do you like to go?"

"I'm a member at Hard Corps. It's one of the city's most popular gyms."

"I get to use the police department's gym," Mike said. "It's a perk. Comes with the job. What do you like about Hard Corps? I've heard people talk about it."

"It's a large gym. They have plenty of free weights, so you don't have to wait so long. The other gyms focus more on machines and big rooms for group stuff for ladies like Yoga, Pilates, and Zumba and have less square footage dedicated to the free weights and things the men go for."

"I heard some of the guys who frequent Hard Corps use anabolic steroids. Do you use steroids?"

"Oh, no. Never have. Never will. I know they're used by some of the guys there. But not me. Too dangerous for me. I don't want to get ripped anyway. I just like to stay in shape."

"You've heard the guys there talking about steroids?"

He nodded. "Oh, yeah. It's fairly common knowledge. It's talked about quite a bit among those involved with them. They're not bashful about discussing the drugs. The guys use nicknames, but you can tell what they're talking about. You can't get the kind of cut some of these guys do without some type of—chemical assistance."

Mike made more notes. "Do you know any of these users personally?"

"Just enough to nod or speak when I see them. The same guys are usually there whenever I go in."

"Have you seen any displays of aggressive or violent behavior there?"

"I've seen a few occasions when two of the large guys exchange epithets, threats or maybe pushes. Nothing I'd call violence. They never came to blows or anything."

"Any of them try to sell you drugs before?"

"Oh, yeah. A few times. They don't bother me anymore. They know I'm clean."

"Good. That stuff will screw up your manhood and your future."

"That's what I hear," LeBlanc said.

"Marc, I need you to understand something. When I asked you at the bank about the overheard conversation between you and Darin Gray in the men's room, I could tell you were lying to me."

"Oh, no sir."

"Let me finish. Marc, I've been interviewing and interrogating people for over twenty years. There are signs given off by people when they lie and they don't even know they're doing it.

"What if I told you I ran a search and found the investigator you hired to collect dirt on Brooke Cole's background? What if I told you he admitted he ran her history and gave it to you? Also, he will gladly testify in court if needed. Would all this help your memory?"

Mike believed there were times when fabricating stories to help folks be honest were simply necessary. The fact these lies by law enforcement were allowed by law was also helpful.

LeBlanc sat forward and looked down between his legs at the floor. He was silent for several minutes. Mike waited without comment as LeBlanc searched for a way to backpedal his way to the truth. He finally decided to speak.

"She had the job sewn up. If Thomas Green wanted her, the job was hers. I felt like I needed to do something to level the playing field. If she had something about her which might negatively impact her ability to do the job, I felt like it needed to be common knowledge, not swept under the rug."

"How much did your investigator tell you about his discoveries?"

"He said she had a prescription for anti-anxiety drugs, Xanax to be specific, and had been taking them since her mother's passing. I felt this information could sway the board's decision and give me a fair chance. We didn't need someone on the fast track to upper management who was covertly using drugs. I was thinking about the bank as much as myself."

I'm sure you were.

"Tell me about Darin Gray."

"I'll be honest about Darin. God rest his soul."

"I'd prefer you were honest with me about everything," Mike said.

"It's an expression."

"Go ahead."

"Darin wasn't management material. I don't know how he made the list of potential Assistant VPs, but—he did. He and

Patrick Nichols have always had a connection. Nichols wanted him in the job. I think he felt Darin could be manipulated in ways to benefit him."

"I thought Nichols recommended you for the position as well as Gray."

"He did. He was hedging his bet against Brooke."

"Why?"

"Like the rest of us, he knew Brooke was good at her job. But, Nichols has a thing about women. He thinks they all should be in admin support, not management."

"I heard a similar opinion from Gray."

"They do have things in common."

"So, who killed Brooke?"

"I don't know. I didn't kill her."

"What about Darin Gray? Did he do it?"

"He couldn't do it. He was with me at the time. If he did, he'd have to have it done by someone else. I don't think he could go through with it. He's too much of a wuss."

"Who could do it? Nichols?"

"I don't know."

"Who's left?"

"I don't know."

"Who could have killed Gray?"

"I don't know that either, but I assure you, Gray's list of suspects will be longer than Brooke's."

"Explain."

"Brooke was sorta stiff, what some of us call a tight ass. She was by the book and inflexible. Brooke was in the right job, as Manager of Internal Audit. That's for sure."

"So, she wouldn't have made a good Assistant VP?"

"Not if she required drugs to handle anxiety. I've always heard the higher up you go in your career, the greater the stress."

"I can confirm this," Mike said, thinking of his own work.

"Has the bank never done any drug testing?"

"Not since I've been there. I'm not sure Mr. Green has a good understanding of today's young people. Or else, he's afraid he'd lose several members of his team."

"The use of drugs today is even more pervasive than in years past," Mike said, "but many folks turn a blind eye, rather than deal with it."

"I don't think our board would allow her the promotion if they knew about the drug issue."

"Marc, are you aware a man about your size was seen in the area of the Cole home the night and at the time of her murder?"

"No. I didn't know. I told you where I was at the time you gave me for Brooke's death. Darin Gray and I were at the Benchmark Bar & Grill eating wings, drinking beer and watching the Predators beat the Blues. I'm sure they have video cameras at the bar if you'd like to verify our presence there."

"I remember. Thankfully, Gray confirmed it and you confirmed his alibi. I'm sharing with you what we know from our investigation. Can I assume you realize much of all that's transpired, at least in the minds of some, points to you as a potential, and quite believable, person of interest?"

"I didn't kill anyone, Sergeant. And, I didn't arrange for anyone to *be* killed. Surely you would agree, exposing her drug issue to interfere with her chances at the promotion and killing her are quite different."

Mike looked at LeBlanc, but said nothing.

"I understand I'm the only one left of the three in consideration for the promotion, but it doesn't mean I killed someone or would kill someone for a damned promotion. Seriously? It's ridiculous to even consider it."

"I tend to agree," Mike said, "but people sometimes get wrapped up in their ambitions and do things out of character, things they wouldn't normally do. You, more than anyone, appear to be in a position to benefit from both their deaths. Most often, motivation for homicide comes from either greed or passion. Both murders were committed with a significant display of violence and passion."

"Not me. The Assistant VP, or any other job, isn't worth it."

"Fortunately for you, I can't build an air tight case against you. However, it could be just a matter of time, or information until this changes."

Mike wasn't convinced LeBlanc was involved in either murder, but he wasn't ready to let him know it.

Chapter 45

Criminal Justice Center
Nashville, Tennessee

Mike's phone vibrated in his pocket. He decided to ignore it for the moment and continue the review of his and Cris's notes from the Cole investigation. He hoped whoever was calling would leave a message.

The vibration stopped, but only for a minute. It started again. He pulled out the phone and saw it was Jennifer Holliman calling.

"Hi, Jennifer."

"I got a call from a lady who says she's Mr. Hinkle's attorney."

"He has an attorney?"

"Mike, he's been taken to ICU."

"Geez." Mike looked at his watch.

"She said he was in rough shape and he asked to see you and me."

"Oh. Can you get away?"

"Sure. I'll tell Murph so he can finish my list of skip traces."

Daniel Murphy, owner of Murphy Private Investigations was not only Jennifer's boss, but also a retired MNPD detective and one of Mike's friends.

"Meet me in the ER lobby of St. Thomas West in thirty minutes."

"I'll be there."

The old guy was so tough, Mike thought he might even outlive him. Obviously, his cancer was pulling him down. Mike knew Mr. Hinkle had little or no family. They'd discussed each other's families in years past. He told Mike he had no one left to care about or to care for him.

Mike parked in a first responder space outside the Emergency Room away from the ambulance entrance and tossed his neon yellow Police vest on the dash so no one would question the car.

"Hi." He said to Jennifer as he cleared the over-sized automatic door. "Been here long."

"Couple of minutes."

"Did the attorney say anything about his condition?" Mike held out his arm so Jennifer could board the elevator ahead of him.

"She said it was grave."

"Why do they use the term *grave* when they talk about seriously ill people? Who is she anyway?"

"She said she's his lawyer and executrix of his will."

"Does she think he's dying?"

"I don't know. She said he wanted to see us, soon."

Mike's brow wrinkled. He closed his eyes as he waited for the elevator to open.

"Okay. This way." He gestured to his right.

They encountered a nurse in scrubs and asked if they could get in to see Mr. Hinkle in ICU.

"Are you family?"

"We're all the family he has. We're his next door neighbors. He asked to see us. We were told his condition was worsening."

"Follow me."

Mike's next step, if the previous request hadn't worked, was to pull out his badge.

The nurse escorted them to a long curved desk inside the Intensive Care Unit where she asked for Mr. Hinkle's room.

As they entered the room, it was easy to tell Mr. Hinkle's condition was not good. He had tubes going into his nose, into his arms and others going beneath his sheets into the lower regions of his wrinkled body. The nurse stepped outside the curtained entrance to allow some privacy.

"He doesn't look so good." Jennifer whispered as she grabbed Mike's arm.

"He's not doing well," the voice came from behind them. "Hello. My name is Joyce Hager. I'm Mr. Hinkle's attorney."

"Mike Neal," he said, "and this is Jennifer Holliman. We're his neighbors."

"I know. It's a pleasure to finally meet you."

Mike looked at Hinkle and said a prayer under his breath.

"You have a teenage son named Mason?" Hager asked.

"I do," Jennifer agreed.

"Mr. Hinkle's told me quite a bit about the three of you."

"He never mentioned you to us," Mike said.

Hager smiled. "I'm not surprised. He is quite an interesting man. I've known him almost as long as you."

"He is a private sort of guy," Jennifer said. "Quiet and keeps to himself. We've enjoyed him as our neighbor."

"What's going on?" The gruff, but weakened, voice of the eighty-something old man began to cough. As the three of them moved toward his bed, the nurse came in and separated them in order to reach her critical care patient.

"Are you okay Mr. Hinkle?"

"Just peachy." His mumbling was barely audible.

Mike had to smile. That was Mr. Hinkle, ornery as ever.

"When are you gonna yank some of this crap outta me so I can go home? What are you pumpin' into me anyway? And, for that matter, what are you taking out? If you're selling my blood, sister, you're gonna be in big trouble. This one here is my lawyer." He attempted to raise his finger and point at Ms. Hager.

"She'll sue the hell out of this place. And him? He's my detective with the Nashville Police Department. I wouldn't mess with him either. He carries a gun."

The nurse looked at Hager and then to Mike. She shared a caring and understanding smile with each.

"Honey, we're giving you oxygen to help you breathe, some meds to keep you comfy and liquids to prevent dehydration. It's all good stuff. I assure you. The only thing we're taking away is your body's waste, so you don't have to go to the restroom." She patted Hinkle's hand.

"Bullshit. I know better," he muttered as she walked away, smiling.

"Mike." The old man squinted. "If you're in here," he hesitated, "who's out saving our city from all the murderin' SOBs?"

"I'm 10-7 long enough to visit my friend."

Hinkle tried to raise his left hand in Mike's direction and Mike stepped toward him to take it as it started back down toward the white blanket.

Hinkle began to speak, but became strangled and coughed until he cleared his throat. "You're a good man, Mike Neal. And—"

He began to cough again.

"Here," Mike said, offering him a drink of water from the cup on his tray.

Hinkle sipped from the straw, sighed, then shook his head in disgust. His coughing finally calmed again.

"And," he turned toward Jennifer. "You are a damn fine neighbor, both of you and Mason, too."

"Thank you Mr. Hinkle. We love you too." Jennifer said.

"Ahh, don't get mushy on me."

Mike and Jennifer both laughed.

"Listen. I'm not sure how long I'll be in here, or for that matter, how long I'll be anywhere. I need you to know—" Hinkle took some deep breaths. "how much I appreciate what you've done for me over the last fifteen or so years."

He blinked twice and a tear dropped from both eyes and ran downward into what was left of his thinning grey hair.

"It won't be long before you'll be back home fussing at the squirrels for making noise as they wrestle with each other on your roof," Jennifer said.

"I hope so. Damn squirrels. You sure we can't shoot 'em inside the city?"

"I'm sure." Mike smiled at Hinkle's straight face.

The nurse came around the curtain. "I hate to break up such a fun party, but Mr. Hinkle needs his rest."

"Oh, come on." Hinkle looked at Mike. "They're always spoiling things. They act like I'm sick or something. It's ridiculous."

"I'd say they also do a bang up job taking care of you," Mike assured him.

"Don't tell her that. She'll get the big head." Hinkle coughed.

The nurse began to laugh and stepped toward the bed.

"We'll see you again soon, okay?" Jennifer said.

"Hang in there, buddy." Mike took Hinkle's hand again. "And

don't pick any fights you can't win. These nurses at St. Thomas are a lot tougher than they look. They get hand-to-hand combat training, you know."

"I'll call you if I need backup," Hinkle said.

Mike laughed. "10-4. I'll be here. Code 3."

"You take care of Jennifer and Mason," Hinkle said. "And that good lookin' brunette, too. Where is she anyway?"

"Carol's visiting her sister, helping with her new baby niece."

"She's getting in some practice, mister. You better get ready, 'Dad'." Hinkle started coughing again.

"Yes, sir." Mike laughed.

Mike and Jennifer waved as they exited the ICU. Both had tears in their eyes. As they turned toward the elevator, Mike realized Ms. Hager was behind them and he slowed to acknowledge her.

"He's a little hard on the outside, as I'm sure you both know well, but the inside is quite soft."

"Yes." Mike nodded. "That describes him pretty well. He's seen a lot in his life to harden the outside."

"You two should know something else about Mr. Hinkle."

"What do you mean?" Sensing the importance of the attorney's words, Jennifer stopped. Mike and the attorney did as well.

"He prepared his will a couple of years ago and recently asked me to verify it clearly states his wishes."

"Okay. Is there something we can help with?" Mike asked.

"Mike, he has decided to leave everything he owns to you and Jennifer."

"What? Why would he do this?" Mike asked.

"I think it was made clear to all of us in the last few minutes. He has no heirs, at least none he'll acknowledge. He wants his estate to go to the ones who've cared for him the most."

"Wow." Mike looked at Jennifer who took his hand and began to cry. "I, uh, don't know what to say."

"Me either," Jennifer said. "He is such a sweetheart."

"One more thing. The doctors say he won't be with us much longer."

Jennifer put her hand over her mouth.

"He knows," Hager said. "It's why he wanted you two to come today."

Mike dragged the back of his finger across the corner of his eye and blew out a large breath. "Thanks for calling us."

"Yes, thank you very much," Jennifer said.

"My pleasure. He insisted I get you here. I can tell. He's happy now."

"God bless him." Mike wiped another tear.

"I'll be in touch," Hager said, as she shook their hands.

Chapter 46

Criminal Justice Center
Nashville, Tennessee

"Hey, partner," Mike said as he raised his phone to his ear. "What's up?"

"After the massive apple fritter I ate, probably my blood sugar. That joker was the size of Jonathan Lucroy's catcher's mitt." Norm belched.

"Whoever that is."

"Hey. He's arguably the best catcher Milwaukee Brewers have ever had."

"I thought Cheryl still had you on a diet."

"A man has to eat to stay alive. It's not my fault there's a bakery down the street from Reed's house. Besides, Wendy was famished."

"Oh, I'm sure. Blame the little girl. Give me some good news. Okay?"

"Reed has two vehicles, a 2015 Lincoln MKX and a 2001 F-150. The Lincoln was clean. No evidence and no sign of bumper damage."

"And the truck?"

"Patience, partner."

"The pickup was more—cooperative."

"What did you guys get?"

"Not much." Norm kidded with Mike. "Just some poorly cleaned carpeting."

"Blood?"

"Yep," Norm said, dragging out the sound of the single syllable in his feeble Milwaukee attempt at a southern accent.

"Darin Gray's blood?"

"Yep," Norm drawled it again.

"Al—right. That's great."

"Wendy sprayed Luminol on driver's side carpeting and pedals. The reaction was immediate. He must have 'stepped in it' as they say. We got some great photos. He tried to clean it, but fortunately, he's not as good at cleaning as Wendy is at searching."

"Thankfully, that's often been the case."

"True. But—this is not all we found."

"What do you mean?" Mike asked.

"We found scratches and cracks in the paint on the truck's lower front bumper. Wendy took some samples and you'll never guess?"

"The paint samples matched the ones you collected from beneath the rear bumper on Gray's Acura?"

"Winner-Winner, chicken dinner."

"Are you kidding?"

"Nope."

"Excellent. Reed's ass is toast. Tell Wendy we owe her a steak dinner."

"I already told her. I learned that trick from my old partner." Mike laughed.

"By the way, all these food references are making me hungry."

"Gimme a break. The wind blowing makes you hungry. So, where do we stand at the moment?"

"Wendy is headed back to the lab with the evidence. Once she completes her reports and I do mine, we'll let you know and I'll get you copied."

"Great. Thanks, partner."

Chapter 47

Criminal Justice Center
Nashville, Tennessee

The layout drawing of the Hard Corps gym and the walk-through of the planned takedown, although simple compared to some, was discussed for nearly an hour by the five MNPD officers and detectives who were involved. All but one.

Norm Wallace was in the middle of an unexpected suspect interview from an unrelated homicide investigation that he couldn't postpone nor interrupt. Mike brought him up to speed on the plan in the hallway during a restroom break. He stressed the need for Norm's assistance in the takedown. Norm assured Mike he would be on site at the gym and on time.

Already familiar with the plan and the physical profile of the gym, Cris left the meeting ahead of the others in order to touch base with the gym's manager one last time on his role and her signal to him in the beginning of the takedown. She needed to make sure the suspect was on site, and begin the guise of her workout. She wanted to select a good location from which to observe the suspect and be able to quickly follow him out the front door and into the hands of the MNPD team.

Cris was riding a stationary bike and facing the mirrored wall which reflected the swollen images of the drug enhanced males. She appeared to be listening to music on her cell phone and paying little attention to anything other than her own workout, but she was using her ear buds to maintain communication with Mike. Whenever she needed to speak, she leaned forward and bowed her head so her face was hidden from view. The inline microphone on the earbuds hung conveniently near her mouth.

"Cris, I'm here," Mike said. "Waiting on one other officer and Norm."

"Norm did know when we needed him to be here, right?"

"I told him in the hallway about two hours ago when he took a porcelain break."

"I hope he gets here soon," Cris said. "I don't know how much longer our suspect plans to be here."

"I'll see if I can reach him. Hold tight."

"10-4."

Cris rode her bike and kept an eye on the suspect's movements as best she could without being obvious. She knew, if he was Edgar Fletcher, there would be a struggle once he saw the uniforms approach him. This jerk had an attitude and didn't mind showing it to anyone. She suspected the *Roid Rage* from using the Trenbolone could ramp up his aggression.

She rode the stationary bike another few minutes before she received Mike's call.

"Cris."

"Yeah."

"Our second officer is here. Norm's phone went to voicemail."

"Damn it."

"I told him to haul ass. We may need his size for this takedown."

"Are we good with two uniforms and us in case he doesn't show?" She asked.

"Should be. You can always use your Brazilian Jiu Jitsu, right."

"Not always. The element of surprise will be out the window when he sees blues and badges. Besides this animal has his own set of rules. I've seen him in action."

"Let's go for it. We need this gorilla locked up before someone else pisses him off."

"I'm ready when you are."

"Are you guys ready? Mike asked the two uniformed officers.

"This jackass won't be an easy target, so ramp it up so we can get him on the ground quickly without anyone getting hurt."

"Okay, Cris. Give the manager the signal. We're ready out here."

"10-4."

Cris tucked her phone away inside her jacket pocket and kept the ear buds in place and the line open to Mike. She focused on the activity at the gym's front counter until she saw the manager finish helping a customer. He looked at her. Cris gave him an exaggerated head nod and immediately returned her attention back to the suspect.

The manager walked to the public address system, which was kept on a shelf beneath the counter, and picked up the microphone. When he pushed the talk button, the steady pulse of rock and roll music, which normally filled the gym, was muted and the only sounds were from the clanging machines and free weights until he spoke.

"May I have your attention please? Edgar Fletcher, your ride is here. Edgar Fletcher," he enunciated clearly the second time as Cris had requested. "your ride is out front. Thank you."

"It's him."

"What did he do?" Mike asked when he heard the manager's announcement come over his cell phone.

"Everything we needed him to, except put his hands on his head and march to the front door. He stopped his lift abruptly, dropped the weights and turned toward the manager. He looked at the front entrance and back to the front counter. No one else in the gym paid any attention to the manager's announcement."

"Great. Get ready guys. He *is* our suspect."

"Mike. He's one of the guys I told you about and he's the most belligerent jerk in here. He'll fight if we let him."

"I'm not sure we can convince him not to fight," Mike said, "but if he does start fighting, we can give him a few reasons to stop."

"He looks to be headed for the lockers. Probably getting his bag and coming out. Get ready."

"No doubt, he's anxious to see who his ride is," Mike said. "Okay guys, it's show time."

"Is Norm here?" Cris asked.

"No. And, I may kick his big ass when he gets here."

"Okay. I'll be coming out right behind him. Here he comes. He looks pissed. Hell, he always looks pissed."

Cris stepped from her bike and quietly fell in behind him, but not too close.

As he cleared the front steps and began to scan the parking lot, Mike and the two uniformed officers stepped from between parked cars across from the entrance. They stepped toward the big man from three different angles, so he would have to keep his head on a swivel to watch them all. Mike faced him from straight ahead and the officers moved in from Fletcher's three o'clock and nine o'clock.

"Edgar Fletcher," Mike spoke in an authoritative tone. "Drop the bag and put both your hands behind your head." Mike looked at the man's arms and wondered briefly if he could even put his hands behind his head.

No one had yet pulled any weapons, but their hands were in position to do so if necessary.

"You must have me confused with someone else." He smiled. "My name is Edward Morris. I don't know any Fletcher."

"Drop the bag and put both your hands behind your head."

"Maybe you didn't hear me. You got the wrong guy, slick." His voice reflected his attitude. "I'm not Fletcher," he yelled. He looked from Mike to each of the officers.

"This is your last warning," Mike said.

Both uniformed officers moved in closer. They drew their tasers and held them at an angle slightly below their target, ready to aim and fire.

"Drop the bag and place both your hands behind your head."

Fletcher pulled in a deep breath and flipped the bag's strap off his shoulder and onto the pavement. His hands did not go behind his head. He clenched his fists. His body tensed, sending a clear signal. He was ready to fight. He began to stomp toward Mike, who was the closest to him.

Cris gripped the expandable steel baton firmly with her right hand, removed it from her jacket pocket and gave it an outward sling. The inner two sections slipped from the base and locked to form a substantial twenty-four inch weapon. Fletcher's focus on Mike must have prevented him from hearing the odd metal on metal scraping sound behind him.

She stepped toward his back and used a cross-body swing to land a hard blow to Fletcher's left leg just above the knee. On impact he shouted in pain and dropped to the pavement, onto the knee. He looked back to see where the blow came from.

Cris was out of his reach, poised for another blow.

"You. You bitch!"

"Tase him," Mike shouted. "Now."

Both officers took a step toward Fletcher as they aimed and fired their tasers at his bulky chest. The electrodes tore through the man's clothing and into his skin. His body jerked and stiffened as he fell onto the pavement and shook. After a moment, the voltage stopped surging through him, but his chest was still rising and falling at a rapid rate.

Mike reached for his handcuffs and approached the big man with caution. As he took hold of an over-sized arm, Fletcher yanked it away and pushed Mike backward.

He screamed as he stood, tearing the electrodes from his clothing and his flesh.

Mike climbed to his feet, as both officers fired their reloaded tasers. One set of barbed electrodes struck him in his abdomen and the other in his thigh. Fletcher cursed and gritted his teeth at the cops. This time the voltage seemed to have little effect other than to make him angrier.

Both uniformed officers and both detectives closed on the angry beast at the same time, attempting to take him to the pavement. Mike was trying to trip him and Cris was beating the hell out of his ankles with her baton.

Fletcher kicked at Cris and pushed the two uniforms to the pavement. He pulled Mike into a bear hug. As he did, Mike's abdominal pain struck.

Between his pain and Fletcher's grip, they took away his strength and most of his breath. As Fletcher squeezed, the pain worsened.

He was sure Fletcher was close to breaking his ribs when he heard an unsettling sound. It was a sound like a stick of wood breaking. Mike prayed it wasn't his ribs.

The overwhelming force constricting his body was released. He was free and fell to the pavement as he heard Fletcher howl and fall next to him.

Fletcher was rocking back and forth screaming and holding his leg, now at an odd angle.

Next to Fletcher Mike saw a towering figure. He shaded his eyes.

"You're late." Mike stood holding his abdomen, his own pain still his focus.

"Nashville traffic." Norm shrugged.

"What did you do to him?"

"I took out his right knee from the side. You need to stomp it kinda hard when the person is his size. He looks to have quite a bit of muscle above and below the knee, but his knee joint is not much more protected than mine. It's a damned painful move. And it's also, as you can see, incapacitating. Yeah." Norm nodded. "He collapsed like a three dollar umbrella."

Cris stood over Fletcher. She smiled up at Norm and winked. Had Mike not been there, she would have attempted a high five.

Fletcher continued to groan and rub his leg. "You son of a bitch!"

"*Wallace* is the name, thank you."

"You know, he could have whipped my ass while I was waiting on you—*partner*." Mike punched 9-1-1 into his phone.

Norm turned back to Mike. "Hey, I'm here." Norm held out his arms. "Besides, you looked like you were holding your own when I walked up."

"When you *walked* up?"

"I'm not supposed to run." Norm tapped his chest. "Heart patient, you know."

Mike closed his eyes and moved his head slowly from side to side.

"This is Sergeant Mike Neal with the Nashville Police Department." He gave the dispatcher his badge number. "I need MedCom. Location is the Hard Corps Gym on Fifth Avenue North. I have a single suspect with what appears to be a severely damaged right knee, likely dislocated, maybe torn ligaments. Yes. It's bent at what I would call," Mike looked at Fletcher, "a painful and unnatural angle. Yes ma'am. Thank you."

Mike rolled his eyes at Norm. "Heart patient? That was fourteen years ago."

The officers began handcuffing Fletcher. He moaned, and cursed as they tried to get his hands together behind him.

"There's no way one set is going to pull those larger caliber guns together behind him." Mike said. "Norm, help us sit him up."

As Norm grabbed one of Fletcher's huge arms and pulled him into a sitting position, the long sleeve of his knit shirt was pulled up on his arm. Mike noticed three parallel scratches on his forearm.

"Where'd you get these scratches, Fletcher?" Mike was suspicious he already knew the answer.

Fletcher didn't respond.

"Answer the Sergeant." Norm nudged him with his size eighteen shoe.

"From my girlfriend. We like it rough."

"Really? Then you must be enjoying the way Norm rearranged your knee."

Norm chuckled.

The officers secured one side of each handcuff set to the big man's wrists, and clicked the two sets together.

Norm released him. Fletcher grunted and cursed again before he fell back onto the pavement and started groaning.

"Edgar Fletcher, you have the right to remain silent," Mike began the Miranda. "Anything you say can and will be used against you in a court of law. You have the right to an attorney. If you cannot afford one, one will be provided for you. Do you understand these rights as I have explained them?"

He groaned. "My name is Edward Morris and I need a doctor."

Norm lifted his right leg and acted as though he was about to stomp on Fletcher's disfigured knee.

"All right, damn it. Yeah, I understand my rights."

"Good answer, asshole." Norm stepped back and folded his arms across his fifty-four inch chest.

Chapter 48

Vanderbilt Hospital
Nashville, Tennessee

It was late. However, in an effort to move the investigation along while valuable information was flowing in their direction, Mike and Cris decided to talk with Fletcher in his hospital room where a uniformed officer would be stationed outside the door at all times. As soon as Fletcher was coherent and not addled to the point of confusion by drugs, Mike informed Fletcher's doctor of their intentions.

"Sergeant," Fletcher's physician said, "we can't stop our care for a patient, not even one who is under arrest."

"I understand your intentions are for Mr. Fletcher's good health," Mike said. "We can appreciate that. However, so we're clear, Detective Vega and I are investigating the murder of a healthy young woman whose life and good health were snuffed out, ended by this man. She won't get the chance to live a full life. She won't get the chance to become a mother or a grandmother. She won't even see thirty years old because this man decided his greed was more important than her life. I don't believe his comfort is more important than justice for her and her widower husband.

"We're here tonight, working for the victim. We can't wait until Mr. Fletcher heals in order to do our investigation, so we'll be turning his hospital room into an interview room. I need you to let all the nurses know they must get their work done for him and be prepared to stay away until we come out. The door will be locked. An officer will be guarding the door on the outside."

"For how long?"

"We don't know. It's up to Mr. Fletcher."

The doctor thought for a moment. "I have a request that could satisfy both our intentions and your victim's justice as well."

"What?"

"I'd like to station a nurse inside the door of his room to monitor his vitals and be available in case of any unforeseen issues."

"Sorry. Put the nurse outside the door and we have an agreement."

"You drive a hard bargain, Sergeant."

"We can inform your team of any issues when and if they happen. My interest is our victim's interest. We have enough evidence to prove Fletcher's guilt. We have to try and see everyone involved in the crime receives what they deserve."

"I can appreciate that. I'll inform the nurses' station. Can you give us fifteen minutes to check his knee, his vitals and his IV?"

"Yes sir."

"Please don't hesitate to call us if anything requires our attention."

"Will do. Thanks for your understanding."

Mike pulled open the door to Fletcher's room. "Cris."

"Yeah."

"We're good. We're going to give the nurses fifteen before we secure the room and begin."

"Got it. I'll wait inside."

Mike stepped across the brightly lit hall from Fletcher's room and reviewed his notes. Two nurses entered Fletcher's room and stayed no more than ten minutes. When they came out, Cris was with them.

"They say we're good to go, Mike."

Mike nodded to the officer outside the room who also heard Cris's message. "Hopefully, it won't take long."

"I'll be here, Sergeant. Good luck."

"Thanks." Mike reached for his digital recorder and turned it on as he stepped into Fletcher's room.

In his hospital gown, the big man looked much less imposing than before. His leg was immobilized in a plaster cast from his foot to his mid-thigh and supported on the bed by an oversized pillow.

"Edgar, it's time for us to talk." Mike came closer to the bed and brought a straight back chair with him. "You should be aware this conversation is being recorded." Mike spoke into his digital recorder identifying his location, date and persons present, then placed it on the bedside table next to Fletcher's bed.

"I explained your rights earlier outside the gym. I'll ask you again if you understand your rights or would you like me to repeat them?"

"I'm not in the mood."

"Mood is not a requirement," Cris said, as she leaned against the window sill next to the bed.

"Do you understand your rights as they were read to you?" Mike asked.

"Yeah. I understand," Fletcher replied with a disgusted tone.

"Why did you resist our efforts to talk with you outside the gym?"

"I told you I was not the guy you were looking for. I don't know what you two are talking about. I finished my workout. I was minding my own business and attempting to leave in order to go to my job when you people attacked me. It's all on video there at the gym. They have cameras inside and out front. I'm sure they caught everything. It'll show what happened. It was clearly police brutality. I was complying with your requests when you people damaged my knee for life. You're gonna hear from my lawyer. This police brutality is gonna cost the city big time."

"You didn't comply with any requests we made," Cris said. "We requested your cooperation three times. You resisted from the beginning and could have seriously injured Sergeant Neal had it not been for the actions of Detective Wallace."

"You're still pissed off because I grabbed your flabby ass." Fletcher refused to look at Cris when he spoke to her.

Cris held her tongue, but her facial expression spoke volumes.

"Where's the big fat jackass that gave me the cheap shot on my knee? I'd like to even the score with the jerk when I get out of here."

Cris pulled out her notepad. "I'll put this down as an additional charge of threatening a police officer?"

"I don't give a damn how you put it down." Fletcher persisted with his bravado.

"Edgar, I suggest you forget about any uneven scores and focus on minimizing the time you'll spend in prison," Mike said, as he took off his sport jacket and draped it over the back of his chair.

"We know who you are. We've run your photo and your fingerprints. You are Edgar Aaron Fletcher," Mike read from his notes. "Born in Cape Girardeau, Missouri on February 12, 1983. You were arrested while a juvenile for shoplifting, and for simple possession. At seventeen, for forgery and identity theft. As an adult, you were arrested at nineteen for possession with intent to distribute marijuana and crystal meth, as well as for contributing to the delinquency of a minor. At twenty-two, you were arrested and convicted of armed robbery and assault. You served time in the Missouri prison system and at the age twenty-seven, well after your release, you were arrested outside a Saint Louis high school, along with one other male, for selling steroids to children. And, you were returned to prison."

"They weren't children," he said. "They were teenagers. Football players, wanting to elevate their game."

Cris stood, both hands gripped the bedrail, and said, "Teenagers *are* children, Fletcher." She shook her head. "And the only thing you were trying to elevate was your net worth."

Fletcher stared forward ignoring Cris's recrimination.

"Okay. Let's cut through all the crap and move this thing forward," Mike said. "As you were told earlier when you were booked, we aren't trying to determine *if* you killed Brooke Cole. Okay? We *know* you killed her.

"We have a number of your head hairs from the crime scene which fell out at a rapid rate due to your use of the steroid Trenbolone. The substance was found in each of your hairs during the crime lab's analysis.

"We also have your DNA which was found beneath three of the victim's fingernails." Mike was anticipating the DNA confirmation within days and felt comfortable at this point stretching the truth.

"But, most importantly, we have four partial fingerprints from within the Cole home which match your right index finger. Our county Medical Examiner found, inside the victim's mouth, a piece of a Nitrile glove you wore. Thanks to this mistake, you were able to leave us these partial prints which offered unique patterns for our Crime Scene Unit to key on. By the way, the unit has already pulled your fingerprints from the FBI's database, as well as from your gym bag, confirming they match those taken from the Cole home."

The big man compressed his lips and exhaled his frustration.

"And, the alibi you provided us is worthless. Your manager at The Hiatus said your timecard shows you didn't report to work on Tuesday night until eight-thirty. The M.E.'s estimated time of death is between six o'clock and eight o'clock.

"So, you see Edgar, we have you in the Cole home the night of the murder. We have your hair on the victim's clothing, your DNA beneath her nails and your bogus alibi tells us you cannot prove you were anywhere else at the time of Brooke Cole's death. This is more than enough to enable the DA and the Grand Jury to issue an indictment for murder.

"Face it, Edgar. You are in a situation where you must make a decision. Do you go down for this murder all by your lonesome? Or, do you share with us the name of the person who supplied you the incentive to even consider such a horrendous act, and let them share in the retribution? Thus, lessening *your* punishment.

"Allow me to let you in on some inside information."

Fletcher cut his eyes toward Mike without moving his head.

"Cris and I have been homicide detectives for about twenty years. I won't say we've seen it all, but we've seen most of it. We know how the system works.

"The great majority of our investigations end in a plea. That means most of our suspects are wise enough to understand their situation, realize they're in a bind, and look for ways to benefit themselves and reduce their prison time. This is what we're offering you today. If you give us the person who got you to murder Brooke Cole, we can work with the District Attorney and get your sentence reduced. Why would you choose to shoulder the entire blame for this murder by yourself, when it's not necessary? Why protect someone who is the primary reason all this happened in the first place?"

Fletcher was quiet. Likely, trying to determine his best next move.

Mike sat, watching him and waiting for his answer.

Cris knew the process. She stared at Fletcher without comment.

Mike posed questions like this on numerous similar occasions with other suspects. He never spoke after he asked the questions. No matter how long it took. His silence eventually pressured the suspect to respond.

The onus was on Fletcher. He took several minutes before speaking.

"Okay." He paused his response and looked at Mike. "I need some guarantees if I'm gonna talk to you."

"We're not allowed to offer guarantees. That's the District Attorney's job."

"Then I'll need to see him before I talk to you."

"Not gonna happen," Mike said. "You don't help us tonight with the name of whoever solicited you, paid you or whatever they did to get you to kill Brooke Cole, and the deal is off. You'll go down alone for this murder and whatever additional charges the DA comes up with."

"Bunch of assholes," Fletcher mumbled, then jerked his arms in as attempt to cross them over his chest, but the handcuffs on both wrists clanked against the stainless steel bed rails and held.

"Damn it." He dropped his arms back to his sides.

"The law is the law. You have an opportunity to arrange things for yourself in a more favorable way if you help us today. If not, then they will fall as they may and you'll pay the price, alone. It'll be too late to alter anything."

Fletcher took several deep breaths and looked from Mike to Cris, as if unsure of whether he could trust either of the detectives.

Chapter 49

"Okay. You asked me who he is. I don't know who he is. He told me his name was Lester. I didn't ask his last name. I didn't care. He came into The Hiatus two, maybe three times a week for over a month. He always sat alone toward the rear of the club, except when Tiffany would dance. Then, if there was room, he brought his drink and moved up to the front on the rail where he could tip her."

"Who is Tiffany?" Mike asked.

"She's just one of the girls." He held up open palms until the handcuffs hit the bed rails.

"Anything about her stand out?" Cris asked, then watched his response.

He was quiet for a moment. "Nothing special. She's small, dark hair, dimples. She's one of the dancers. There's like twenty-five or more others. They come and they go.

"He got too close to her one of the first nights he was there. I grabbed his arm and warned him. We give them one warning. After that, they leave for the night.

"He apologized and then he was cool. We talked a few times after that night. He became a regular customer."

"What time of day did he normally come in?"

"Seems like it was always around eight or eight thirty. I normally got to work about that time and he told me a couple of times he'd just got there."

"Describe this guy," Mike said. "Age, weight, height, facial hair, clothing, shoes, scars, tattoos, moles, warts, missing appendages. Tell me all about him as if he just stole your life and you want us to get it back."

"He always wore a cowboy hat."

"What kind?" Mike asked.

"What do you mean what kind? A freakin' cowboy hat."

"Was it made of straw, made of felt? What color was it? Was the crown creased, not creased? Was it a large brim, small brim, flat brim, broken brim, decorative hatband, plain hatband, no hatband? Think Edgar. Do you want some portion of your life back or not? We never saw this guy. You did. Help us find him."

Fletcher exhaled and closed his eyes. "Okay. His hat was large, I guess a large brim? I'm not sure, but it was a dark color, maybe black. It's dark in the club. He wore the hat low on his forehead. It kinda shaded his face and made it hard to see him clearly. He looked down a lot toward his drink when he talked. When he wanted to look at me he tilted his head to the other side. I remember because I thought it was peculiar. He reminded me of a cowboy in one of those spaghetti westerns Clint Eastwood used to make."

"He was keeping his face covered so the club's security cameras couldn't get a clear image," Mike said. "What about age, weight, height, facial hair?"

"He had a dark mustache."

"Did it look real?"

"To me, it did. Sorta thick. Came down over his upper lip." Fletcher hesitated. "It was hard to judge his age. At least thirty, maybe thirty-five. He was sitting most of the time, but I'd say he was less than six feet tall and around a hundred and," he paused, "seventy-five."

"What did he wear?"

"I don't pay attention to what other men wear. I prefer to watch the ladies." He glanced at Cris then looked away.

She rolled her eyes. "I doubt, if you work in a place like The Hiatus, you're looking at what the ladies wear."

Fletcher smiled his agreement.

"I like to look at ladies as much as anyone," Mike said. "But, this isn't getting us anywhere in our effort to shorten your prison sentence."

"I'm pretty sure he wore jeans and western boots," Fletcher said. "Seems like he always had on a jacket, so I don't remember any shirts. Probably plaid?"

Mike began to speak, but Fletcher interrupted him.

"I know, I know. Color. The jacket was a dark color, black, brown, dark green. It wasn't a heavy jacket. It was like a baseball jacket, you know, short. Waist length."

"Any printing or logo on the jacket?"

"No." He tilted his head. "Wait a minute. Can't you look at the video recordings from the club? I've seen Joey, the manager, viewing them in the past when he suspected a bartender we had of pocketing some cash."

"Edgar," Mike said. "Do us a favor. Let us be the detectives. If you can tell us what he looks like, it will help us spot him on the club videos and other cameras outside the club, like parking lots and businesses around the club when maybe he isn't trying so hard to hide his face. Okay?"

Fletcher nodded.

"What about scars, tattoos, earrings, piercings, anything like this to help identify him?"

"No piercings. I'm not sure how many cowboys have piercings."

"You might be surprised," Cris said.

Fletcher squinted at Cris.

"His arms were covered by his jacket. I don't recall any tats on his hands or what I could see of his neck and face."

"What else can you remember about him?" Mike asked. "Did he have an accent? Did he sound like he was from this area, or up north? Midwest? You said you talked to him a lot. Did his speech and accent remind you of anyone else you know?"

"I hadn't thought about it. He was definitely not from the north or upper midwest. His accent was southern. Definitely, southern. He sounded like us. I guess it didn't register since damn near everybody I talk to in the club is from around here."

"Did his accent seem forced, like he was acting or was it easy and natural?"

"I think I would have noticed if it was exaggerated or fake.

"We talked a few times after he started coming in regularly. One night we were talking and laughing at some of the other customers before it got busy and he asked if I knew anybody who would be interested in making a significant chunk of money.

"At first, I thought he didn't look like someone who might have a lot of money. I said 'maybe'. I told him I knew several folks who like money and a few who would do most anything for it, if there was enough of it. He told me he had a need for someone to do something ugly. It was important and it paid a lot of money.

"I asked if it was legal and how much he was talking about. He told me no and maybe ten thousand dollars. I asked how ugly it was, since it wasn't legal. He said there was a woman who needed to die and it didn't matter so much how she died. I asked him who she was and why she needed to die. He said it didn't matter, it wasn't part of the job.

"Then, after a few minutes, he asked if I was interested? I told him it wasn't enough money for something so risky. I had to leave him for a while to escort some clown, who wasn't following the rules, out the door.

"I came back to his table later. He said he could try to get more. I told him I knew a guy who might be able to help him. But, I was sure he would expect more money for something like this. I also told him, I didn't think he could get anybody to do it for ten. The gamble wasn't worth it.

"He asked how much I thought my friend would need. I told him I was sure it would take at least twenty-five thousand.

"I didn't see him at the club again until a couple of nights later. When I had the chance, I went to his table. We talked a few minutes about one of the new girls on stage. I was wondering if he would bring his offer up again or if he'd decided to drop it. He opened his jacket and showed me the fifteen thousand dollars. He said he'd have another ten thousand once the job was done.

"I told him, we'd talk again later. I went back to work. I was pretty sure he or whoever he was working for must want this done enough to pay what I'd asked. When we spoke later that night, he said he would bring everything I needed the next night.

"The next night he brought a map showing the location of the woman's home and a list of what he called important things for whoever took the job."

"Do you still have this map and list?"

"No. I trashed them in a dumpster."

"What was on the list?"

"It had a description of the woman, where she lived, what time she came home on weeknights, the fact she'd be home alone some nights, the place where she worked in case I wanted to follow her home, things like that.

"Oh, it also said I could take anything of value I found in order to make it look like a home invasion and robbery, but I couldn't take her phone. It said specifically not to take her phone. This part I didn't understand. I could get fifty to a hundred bucks for a decent iPhone any day."

"Assuming you didn't get tracked down before you could sell it?" Cris said.

"What do you mean?"

"An iPhone can be tracked to within a few feet by an Apple software app. I wish you'd taken the phone," Cris said. "It would have made finding you much simpler and your knee would still be intact."

Fletcher frowned.

"I still want to know why he came to *you* with this offer in the beginning?" Mike asked.

"I don't know. I don't. Maybe he was checking me out all those times he came in and saw me as the type who might be interested in the money. I don't know."

"I don't buy this. There has to be a reason he chose you to open up to and comfortably make an offer that alone could put both of you in prison. How did he know you wouldn't go to the police? What gave him the comfort level to approach you about it? There's something you're not telling us. We've seen your police record, we know your background. We know why *you* wouldn't go to the police. But, how did he know?"

"I—don't—know. How many times do I have to say it?

Fletcher sat thinking. "I try to be seen by everyone as someone you don't want to cross. I'm not known to have the best attitude. Some say I have a short fuse. This keeps most folks away. I like it like that. I don't want a bunch of needy ass friends, always hanging around, wanting favors or borrowing money. I'm not the friend type. I don't do *friends* well."

"What gave him the impression he could talk to you and get what he was looking for? If you're so tough and you don't *do friends*, then what made this guy think he could get to you, make a connection and convince you to take care of this especially ugly job, as he put it?"

"I—uh."

"Think back. What did he say to you that caused you to see him as not just some dumb joker in the strip club, but someone you could relate to and maybe even trust?"

"The first time we talked was the night after I pulled him off the rail. He came in and went straight to his favorite table and ordered. After a few minutes, I had to walk by his table in order to get to the back and bring up more beer. He said something as I passed. I could tell he was talking to me, but I couldn't hear over the music what it was he said, so I stopped and stepped closer to his table. He said, 'I'm sorry about last night. I got kinda excited.' I told him no problem. He thanked me and I went about my job. It seemed like nothing at the time."

"Was that it? Was it normal for a customer to apologize to Security?"

"I wouldn't say it's normal. Most customers try to avoid talking to the security staff. They look at us like the cons look at the corrections officers in prison. Some customers lose control when they get drunk. Then, after the security team gets involved and brings them back down to Earth, they usually get their brains back. It happens all the time."

Fletcher stopped and stared across the hospital room. "Wait a minute." He turned to Mike. "I remember one night, maybe a week or two after he started coming in, I had to get between a couple of idiots on the rail. They got in a fight while three of the girls were on stage at the same time. I think both guys were trying to tip the same girl. Neither man liked the competition from the other one.

"I stepped up when they started yelling at each other. One of the drunks swung at the other while I was trying to keep them apart. The guy missed and hit me. His ring put a cut under my eye. Needless to say, this pissed me off big time, so I focused my attention on him.

"Once I got him in a head lock I turned to see where the other one was. I found the cowboy had him pinned to the rail with a chair. I remember thinking he looked like a lion tamer. The drunk kept trying to slug the cowboy, but he couldn't reach him because of the chair. It looked pretty damn funny.

"After I got both guys outside, I headed for the back to get cleaned up and stop the bleeding. When I came out, I stopped at the cowboy's table to say thanks. He smiled at me and offered his hand. I guess that's when, like you said, we made a connection."

"So, it was after that night when he came to you with his proposition?"

"Yeah. Best I remember, it was a couple, maybe a few nights later."

"Which three girls were on stage when the fight broke out?" Cris asked.

"I'm not sure. Let me think. I know Crystal was one of them. She was the one they were fighting about." He closed his eyes. "I have no idea who the others were. They all ran off stage when the scuffle started. Crystal was really the only one involved."

"Could one of the other two have been Tiffany?" Cris asked.

Mike looked at Cris.

"I guess. I have no way of knowing. It could have been any of the girls working that night."

Cris looked at Mike and nodded.

"Edgar, you need to get us the DVDs or digital files from your boss which were recorded on all the nights this guy came in.

"Also. Let him know we will have a search warrant for these items by tomorrow morning, but he shouldn't wait. The sooner we acquire the files, the sooner we can review them, find the cowboy and convince the DA you weren't alone in this crime."

"I'm not sure I can remember which nights he came in," Fletcher said.

"Then I suggest you either get us *all* the recordings for the period of time he was coming in, beginning to end, or else pack your bags and say your goodbyes to all your non-friends at the gym.

"Let your boss know how important this is. He may be short-handed with you in the hospital, but he's going to have much bigger problems if he violates the search warrant and we don't get these videos.

"Cris and I are taking this investigation forward to a conclusion in the next couple of days. How it ends will depend primarily on how much good information we get from you and your boss's Digital

Video Recorder. You may want to give him a call as soon as we leave so he has plenty of time to collect the videos that will help you avoid a lifetime of prison time. Are we on the same page, Edgar?"

Fletcher nodded. "Yes. I'll call him."

"A couple of other loose ends. What happened to Brooke Cole's laptop computer?"

"I gave it to my girlfriend."

"Does she still have it?" Mike asked.

"As far as I know. The last time I saw it was a couple of days ago at her apartment."

"We have to have it. Before we leave, give Detective Vega her address and call her so she knows we're coming. We'll pick it up tonight. It better be there."

"It will. She was excited to get it, but hasn't yet learned how to use it."

"What about Brooke Cole's jewelry? Wedding rings and earrings?"

"My girlfriend."

"The prescription bottle of Xanax?"

"What?"

"Don't lie to me," Mike said.

"I sold them."

"What about the nine millimeter semi-automatic pistol you took from the nightstand?"

He hesitated answering.

"Edgar. This is a stolen gun we're discussing. You will be held jointly liable for any and all crimes, *any and all crimes Edgar*, the gun is ever involved in. Are you prepared to add additional years in prison to those you are about to receive for a murder conviction. If you receive additional years for this, you'll certainly die in prison."

"My girlfriend has the gun too." He shook his head. "I liked that gun."

Mike looked at Cris and rolled his eyes.

Chapter 50

The Hiatus Club
Nashville, Tennessee

"Can I assume you've never been to one of these clubs?" Mike smiled.

"You cannot. Like you, I've sought and followed the truth wherever it took me. In fact, I've been to *this* place before. It's been over a year, I think. Not long after Jerry and I became partners, we came here to interview one of their dancers who was a witness in our investigation."

"Hi. Is your manager here?" Cris asked.

"He's in the back. Can I get him for you?"

"Sure. Thanks."

After the young girl walked away, Cris turned toward Mike. "You think her mom and dad know where she is? She looked like she was underage."

"Not likely on either count. The clubs are particular about the things that can get them in trouble with the law. Of course, if the girls show the manager an ID that appears valid, he's off the hook."

Cris nodded toward the rear of the club to let Mike know the manager was coming.

"Can I help you?" The forty-something man said as he walked up.

As if practiced, Mike and Cris held up their credentials at the same time.

"I've been expecting you. Ed called me earlier."

"Can I assume you have the videos we're looking for?"

"I do. But, they're on my computer. The files are pretty large, so I wasn't sure how you'd want to receive them."

"I'm going to have a gentleman call you so you can discuss this with him and send them directly to him right away. His name is Dean McMurray. He works with us at the police department. He will be calling you shortly after we leave."

"No problem. I would like to be sure you're aware of something before you see the video. The club is dark. The stage is the only part that's well lighted and it shows on the recordings. I wish they were better, but our budget doesn't allow us the funds for low light cameras."

"Okay. I understand. We'd like to ask you a few questions."

"Sure. There's a table in the back room if you'd like to sit somewhere away from this music. Sorry, but the girls practice their routines in the mornings."

"Okay," Mike said.

Mike and Cris followed the man through the club and into the back room. For the sake of both his and Cris's embarrassment Mike was glad the practicing dancer had her clothes on.

"Here we are." He gestured toward a folding table that looked to be ready to collapse at any moment.

"Is it Joey?" Mike asked.

"I'm sorry. Yes. Joey Martinez."

"Joey, when we finish we'd like to talk with Tiffany."

"I would too. She hasn't shown up for two days. No call. No nothing." He looked from Mike to Cris. "I wish I could say this is uncommon behavior for dancers."

"Do you have her home address?" Cris asked.

"All our dancers are independent contractors. 1099's, not employees. They come and they go. We don't ask for personal information and they don't want to share any. Some have questionable pasts they want kept to themselves.

"They're paid in tips from the customers. If they're good at what they do, build a clientele of interested and happy men who come to see them, everyone wins. The girls make more tips. We sell more drinks and covers. It's how most successful clubs work."

"So, no one's heard from her? None of the other girls?" Cris asked.

"Not according to what they're telling me."

"What was Tiffany's last name?"

"No idea. My guess is, Tiffany wasn't her first name either. Few, if any, of the dancers use their real names. They usually choose something that sounds sexy or more interesting than Susan or Janet."

"Did she leave anything behind? Any personal items?"

"I can have one of the girls look, but I doubt it. The girls come in each night with the costumes they're going to wear, their makeup, wigs, etc.. They don't leave them or anything personal here."

"Do you have any photos of her?"

He hesitated. "There should still be an eight by ten in the inner lobby up front where we have several of the most popular dancers' photos."

"Are you telling us you have no personal information at all on the dancer who called herself Tiffany?" Mike asked.

"That's right. And, as if that isn't bad enough, out of twenty-eight dancers, we have—or had, two who called themselves Tiffany. We referred to the newest one as Tiffany Two in order to avoid confusion."

"Was the one we're looking for Tiffany one or Tiffany two?" Cris asked.

"She was Tiffany one. For a dancer in a gentleman's club, she'd been here quite a while."

"How long?"

"Ten months."

"That long?" Cris said, with a thick touch of glibness in her voice.

"For this line of work, it is a long time. She was here long enough to make friends with some of the folks who work here regularly."

"Other dancers?"

"Yes. And bartenders. And even Ed."

"Edgar Fletcher?" Mike asked.

"No. Ed Morris. The one you spoke with. He was part of our

security team."

"Okay. Ed Morris." Mike and Cris shared a look.

"Shortly after her arrival, she and Ed dated for a while."

"Really?" Cris looked at Mike, her eyes were smiling. "What's a while?"

"Couple of months, maybe longer? I think sharing the view of her body with all the other men in Nashville got to Ed. They had a big falling out. You may know, he's not the most understanding and tolerant man in the city.

"He wanted her to quit and find another line of work. She, like most of the dancers, got used to the money and realized she couldn't make anywhere near this much in most other jobs she could qualify for."

"Was their parting as consensual as their relationship?"

"I don't think so. I heard Ed got so mad he called her some truly nasty names. One of the girls said she overheard the fight. She told me she'd never heard so much cursing and ugly names from both of them.

"Tiffany called in sick for three days afterward. When she returned, one of the girls said she saw bruises on Tiffany and saw her putting makeup on them. I never saw them myself.

"When she came back she refused to even look at Ed. Afterward, when she was on stage, she was an even better dancer than before their split. She worked hard at drawing the customers' attention to her. In my opinion, it was mostly to hurt Ed. She was good at bringing the guys in and bringing them back. It had to hurt him."

"Do you think Ed fell in love?" Mike asked.

"I'm no psychologist, but I'd say yes. He seems to be over it now, or at least he acts like he is most of the time, but I've heard things he's said recently to and about her."

"So, she wasn't over his abuse," Mike said.

"No. It takes girls longer." Cris said, looking from Joey to Mike. "It leaves scars. Love hurts."

Both men offered her a compassionate nod.

"I'd like to get her photograph now," Cris said.

"Sure. Follow me. By the way, here's my card with the number for your man to call me about the video files."

"Thanks," Mike said.

"Here we are," Joey said, as the three of them entered the inner lobby. "Well." He scanned the wall of photos. "I don't see her photo."

"It looks as though there's one missing here." Cris pointed.

"Hmm. Maybe she took it when she left."

Mike and Cris exchanged looks.

Chapter 51

"Dean, what are you working on?"

"The Lieutenant's laptop. This thing has more viruses than a Dickerson Road hooker."

"Have you received the video files I called you about?" Mike asked.

"I'm not sure," Dean said. "I called the man at the number you gave me and told him what to do. I've been covered up as usual and I haven't checked to see how well he followed directions."

"What did you tell him to do?"

"Do we seriously have the time for me to explain the ins and outs of Dropbox and large file transfers? Instead, why don't I check to see if we have at least some of the video files, so we can get started reviewing them. Okay with you two?"

"Sure," Mike said, before smiling at Cris.

Mike and Cris were both used to Dean's persnickety nature and love of sarcasm. His knowledge of technology and his perfectionist tilt helped them resolve numerous investigations.

"Watch your toes." He grabbed the push rims on his wheelchair and quickly moved himself in front of another large monitor and keyboard.

"Let's see. This is good. I have several files from your friend—Joey. Isn't that a young kangaroo? A Joey?"

"Yes. Once again. You are right."

"I thought so. Thank you Cris."

Dean opened the file with the oldest date first.

"Oh. The image is bright in some spots and dark in others. Let me try to adjust the light a bit. That didn't help much."

"What's the time of day on this?" Mike asked.

"17:00. What time does your suspect show?"

"Let's start at 19:30 and see if we can find him," Mike said.

"The person we're looking for will be wearing a large dark cowboy hat and sitting at a table alone in the rear of the club."

"Which side of the image is the rear?" Dean said as he clicked on fast forward.

"Based upon our visit today I'd say the rear is at the top of the monitor from this camera angle."

"Are all the cameras mounted near the ceiling?" Dean asked.

"I'm not sure," Cris said, "but this angle won't help us to see the cowboy's face."

"Okay," Dean said. "We're at 19:25. Close enough. Play." He clicked the play button on the software and leaned back in his wheelchair. "Oh, my! Uh, I wasn't ready for that. Sorry, Cris."

"It's okay Dean. I've seen boobs before."

"I, uh guess you have. Cowboy hat. Where are you?"

"We aren't sure which nights the suspect came in, so we requested all nights from about the time he started his visits. My suggestion is we key on the area here at the rear of the club and watch for the dark cowboy hat. What do you think?"

"Works for me," Dean agreed. "But, I would like to make a suggestion."

"Shoot," Mike said.

"Why don't I set up each of you on a different computer, with a different file on a different date and the three of us can work in triple time? Also, I'll show you how to move forward in time by half hour increments each time you click. This way, you can focus on the area of the rear of the club and watch for changes resembling a dark hat. I'll load the DVR viewing software on the two PCs and then the video files. Give me fifteen or twenty minutes. You can grab some coffee."

Mike looked at Cris. "This is why we pay him the big bucks."

"Him, who? What big bucks? There are no big bucks paid in this lab, I assure you."

"Thanks Deano. Can I get you a cup?"

"Maybe later. I don't want to spill it on my keyboard. And, you shouldn't either."

"10-4," Mike said. "Cris, keep the cups away from the PCs. Orders from the A/V lab supervisor."

Mike and Cris had returned from getting their coffee and were busy reviewing videos. Both had spotted the cowboy, or at least his hat, in one or more of their files. None turned out to be the nights when Tiffany's dancing pulled him forward to the rail or the brawl caused him to grab a chair and help Fletcher.

"I've got it," Cris shouted.

Mike paused his video and rolled his desk chair until it was beside Cris's.

"Okay. Start it. He could see a partially clad attractive dark-haired young girl dancing on stage and the top of a dark cowboy hat at the edge of the stage with the owner's face completely hidden below it.

"Damn it. We can't see him any better on the rail than at the table," Cris said. "This sucks."

"Let's keep looking at the others. Maybe the fight night will offer us a better angle. At least we can now see something of what Tiffany looks like." Cris printed the blurry image of the girl.

Mike watched his next video wondering how many were left to review.

At 20:10, the cowboy walked into the image from the bottom of the monitor and went straight back to the same table as before and sat. The table was at the edge of the camera's field of view and in one of the darkest areas of the club. Something told Mike the cowboy may have suspected this.

When the waitress came to take his order the cowboy looked up at her right before she shifted to her other foot and blocked the man's face from camera view. Mike backed it up and froze the image before she'd moved. It was dark, fuzzy and impossible to determine facial features other than the dark mustache, but he could see a man's face.

He printed it though he knew it would be little help if any. He continued his viewing and hoped for an epiphany that would direct them toward who this cowboy was.

"Are you getting anything that's legible?" He asked Cris.

"No. The quality is really bad. I can make out Fletcher because of his size and the fact he's moving around, in and out of the light. I can make out the ladies because the lights are on them and I can make out someone wearing a dark cowboy hat and sitting at a table alone. Except for the occasional spotting of dark hair on his upper lip, I can hardly be sure this person is even male. This crap doesn't look like anything that's going to help us."

They continued to view the videos, only faster now. They were searching for something, anything they'd not yet seen.

"Hey guys," Dean shouted. "I think I have the brawl you were looking for."

Mike and Cris paused their screens and went to see what Dean had found.

"This may be the fight you were talking about. These two stood and appeared to be shouting at each other. Then this big guy walks over and gets slugged by this one. While he's wrestling with the one that punched him, your cowboy comes over and traps this one against the stage with a chair. Let me run it back."

Dean played the fight segment over and all three watched to see if the cowboy's face turned toward the camera. It didn't.

"Damn it!" Dean said. "It's like the fool knows the cameras are watching him."

"He's no fool. He does know. And, he's sharp enough to prevent us from identifying him. This is why he has the big brim hat."

"There are a lot of cowboys in Music City," Dean said.

"Like most of them," Mike added, "this boy may be all hat and no cattle."

Mike sat, staring forward, thinking.

Cris knew he was mulling over something.

"What is it?"

"Wait a second. We're missing something here," he said, as he scratched his head. "Think. We can see Fletcher here in the fight scene video." He pointed to the monitor. "So, we can tell how big he is in relation to the other men. We *know* how big he is and how tall he is.

"We can't see the cowboy's face, but we can see his size in relation to Fletcher. Who of our potentials would appear the size of the big hat cowboy if he were alongside Fletcher? My list would say Nichols, Reed or Gray," Mike said. "I think Gray was too small to match up with the cowboy. Nichols and Reed didn't know about the audit until after Brooke was killed. Marc LeBlanc is much too tall."

"I think my list of similar size men is longer," Cris said, "but I'm not sure they all had sufficient motive."

"If their monetary success was tied to Jon Cole's success, most of your list would fit here as far as motive is concerned, unless of course their size eliminated them. Like you say, *sufficient motive* is a key element. Pissed off is one thing. Willing to murder someone is another.

"Correct me if I'm wrong," Mike said, "but the way I understand it, Jon and his career owe several people or companies more money than he can pay back any time soon. His small venue events don't offer anything in the way of remuneration for his investors. These gigs keep him in the public eye and feed his fans their dose of Jon, but only pay barely enough to feed and house him and the band."

"True."

"And, at some point, unrewarded commitments drive attitude changes, a reduction in patience and force relationship pressures to rise. I don't know much about the music industry other than the ugliness Scott Lindsey shared with us the night Brooke was killed, but I have learned a good bit about human nature over the years.

"These folks are gonna eventually expect their money back along with something resembling a reward for risking it. He owes them that much."

Cris said, "That reminds me of what Bill Sands told me when we were discussing his years with Jon before they came to Nashville."

"What did he say?"

"I told you. Remember?"

"No. I'm getting old and forgetful. Tell me again."

"Sands told me, back in the day when they were playing regular gigs around East Texas, he felt Jon saved his life by helping him to get off drugs. They were much younger and dumber then, in their early twenties.

"Jon helped him get into a program in Tyler, Texas that allowed him to break his addiction. He stayed for over a month and got clean.

"Sands said he would do almost anything for Jon. He owed him that much."

Mike sat for a minute, staring at Cris and thinking. "So, if he felt he owed Jon, does that include preventing Jon's wife from ruining his *and* Jon's lucrative music careers?"

Cris pursed her lips. "Possibly?"

"Is the big hat cowboy the right size?"

She looked at the monitor. "He looks bigger than Sands, but it could be the jacket."

"Go back through your notes and re-visit the video of your interview with Sands. You did talk to him at the CJC didn't you?"

Cris nodded. "Yes."

"Let me know what you see and hear, including anything you may have missed before and then we'll review it together."

"Gotcha."

"Dean," Mike said. "You're the man."

"I didn't do anything." He turned his palms up.

"You're still the man," Cris said. "Thanks."

Chapter 52

Franklin, Tennessee

The cell phone's ringer played the classic *Hello Darlin'* by Conway Twitty.

"Hello."

"Looks like the worst might be over."

"What makes you think so?"

"For starters, I'm not in jail. If they were getting close, I believe I'd know it."

"You may be too optimistic. Or, they may be quietly circling the wagons and loading their guns. You just don't realize it."

"Yeah. Let's hope not. There was a lot of effort and money put into this in order to make it work."

"A hell of a lot of *my* money." He took another sip of his Tennessee Whiskey. "What about the stripper girl?"

"She's moved back to her hometown outside Cincinnati with enough money to kickstart her new life without taking her clothes off. She doesn't know my name or anything about what's happened here other than gaining her karma with the big guy and a chance to start her life over."

"She did a good job for us."

"She was driven by her revenge. He treated her badly. We were lucky our friend Cherry at The Country Tradition used to tend bar at The Hiatus and knew the girl's story. It helps to know folks."

"I wonder what, if anything, the cops learned from the big man."

"He didn't know anything. The cowboy he was dealing with doesn't exist. Besides, he was blinded by the money I offered him."

"So. If this thing goes south, are you going to be able to hold up your end of the agreement?"

"Don't worry. I know what I agreed to. You're safe." He paused. "If I'm caught, the story is: I sold my dad's 1961 Fender Telecaster to get the money. He left it to me in his will."

"Sold it to who? They'll ask, you know."

"To you. Who else do I know who can afford a $30,000 guitar."

"Well. At least I know the story in case they ask me."

"You will need to figure out where the high dollar ax is now."

"Easy. It was stolen from my Corvette." He laughed. "I'll call my insurance agent."

"I hope it doesn't come to it, but if it does, I'll go down for this. I owe him." He paused a moment. "I'm glad I had the opportunity to pay him back. Hopefully, if I'm lucky, the cops will file this one away in the cold case storage, we can move on and he'll never know. But, if things turn out differently—so be it. At least he's free now. He's gonna be so big and I'm gonna be so proud of him."

"Yes. He will." He swirled the ice in his Jack Daniel's, held the cell phone away from his mouth for a moment, and emptied the glass. "There's been a lot invested in Jon and a lot done to save him, but I still feel the money was well spent."

"Yep, me too. I'll hope to see you at Brooke's funeral, assuming I don't get a visit from the cops first."

"Call me if you find you're gonna need legal support. I can help. Hell, we may be able to plead this thing down to jaywalking."

"I wish." He hesitated. "Thanks. Really, thank you for everything. Especially for sticking with Jon and helping him fulfill his dream."

"Thank you for your willingness to sacrifice yourself to save his future."

"What are friends for?"

Chapter 53

Outside a Suspect's
Apartment Complex
in South Nashville

"Did you get the word yet on the contents of Brooke's laptop?" Cris asked.

"The bank's IT System Administrator who searched it said it hadn't been booted up since the day Brooke was killed. Fletcher's girlfriend didn't even turn it on."

"I doubt if it would do her any good. I'm sure Brooke had it password protected."

"Likely. Brent Spangler from Fraud has it now and will be going through it with President Green and his IT guy to determine to what extent Patrick Nichols and Reed perpetrated fraud against the bank. Brent said he'd contacted the FBI. The local office is sending an agent to the bank today."

"Strange stuff," Cris said. "Has the District Attorney issued indictments yet for Reed and Nichols?" Cris asked.

Mike checked his rearview mirror. "Reed's being indicted for first degree murder. The DA is waiting for the data from the PC before he moves forward on the embezzlement charges.

"Nichols will also be indicted for embezzlement once the data is in, but the DA agreed to give him some degree of consideration for his coming forward on his own, exposing the fraud and also exposing Reed as Darin Gray's killer."

"The guy in competition for the job at the bank who hired the PI to find dirt on Brooke, what ever happened with him?" Cris asked. "Surely, he didn't get the promotion."

"President Green decided to pass on Marc LeBlanc for the Assistant VP position and leave him where he was. I think Marc's lucky to keep his current job. He may find he has to change employers in order to satisfy his ambitions."

Once again, Mike looked in his rearview mirror.

"Mr. Green chose to go outside the bank to a recruiter in order to fill the Assistant VP, Brooke's Manager of Internal Audit position, and Darin Gray's job. He said it may take him a while to fill Nichols's Vice Presidency. He told me he'd like to promote from within for most of the openings, but wasn't confident he had the caliber of folks he needed."

"Edgar Fletcher's indictment for First Degree Murder does include a charge of Conspiracy. Right?"

"It does," Mike said. "His willingness to assist our investigation and his attempt to expose the one who paid him is supposed to benefit him with the District Attorney. The DA hasn't made that promise yet, but he said he was willing to give it consideration should everything promised be realized."

"You sure ask a lot of questions, Detective Vega."

Cris smiled. "Yes. My boss tells me I should ask open-ended questions and keep people talking in order to learn all there is to know. Possibly even get all the facts to eventually point me to the truth."

"Sounds like a smart man. You need to listen to him."

Cris laughed. "You'd like him. He's pretty sharp for an old guy."

"Ouch. Now, it's my turn. What do we know about Jon's status? Is he getting back to his songwriting and performing yet?"

"Jon received a call from the life insurance company. They asked him to mail a copy of Brooke's death certificate so they could do an EFT into his account. He said after he takes care of Brooke's funeral expenses he plans to sit with Scott and decide how best to use the money to further his career.

"He's still on his break from trying to write songs. His emotional state appears to be improved from our last meeting, but he's not yet ready to turn the sound back up on his career. Give him a few more weeks and he should be better able to handle the outcomes from all these negative events hitting him at once."

"Since this investigation began," Mike said, "I've been reminded of something my mom said way back when I was a senior in high school. I'll never forget it. She said, 'A man marries a woman hoping she'll never change. A woman marries a man hoping he will.' This expectation from both parties has, I'm convinced, created considerable disappointment in an awful lot of lives."

"No doubt. I think we all expect too much from our significant others."

"So, you've not met your knight on a white stallion yet?"

"No."

"This leads me to one last question." Mike smiled. "What's the status on Goodrich and Vega?"

"What?" Cris sat with her mouth open. "How do *you* know about it?"

"You're not the only detective around here, lady. So, as Norm says, *Spill it.*" Mike laughed.

"We've talked. He asked me out. I agreed to meet him at Stoney River for dinner tomorrow evening. He's a gentleman."

"You're going to meet him there? You aren't even going to let him pick you up and take you home? Oh, Cris. *Come on.*"

"What? We just started this thing. Gimme a break. I'm not even sure dating a patrol cop is best for me."

Mike laughed. "Hey. What the hell difference does that make anyway? So, he's a patrol cop. Is he not good enough to date a detective? You and I were patrol cops before we were promoted. It's not been *that* long ago. Wouldn't you have dated a detective back then?"

Mike looked in his rear view mirror. "They're here." He started the car. "We'll have to continue this line of questioning at a later date." He chuckled.

Cris shook her head.

Mike drove two blocks into the apartment complex where their suspect lived. He parked outside the unit blocking residents' cars. The two patrol officers' marked units parked behind him."

"Detective Vega, I believe this arrest is yours." Mike gestured toward the building.

"Unit is Apartment #448. Up here guys," Cris said, as she took the lead.

The four cops climbed the metal staircase, making considerable noise as they went.

Cris stepped to the door of the apartment and knocked as if she was hammering a nail. She waited no more than five seconds. As she was about to knock again, the deadbolt was thrown back and the door opened.

"Bill Sands, step out here please," Cris said.

Sands's eyes widened and he took two steps through his doorway. He didn't ask what was going on. His facial expression said he already knew.

"Turn around. Put your hands behind you."

One of the uniformed officers put her handcuffs on Sands and turned him back to face Cris.

"Bill Sands, you are under arrest for conspiracy to commit first degree murder in the death of Brooke Ashton-Cole.

"You have the right to remain silent. Anything you say can and will be used against you in a court of law. You have a right to an attorney. If you cannot afford an attorney, one will be appointed for you. Do you understand these rights as they have been explained to you?"

Sands looked from cop to cop. "Yeah, I understand." His look was not one of surprise or confusion, but one of conclusive realization.

"Bill, is there anything we should turn off or shut down before I lock your door?"

"Can you turn off the stereo?"

Cris stepped inside the apartment. The stereo was playing what sounded like a George Strait tune. She pushed the power button. That's when she spotted it. Atop one of the stereo speakers sat a cowboy hat. It was a wide-brimmed black hat like George Strait was famous for wearing and one like Edgar Fletcher had described to the detectives during his hospital room interrogation.

"Mike."

He stepped inside the apartment and shifted his gaze in the direction Cris was pointing. He chuckled as he stepped toward the hat.

"That was thoughtful of him." Mike smiled as he pulled on the pair of Nitrile gloves he'd taken from his jacket pocket. "We never have too much evidence."

Cris followed Mike through the door and noticed Sands was focused on Mike and the hat in his hand. She pulled the door closed and checked the lock.

"Done," she said to Sands.

"Will I be coming back anytime soon?"

Cris shook her head. "Not likely. It'll depend on your bail and whether or not it's paid."

He lifted his head, pulled in a deep breath and said, "Can you ask Jon to come over and collect my valuables before someone else breaks in and takes them? Let him know they're his now, assuming he wants them. If not, he can give them to the guys in the band. Jon has a key."

She nodded. "I'll call him."

"Can you—?" He cleared the lump from his throat. "Can you tell him I'm sorry for his pain?"

Cris nodded. She locked the door, pulled it closed and checked it. She followed as the officers escorted Sands down the stairs to the cruiser.

Chapter 54

Nashville International Airport

Two weeks later

He stood across the walkway from the Nashville International Airport baggage claim carousel labeled for Flight 1029 Boeing 737 from Kansas City. After swapping text messages earlier in the day, this was where he and Carol agreed to meet.

He kept running through ideas in his mind on how best to break the ugly news. There was no good way, no less painful way to share this life-altering revelation. He imagined how it would be if the roles were reversed, but it wasn't the same.

The warning bell and flashing light on another baggage carousel announcing the unloading of passenger bags for a different arriving flight interrupted Mike's thoughts of his impending discussion. He checked his wristwatch and again held his gaze at the flow of passengers coming for their luggage. He saw her as she stepped onto the escalator with her bag.

She spotted him. They exchanged waves. Smiles from both grew larger as she rode the steps down and into the baggage claim area. By the time she reached the bottom, Mike was at the last step with waiting arms.

"I sure missed you." Carol groaned. She hugged him as hard as she could.

"I missed you, too."

"They looked at each other briefly and kissed, hard and long."

"Do you have any checked bags?"

"No. It's all in there and here." She indicated her pull behind bag and her large carry on, hanging off her shoulder. "Except for the new clothes I bought in Topeka. I had the two big boxes shipped to your house."

"Only two big boxes?" Mike laughed as he took the handle of the bag on wheels and her shoulder bag. "They arrived yesterday."

"Already?"

"Yep. I was afraid to open them."

"You'd look sorta funny wearing what's in those boxes."

"I figured as much, so I left them unopened in the living room." Mike smiled.

They exited through the automatic sliding doors and crossed the Arriving Flights pickup lanes at the crosswalk and headed for the Short Term Parking garage.

She looked up at Mike. "You seem sorta quiet. Aren't you glad to see me?"

"I *am* glad to see you. I'm just drained. It's been rough lately. Nashvillians are still killing each other at a rapid pace and they're not giving us much time to sleep."

"Will it ever change?"

"I hope so. I'd like to see the day when we're required to transfer some of our detectives due to a lack of work. Instead, today we continue to search for more qualified and promotable officers in order to keep up with demand."

"Part of the price for Nashville's exploding growth?"

"Yes, partly. But, just because our population is escalating, doesn't mean we should try to control it by thinning the herd."

"Agreed." Carol nodded. "I hated to hear Mr. Hinkle passed."

"Yeah. It seemed like his pancreatic cancer took him kinda quick. But, he hadn't told Jennifer or me about it. According to his attorney, he knew about it for quite a while, but didn't share with hardly anyone."

"He was a funny old guy," Carol said.

"He didn't have any relatives who kept in touch with him or he with them, so he left his estate to me and Jennifer."

"Seriously?"

Mike nodded.

"Wow. That was generous."

"The reading of the will is scheduled for late next week. They're required to wait for the death notices to run in the area newspapers. He lived like a pauper, so I'm not expecting much beyond the house and lot.

"He said we'd done more for him than all his relatives put together. We got to meet with him and his attorney in the ICU before he passed. I'm glad we got to do that. I'm going to miss him."

"You and Jennifer must have had a bigger impact on him than you realized."

"I guess." He smiled at her. "By the way, in case I forgot to mention it, you look great."

"I always look great right after a month and a half long babysitting gig followed by a two-hour flight with a hundred other sardines exchanging the same stale breathing air inside a flying can. It's great for the complexion." She patted her cheeks.

"Mike laughed."

"You've lost weight," Carol said.

"Yes, I guess I have. A few pounds anyway. My chef has been out of town."

Mike unlocked the car and loaded Carol's bags. He started the car and pulled out of the garage into airport traffic.

Carol watched him for a while as he drove. "I know you, Michael. You're not just tired. Something's bothering you."

He was quiet for a moment, then said, "I have something to discuss when we get home."

"You sound as though it's serious."

"Yeah. Sorta." He accelerated and merged into traffic on I-40. "I'd rather not get into it while I'm driving if it's okay."

"Okay." She sat quietly for several minutes, no doubt pondering what could be bothering him.

"How's your sister?" Mike asked, breaking the silence after a long period of focusing on Nashville's congested traffic.

"She's much better. She's enjoying Piper now and seeing what a blessing she is to her and Bryan. I have dozens of pictures of Piper to show you. She is such a good baby."

"So, the psychologist thinks your sister is going to be okay?"

"Yes. It'll take time, but she's making good progress. A friend from their church who's a retired nurse is gonna keep an eye on her and Piper. It's amazing what postpartum depression can do to drain a new mom. I'm glad I could be with her and help her through this."

Mike nodded. "Me too. I'm glad she's better. I know it must have been scary there at first for everyone."

"Yes. She was kinda out of it for a while. The counselor from the hospital was a big help. I learned a lot from her about being a mother."

He looked at her and gave a half-smile.

Mike pulled the car into his driveway and parked.

"I'll get the bags."

As they came into the kitchen, Carol looked around as if she was searching for something. The last time they'd been apart for an extended time, Mike bought a bottle of Cabernet and a nice card for her. With his mind dominated by his full plate at work and his new health situation, he'd not thought to buy either.

"Okay." Carol said, as she walked into the living room and sat in the same place she always sat on Mike's sofa. "Let's talk."

Mike sat on the sofa next to her, but not as close as he usually did. He pulled his right knee up on the sofa so he could face her and see Carol as he spoke.

"Your look has me worried, Mike."

"I understand. I'm a little worried too."

"What is it?"

He exhaled a large breath. "Shortly after you left, I began to have a pain in my lower abdomen. I may have had it before then, but didn't pay it much attention. I was convinced it was another pulled muscle from an over-active workout at the gym. But, it lingered. So I started taking some extra-strength acetaminophen after a few days."

Carol watched him, with a puzzled look.

"It didn't seem to help. I started thinking it could be another kidney stone, but the pain was sorta low and more in the front. So, after a week or so, I decided I would let Dr. Fairchild take a look and see what he thought."

"You're scaring me."

"Sorry. So, I made an appointment. By the time I got in to see him, it was hurting pretty bad."

"Were you still working all this time?"

"Yeah. We've been short-handed lately due to vacations, so I was mainly helping Cris and Norm with their cases.

"Anyway, Dr. Fairchild sent me to a radiologist so he could run an MRI. He said it was the best way to be sure of the cause."

"How long ago was this?"

"About two weeks, or so."

"Why didn't you call me?"

"What? So you could have me and the baby both to worry about?"

"What did the Radiologist say."

Mike hesitated. "He said I had a tumor near my groin."

Carol gasped, covering her mouth with her hand.

"So, Dr. Fairchild ordered a biopsy to determine if it was cancerous."

"And?" She cringed.

"It was malignant."

"Oh, my God. Mike. No. She started to cry, and then moved closer to put her arms around him. I love you. Oh. I'm so sorry."

"I'm sorry too."

She kissed him.

They held each other for a minute.

Carol pulled her head back and said, "You said, *was*."

"He said since I was feeling pain from the tumor, I shouldn't wait. So, I had it removed."

"Already?"

"I took his advice. There was no reason to put it off. I didn't want to wait around and end up regretting it."

"What was their prognosis?"

"They started radiation therapy right away. They think there's a good chance with the radiation they can stop any that may have tried to spread to other organs."

She shook her head. "Oh, my God. I—I can't believe this."

"Yeah. They said they should be able to tell pretty soon if things are looking positive."

"That sounds hopeful." She wiped her eyes.

"They said they've had good luck with this kind of cancer before. They think they've caught it before it's spread or become unmanageable."

"How long did you have these pains before you went to Dr. Fairchild?"

"I don't know. A few weeks, maybe. I mean, how do you know? It's a pain. I've had several pains before from overdoing it in the gym."

She nodded. "So, how long do you go for radiation?"

"They said it would depend on the results from their tests. Then they reevaluate and make a new decision."

"How do you feel?"

"I'm okay. I'm still able to work. The whole idea of it all is a bit overwhelming psychologically and it's hard not to allow it to get in the way and dominate your thoughts."

"The Oncologist asked me about my exposures in Iraq and Somalia. I told him what I knew. But, I couldn't be sure. Those countries are not regulated nor monitored like we are. Toxic and virulent areas were not labeled, nor were they shielded. You couldn't be sure what you are being exposed to over there.

"We were suspicious there were toxic chemical and biological agents in the vicinity. There was always smoke from the oil well fires, dust, pesticides in the high ambient temperatures, not to mention all the vaccines we endured associated with Gulf War service.

"He said they were seeing several of these types of issues nowadays. A high percentage, if caught in time and treated immediately, are able to be dealt with successfully and most everything will be okay."

"It sounds hopeful. What did you mean by most everything will be okay?"

"Well, they said the main drawback from the radiation treatments in the lower abdominal area of a male's body is what it does to the patient's reproductive system."

"What do you mean?"

"It appears—. The radiation treatments cause sterility. I won't be able to have children."

Carol's face told a story her words would not tell.

"But, *you'll* be okay. The tumor is gone and *you'll* be okay. Right?"

"Supposedly."

"Okay. That's what matters."

"It's not all that matters."

"What do you mean?" Carol asked.

"You know what I mean. I can't ask you to give up having your own babies. It wouldn't be right. I know how much you want children. The way you talked about it on the phone for the last month, you've been like a kid looking forward to Christmas."

"I don't have to have children, Mike, as long as I have you."

He tilted his head and chuckled. "That sounded derogatory."

"You know what I meant." She punched his arm.

"I know."

"We could even adopt."

"It's not the same."

"I know it's not the same, but it's how people deal with these things. We're not the first couple to face this kind of disappointment."

"I don't know. It's been driving me crazy, dealing with it. Trying to face the unknown future possibilities and know what to do about it without hurting you."

"Mike, it's okay. We have each other. I will always love you regardless of what either of us does because of this Godless monster.

"Life's not fair. You've told me this over and over as long as I've known you. You do the best you can with what you have to work with and you move forward. You always move forward."

"This demon disease took my mom twenty-four years ago." Mike said. "Now it's trying to take me. I can't let it win."

"Exactly. I can help you, Mike."

He pulled her into his arms. "Thank you."

After a moment Carol said, "I don't know this, so I have to ask." They stepped back in order to see each other. "Does the radiation have any other detrimental effects on the body other than sterility?"

"Such as?" Mike said with a curious expression on his face even though he was confident he knew where she was going with her question.

"Well, such as ED."

"Ed? Ed who?"

"I think you know what I mean, Sergeant Neal."

Mike smiled. "I asked Dr. Fairchild about it because, obviously, I was also concerned. He said it should have no effect in that area."

"That's good news."

"I thought so too. After he covered this topic is when he went into this long sermon on the effects of the radiation and what most men my age do when facing the future without the ability to father children."

"Which is?"

"He said they go to the bank and make a deposit."

"The bank?"

"Yeah. The sperm bank where they—."

"I know what they do. Did you—?" Carol's eyes bulged and her mouth made the shape of an 'O'.

"I did. I gave them a bunch of samples so you could have that basketball team."

"Oh, Mike."

"They tested the sperm counts."

"And they were all good?" she asked.

"They told me all the samples were loaded with Olympic swimmers."

She laughed.

"They're currently parked in 330 degrees below zero liquid Nitrogen waiting for your egg to give them the thaw signal so they can get the party started."

"Oh, Mike." She grabbed him around the neck and squeezed.

"Careful. I'm a sick man recovering from surgery."

She released her choke hold, leaned back, smiled and said, "Thank you, Dad."

"You're welcome, Mom."

Acknowledgements

For their unending support, contributions, encouragement and critique, I want to thank Dew Wayne Burris, Steve Teer and Beth Teer.

I would also like to thank numerous law enforcement officers and first responders on duty in Davidson and Rutherford Counties as well as several retired officers and detectives for their service, their role models and the inspiration they provide.

To my wife Sandra, for forty-one happy years, for your undying support and your exceptional graphic design skills. But most especially, for patiently believing in me. Thank you, always.

Authors Bio

Ken Vanderpool began writing Crime Suspense Fiction in 2006 following an eye-opening medical procedure and an intimate encounter with his mortality. He decided it was time to complete the book he'd planned to write. Once finished, he realized writing was his passion. He plans to continue the Music City Murders series and possibly begin a new series as well.

Ken is a graduate of Middle Tennessee State University with his degree in Psychology and Sociology with a concentration on Criminology. He has also graduated from the Metropolitan Nashville Citizen Police Academy, the Rutherford County Sheriff's Office Citizen Academy and three times graduated from the Writer's Police Academy in Wisconsin.

Ken's first novel in the Music City Murders series, **When the Music Dies**, was published in 2012. Second in the series, **Face the Music**, in the summer of 2014. Number three, **Stop the Music**, in the fall of 2016. Currently in the works is number five, **Remember the Music**, scheduled for release in early 2019.

Ken has spent his entire life in Nashville and Middle Tennessee and proudly professes, "There is no better place on earth." Ken currently lives near Nashville in Murfreesboro, Tennessee with his wife Sandra and their Cairn Terrier-ist, Molly.

www.kenvanderpool.com